SEVENTH HEAVEN

ALSO BY ALICE HOFFMAN

Property Of
The Drowning Season
Angel Landing
White Horses
Fortune's Daughter
Illumination Night
At Risk

SEVENTH HEAVEN

ALICE HOFFMAN

G. P. PUTNAM'S SONS
New York

To Jake and Zachary,
to Ross and Jo Ann,
to Carol DeKnight,
to Sherry Hoffman,
to my grandfather, Michael Hoffman,

with love

And to the memory of Houdini

SEVENTH HEAVEN

1959

1

IN THE COUNTRY OF THE KING

*L*ATE in August, three crows took up residence in the chimney of the corner house on Hemlock Street. In the mornings they set up a racket that could wake the dead. They picked up stones in their beaks and tossed them down at picture windows; they plucked out their feathers, which would surface all day long in odd places, in bowls of Cheerios, in the pockets of shirts drying on laundry lines, inside glass milk bottles delivered at dawn.

This corner house was the only one to have been vacated since the subdivision was carved out of a potato farm, six years earlier. Before the builders began working, the town was nothing more than a post office up on Harvey's Turnpike, surrounded by farms. All that first spring renegade potatoes were unearthed when the men on Hemlock Street put down their lawns and planted mimosas and poplars; on trash day there would be heaps of potatoes alongside the aluminum cans. Everything in the neighborhood was brand new, the elementary school, the high school, the A&P, the police station on the Turnpike. The air itself seemed new; it could make you dizzy if you weren't used to it, and relatives visiting from Brooklyn or Queens often had to lie down on a couch with a damp handkerchief pressed to their temples. The bark on the trees left fresh, green patches on your hands if you dared to climb the thin, wavering branches. Each house in the subdivision was the same, and for the longest time husbands pulled into the wrong driveways after work; children wandered into the wrong houses for cookies and milk; young mothers who took their babies out for walks in their new carriages found themselves wandering past identical houses, on identical streets, lost until twilight, when the ice-cream man's truck appeared, and they could follow the sound of his bell, which traced his reliable route past their doorsteps.

To outsiders, the houses might still seem identical, but after six years those who lived here could now easily tell the difference by the color of the trim on the brick fronts, by the flower boxes or the lawn statues or the hedges beside the driveways. Now when the children played kickball on summer nights, they knew exactly which screen door to swing open, and which bedroom was theirs to throw off their damp, sweaty clothes. Mothers no longer tied address tags to their babies' wrists when they set them out to play in backyards. Even the dogs, who were so confused that first year they huddled together on street corners to howl at noon, now knew precisely where their bones were buried, and where they would stretch out for the night.

To have peace with your neighbors you needed to adhere to two unspoken rules: mind your own business and keep up your lawn. And because they all came from the same circumstances, because this was the first house they, and most likely anyone in their family, had ever owned, the unspoken agreement was kept—until Mr. Olivera violated the pact by dying. One day in November, when the sky turned black at four thirty and the children dragged their sleds over to Dead Man's Hill on the other side of the parkway at the first hint of snow, Mr. Olivera climbed into bed, beneath two wool blankets. He turned on his side, breathed deeply three times, thought about adding antifreeze to the radiator of his Chrysler, then went to sleep and never woke up again.

Olivera's wife, who was old-fashioned and made jam from the grapes her husband grew by the side of the house, immediately went to Virginia to stay with her married daughter. While Mrs. Olivera was deciding whether to stay with her daughter or move back to a neighborhood where she would be the only woman over sixty, widowed or not, the house, for reasons no one could fathom, began to fall apart. By Christmas the shutters had split and come off their hinges. By February the concrete along the front stoop was crumbling. Late in the spring, the grass in the front yard grew so tall people swore mosquitoes were breeding there, and they crossed over to the other side of the street so they wouldn't have to pass by. Joe Hennessy, who had been on the Nassau County police force for five years and was up for review, finally dragged out his new power mower and went across the street. Hennessy was six-foot-two, with strong muscles in his back and arms, but after he had cut half the front yard he was so exhausted he had to sit down on the front stoop just to catch his breath. By July, when Mrs. Olivera decided to sell the house, it was too late. By then there was a peculiar smell emanating from it, even though the windows were closed tightly and locked, and the overripe odor, which made people in the neighborhood wonder if a pot of jam had been cooked too long and then forgotten on the rear burner of the stove, drove prospective buyers away.

All through the summer the smell persisted; it grew riper and sweeter each day. The women on the block bought Airwick and they washed their floors with Lysol, but the smell came in through the screen windows and seemed to slap them in the face. Ace McCarthy, who was seventeen and scared of very little in this world, lived right next door to the Olivera place, and although he would never have told anyone, there were times, late at night, after he had turned off his transistor radio, when he swore he could hear someone groaning. Some jokester on another block, on Poplar or Pine, started the rumor that the house was haunted, and on Saturday nights carloads of teenagers parked outside. The boys honked their horns and dared each other to spend the night in the Olivera house; they called each other chicken and kissed each other's girlfriends, and they wouldn't budge until Joe Hennessy went out, opened the door of his squad car, and let the siren rip.

Why this should happen on their block, of all places, no one was sure. Hadn't they raked all their dead leaves into heaps they burned along the curb each October? Hadn't they brought lemon pound cakes and brownies with walnuts to the bake sales at the elementary school? Their children were rowdy, but good-natured; the worst their teenaged daughters would do was slip a tube of lipstick into their pocketbooks in the drugstore, or eat an entire bag of chips while they baby-sat. The neighbors looked to those around them for an explanation. A punishment of some sort had befallen them, but who was it directed toward? Not John McCarthy, who owned the Texaco station up on Harvey's Turnpike, even though he was the most logical candidate since his house was right next door to Olivera's; but perhaps the curse was aimed at his two wild sons, Jackie and Ace, who called their father the Saint behind his back. The Shapiros, on the other side of the McCarthys, certainly deserved something that would knock them off their high horse. They'd been suspiciously lucky with their children; Danny was too smart for his own good, and Rickie liked to comb her red hair right in front of you, just to show off. It was unlikely that the punishment was directed at the Durgins—Donna Durgin's house was so clean she put everyone else to shame—or the Winemans, whose crab apple trees formed a bower of pink blossoms each spring; and certainly it was not directed at Joe Hennessy; you could tell Joe was a good husband and father just by looking at him, you were lucky to have someone like Joe living on your block.

But there it was, punishment all the same, and no one was the least surprised when the crows appeared from the south. People turned off their TV sets and their radios and went out to stand on their lawns just to watch. They were big birds, with eyes like rubies, brave enough to chase cocker spaniels and Irish setters out of the Oliveras' yard. When the Hennessys' boy, Stevie, shot at one of them with his BB gun, the largest of the crows caught the BB in its beak, then chased Stevie across the street, managing to tear a patch out of his blue jeans before the boy could escape into his house, crying for his mother. Ellen Hennessy swooped Stevie into her arms, and after she was sure he hadn't been wounded, she ran into the street, waving her apron at the crow, but the bird simply ignored her and went right back to perch on the Oliveras' chimney.

Finally something had to be done. On a Friday night Phil Shapiro and John McCarthy met in Hennessy's rec room after supper. Hennessy's wife had put out some Fritos in a bowl and made sour-cream-and-onion dip, which she set on the laminated bar. Phil Shapiro and John McCarthy tried to get comfortable on the black vinyl couch. Hennessy took the knock-hockey game off the low coffee table and sat down opposite them. In six years the men had rarely been to each other's houses, and then only for a holiday party or to borrow a siphon or a screwdriver. Sitting down face to face and accepting a beer from

Hennessy didn't make them any more comfortable. The rec room was in a finished nook of Hennessy's basement, and the washing machine was thumping away behind the knotty-pine-paneled wall. Phil Shapiro was the one who suggested the meeting; he was the one who found out that the realtor wasn't even bothering to show the Olivera house anymore. Phil had come directly from A&S, where he was the head of accounting, and although he hadn't taken time to have supper, he wished he'd gotten out of his suit because John McCarthy was wearing his Texaco uniform and Hennessy wore old chinos and a short-sleeved sports shirt.

"God, it's hot," Phil said, and he took off his tie and put it in his pocket. He sipped a Budweiser, to be polite.

"Hot," John McCarthy agreed.

The three men thought this over and swallowed beer. They could still smell the overripe scent of the Olivera house, even here, across the street.

"The way I see it," Phil Shapiro said, "if we don't do anything, our property values are going straight down."

"That's the way I see it," Hennessy agreed.

"Every time I look next door I worry about some child falling in the window wells or getting trapped inside Olivera's garage," John McCarthy said.

Hennessy and Phil Shapiro were silent, momentarily embarrassed by what now seemed to be their greed. Hennessy had heard the McCarthy kids making fun of their father, calling him the Saint, and it was true: when he looked at you you felt guilty no matter how blameless you might be.

"Well, yes," Phil Shapiro finally said. "Exactly. Someone could get hurt. Those crows could find a pack of matches, rub them the wrong way, and poof, up goes the house in flames."

"I never thought of that," John McCarthy said, worried. "And don't forget that someone could cut across the lawn, get tangled up in the weeds, fall down, and break his leg."

"Yep," Phil Shapiro said. "We need to move on this."

Ellen Hennessy opened the door upstairs and called down, "Can I fix you boys anything else?"

"That's okay, Ellen, we're set," Hennessy said. "Or are you interested?" he asked his neighbors. "Cheese and crackers? Coffee cake?"

Both men politely shook their heads; they preferred to eat at home.

"Set," Hennessy called upstairs. "So," he said to his neighbors.

"So we take an ad in the paper," Phil Shapiro said. "And we have the buyer connect with Mrs. O. down in Virginia."

"Who's going to look at that dump?" Hennessy said. "Anyone you want living on your street?"

"A handyman," John McCarthy said. "A fix-it fellow."

Hennessy stood up and brought over the bowl of Fritos, then took a handful for himself. Getting involved in someone else's business just seemed wrong, but before an hour had gone by it had been decided. Phil Shapiro would contact old Mrs. Olivera and get her okay, Hennessy would place ads in the real-estate sections of three newspapers, and John McCarthy would show the house in the evenings.

Across the street you could see the yellow light in the Hennessys' basement, and from where Danny Shapiro and Ace McCarthy sat, on the bumper of Jackie McCarthy's blue Chevy, it was a truly amazing sight. What on earth could their fathers and Hennessy possibly find to say to each other for more than an hour? Neither of their fathers said more than a few sentences a day to their children, unless pressed by an emergency, but there the men stayed until half past eight, when the yellow light was finally turned off. The men came up the basement stairs and lumbered past Ellen Hennessy; their own kitchens were equally small, so they knew to squeeze past the kitchen table.

"Well, I hope you came up with some good ideas," Ellen said to Hennessy after he'd walked his neighbors to the front door—as if they didn't take the exact same path in their own houses every single day. Hennessy watched his wife wipe down the linoleum countertops with a pink sponge. She was wearing plaid Bermuda shorts and a white blouse with a Peter Pan collar; her hair was cut short, so you could see the back of her neck.

"Sure we did," Hennessy said. He had brought the Fritos upstairs and now he held the bowl and tossed chips into his mouth.

They could hear the crows cawing as they nested for the night. John McCarthy had told the other men that he wore earmuffs to bed so he wouldn't have to hear the birds fussing.

"We're going to dynamite the place."

"Ho," Ellen said, "that's a good one."

The crows didn't bother Ellen as much as they did her husband. She set her hair on wire rollers at night, and before she put on the hairnet she tucked wads of cotton over each ear.

"I like your hair when you don't set it," Hennessy said to her. "Just straight."

"Please," Ellen said. "You've got to be kidding."

Hennessy went to her and put his arm around her waist. The house was small, but at times like this, Hennessy could almost forget that the children, already tucked in, might not yet have fallen asleep. "Let's go to bed early," he said.

"Uh uh," Ellen told him. She wiped the burners of the electric stove with even strokes.

Hennessy let go of her. He waited to see if she would turn around, and when she didn't, when she kept on cleaning, he went to the kitchen hallway that led to the garage. He walked into the garage, flipped on the dim light, and rolled open the door. It was cooler here; a circle of moths gathered around the light bulb that hung from the ceiling. Hennessy didn't even feel angry anymore when she said no. He crouched down behind his workbench, and when Ellen came and stood in the doorway she couldn't see him in the dark, searching for a can of gas.

"Joe?" she called.

Hennessy picked up the gas can and pulled his new mower out of a corner.

"I'm going to finish up at Olivera's," he said.

He rolled the mower out past their car in the driveway, then guided it across the street. Ace McCarthy and Danny Shapiro saw him approaching; they knew, from Hennessy's son, Stevie, that he often wore his gun when he wasn't on duty.

"You boys bored?" Hennessy said as he rolled the mower past them.

"No, sir," Danny Shapiro answered right away.

"Because if you are," Hennessy said, "there's a lawn that needs mowing."

"Oh, no," Ace said. "Sir," he added, so easily you'd never guess how the word stuck in his throat. "This being Friday night, we have much, much better things to do."

"Yeah," Hennessy said, because he suspected Ace of following in his brother's footsteps, with a pocketful of fake I.D.s and those pointy black boots. He probably had some bottled beer cooling in the creek behind the high school. "I'll bet you do," Hennessy said.

The half of the lawn Hennessy had mowed had already grown as tall as the wild side. He stopped in the Oliveras' driveway and looked up at the chimney. The crows cackled to one another, then edged out of their nest and peered down at him. Hennessy had to pull on the mower's starter three times before it caught, and when it finally did, the engine started with a roar that sent the crows circling into the sky, screaming. It took Hennessy nearly an hour just to finish the front lawn. At first the crows tossed stones at him, but after a while they gave up and went back to the chimney; they watched him carefully as he worked.

It wasn't a good job, but it would do, although the lawn was still uneven in patches. McCarthy would be showing the house in the evenings, and you could get away with a lot in the dark. Hennessy was sweating hard; he took off his shirt and wiped his face with it, then opened the chain-link gate and dragged the mower into the backyard. He stopped only for a moment, beside the grapevines. In August the grapes always turned purple; because there had been no one to harvest them, they had dropped to the ground in overripe mounds. It was getting darker, already it was difficult to see, and Hennessy had to work fast if he wanted to finish tonight. And even though Hennessy worked without stopping, the children on Hemlock Street fell asleep to the sound of his lawn mower, and on all sides of the abandoned house neighbors could finally throw open their windows, thankful that at last the disturbing odor of the Olivera place had been replaced, at least temporarily, with the crisp scent of newly cut grass, a scent that made your throat tighten and reminded you exactly how good it was to live here.

On summer evenings like these, when the children were tucked into bed, safety hung over the neighborhood like a net. No one locked windows, no one locked doors. The G.E. refrigerators hummed and the stars were a brilliant white. In the morning, the traffic on the Southern State would be loud enough to wake sleepers from their beds, but at night the parkway was nothing more than a whisper, lulling the children to sleep beneath their white sheets and their quilts patterned with rocking horses. The later it grew, the more the hands of kitchen clocks lingered on each hour. A summer night lasted longer here than it did in other places. The chirp of the crickets was slower, and when children fell out of their beds they never woke, but instead rolled gently under their beds, still clutching onto stuffed bears.

In the moonlight you could see that, even after six years, everything still seemed new: lunch boxes and bicycles, couches and bedroom suites, cars parked in driveways and swing sets in the yards; there weren't even any cracks in the cement. When the potato farms were being torn apart and the builders were bulldozing the sandy earth, the fireflies grew so confused that they left one night in a shining cloud. But this year they had returned and had stayed on for an unusually long time to drift through the rosebushes and the crab apple trees. None of the children who grew up here, or even those who moved here from apartments in Brooklyn or Queens, had seen a firefly before, yet they immediately knew what to do, as if their response to the bugs had been tacked to their brain waves. They ran inside for empty pickle jars and filled them with the fireflies they'd trapped in their hands. Beneath these children's beds were green globes of light that never dimmed until morning. Good night, these children had been told, and they always believed it. Sleep tight, they'd been told, and they always did. When monsters appeared in the closets, or under the catalpa trees, the children kept it to themselves. They never told their parents or whispered to each other. Sometimes the monsters reappeared on paper in school, drawn with crayons and colored pencils; they had purple hair and large yellow eyes, and you could tell they didn't believe in good nights or sleeping tight.

In some of the houses on Hemlock Street, good girls slept with their fingers crossed. They believed it was wrong for boys to want to touch their breasts, and luckily for them they never dreamed. They never thought about how babies were made; they wouldn't even tell their best friends if they did. And yet on summer evenings they felt weak in the knees. They sat in the bleachers at the high school and watched the boys play baseball; they chewed Juicy Fruit gum and combed their hair, and suddenly they felt as if they were made of glass, as if they were on the edge of something they knew in their hearts was bad.

And when the sky grew darker, the late blue dusk of summer, boys of sixteen and seventeen stumbled along the bases in the approaching dark. Boys who had never had a thought in their heads found themselves feeling defeated. They thought about their fathers, how they set out the trash cans on the curb, how they could always be found at the kitchen table on Saturday nights, their checkbooks in front of them, stacking up the bills. Water, electricity, mortgage. They had no idea why thinking about their fathers should make them stumble, why suddenly they couldn't stop wondering what a girl's mouth was like, what her fingers would feel like against their skin, how pale a girl's eyelids might seem when she closed her eyes.

These boys' fathers had once felt what their sons felt now, that terrible freedom of a summer night. But lately odd things pleased them; they found themselves grinning when they paid the bills, they found themselves thinking, This is mine, and they didn't mind so much being home on a Saturday night. They had poker games to think about and promotions at work, they had candy-colored cars with long fins in their driveways. So why was it that they were so moved when they saw their oldest sons button their white shirts and comb their hair back with water? Why did the youngest of their sons, the fearless ones who climbed to the top of the monkey bars and begged to stay up past their bedtimes, make their throats grow tight with longing?

On August nights these men's wives no longer looked at themselves as they tissued the cold cream off their faces. Many of them still could not believe they had children; put into a twilight sleep, then handed a baby they hardly recognized as their own, they were suddenly much older than they ever thought they'd be. Just before winter each year they took down the red boots from the top shelf of the hall closet. Just before spring they carried up light jackets and Easter coats from the basement, shook out the mothballs, and hung the coats on lines in their backyards. They had recipes for coconut cake; they had chicken soup with rice for the littlest children, home with sore throats; they had orders in for new dinette sets with laminated tabletops that looked like real wood yet were easily sponged off after a meal.

But this year the women saw that the fireflies had returned. They saw a flash of light at their windows just as they were about to get into bed. The green light formed a net of stars within the grid of silver fences along the backyards. When the women went into their bathrooms they could hear their children's even, sleepy breathing through the thin plaster walls. They sneaked cigarettes while sitting on the rims of the tubs, which they had scrubbed with Bon Ami earlier that day. Then they faced the mirror and took the bobby pins out of their hair and combed out their pincurls, but by the time they went back to their bedrooms their husbands were already asleep, and the fireflies were hidden between the blades of grass on their own front lawns.

It was so hot you had to keep your eye on the road because all along the Southern State the asphalt had buckled and snapped apart. Lately the heat had been fueled by a wind from the west that tore up the last of the brown, matted grass on either side of the parkway. Nora Silk was trying to keep up with the moving van, but every time she stepped down hard on the gas and hit sixty-five miles an hour the Volkswagen shimmied for no reason at all. Nora had to hold tight to the steering wheel whenever the tires edged into the fast lane. She looked past the heat waves and concentrated on driving until she heard the pop of the cigarette lighter.

"Put that down this minute," she told Billy.

He was eight and he couldn't keep his hands off the lighter. Eventually, Nora knew, he'd drop it and the carpet would catch fire and then they'd have to pull off the road. As soon as they did the baby would fall off the backseat and wake up, and Nora would have to climb over, comfort him, and start to search for a clean diaper and his favorite teddy bear.

"This instant," Nora said. "And hand me a Salem."

Billy took the new pack of cigarettes out of the glove compartment and pulled off the cellophane. "Just let me light it," he said.

"Not on your life," Nora said.

"Just this one time," Billy pleaded.

He was a real bulldog about some things. You had to shake him off or, if you didn't have the energy, if the weather was broiling and your mascara was melting and the asphalt was cracking into bits, give in to him.

"This one time," Nora said darkly.

Billy quickly pushed the lighter in and dangled the cigarette between his lips. Nora looked in the rearview mirror to make sure James hadn't fallen off the backseat. He was covered with a cotton baby blanket and he looked as cozy as bread. Nora fluffed up her bangs, then noticed that Billy was inhaling.

"Hand it over," she said.

Billy held the cigarette high in the air. He was a thin child, blond with satiny blond skin, but when he wore his awful taunting look, complete strangers had to fight off the urge to smack him.

"Now," Nora said.

She took the cigarette away from Billy and inhaled. Her hands always shook when she yelled at him, and the charms on her gold bracelet jangled. "And close your window," she added. "Do you want Mr. Popper to jump out and get caught under someone's tires?"

The black cat, who was so lazy he rarely bothered to blink, was curled up on the floor, his head resting on one of Billy's sneakers. The cat wasn't about to make an escape, but Billy felt sick to his stomach, so for once he did as he was told. Nora stole a look at him when she realized he had actually minded her, then she turned back to the road, inhaled, and let out a stream of smoke. She knew that Billy felt like crying—well, maybe she did, too. She had a boy who liked to play with fire, a baby who hadn't the slightest notion of what a father was, and a cat who liked to run his claws up her leg as soon as she put on a new pair of nylons. She didn't have to look at Billy to know what he was doing.

"And stop pulling on your hair," Nora said.

Ever since Roger had moved out, Billy had taken up the habit of twirling his hair so hard he'd pulled out patches and you could see his scalp showing through all along the right side of his head.

"You're going to love the house," Nora said. "You'll have your own room."

"I'll hate it," Billy said in a singsong voice that made Nora want to throttle him.

Nora stepped down harder on the gas; the car vibrated and a high-pitched whine came from the engine. She'd known they had to get out of their apartment when she found the baby at the window, calmly eating paint chips off the sill. She started looking just after Roger had left and the heat had gone off and she'd begun to take Billy and the baby into bed with her, to keep them warm. All night she had felt their small feet, like pieces of ice against her spine, and whenever she managed to fall asleep she dreamed about houses. They began to spend every Sunday looking out on Long Island, and every Sunday Billy stuck wads of gum under the cabinets in the kitchens of model houses, he peed into the bathtubs of newly tiled bathrooms, knowing as he did that Nora couldn't grab him and smack him in front of the realtor. All she could do was grind her teeth and hoist the baby up on her shoulder as they were led through dens with knotty pine paneling and living rooms with shiny oak floors. When the tours were over, Nora would stand on the front lawns of houses she couldn't afford, unwilling to leave until the smell of freshly cut grass sent the baby into a fit of sneezing.

She was about to give up hope when she found the ad for the house on Hemlock Street. She phoned the number listed right away, even though it was a quarter past nine. Once she made sure the price hadn't been misprinted, she carried her sleeping children over to Mrs. Schneck, who had the apartment next door and who made good noodle soup and baby-sat for fifty cents an hour. Then Nora drove out to Long Island. The exit off the Southern State was easy enough to find, but she'd gotten lost in the development for close to an hour, circling Hemlock Street but never quite finding it. She put on her brights, and still she couldn't tell one identical house from another. Desperate and running out of gas, she made a right-hand turn and suddenly there she was, right in front of the house. The next-door neighbor she'd spoken to on the phone was waiting for her in the driveway. He'd worried that she'd had an accident and had planned to give her five more minutes before he called the highway patrol. As he let Nora in through the side door, he apologized for the state of the house. It may have been foolishness, it may have been because the electricity had been cut off and Nora couldn't really see—she had to keep one hand pressed against the wall to feel her way through the dark—but Nora fell instantly in love with the place. At this asking price, she could afford to.

She contacted Roger the next day. He was working in Las Vegas and bothering her for a divorce, and finally Nora was calling to give in, on one condition: Roger had to cosign for a mortgage to make the bank think she still had a husband. Of course Roger agreed. He had so many outstanding loans—including one for the Volkswagen, which, in Nora's opinion, no sane man would have ever bought, on time or otherwise—one more didn't make a bit of difference. As soon as the mortgage came through, Nora signed the divorce papers Roger had sent her. The documents accused her of alienation of affection, and since that could mean whatever you wanted, it was probably true. Frankly, Roger didn't even seem like a real live person to her anymore. Two weeks later he sent back the divorce certificate along with a photograph of himself and his rabbit posed in front of a motel in the desert. He was so thrilled about being single again you could see the red aura of delight all around him, even though the photograph was a black-and-white. The rabbit, whose name was Happy, was a part of Roger's act, but Billy had always thought of him as a pet. After Roger left, Nora couldn't get Billy away from the spot where the rabbit's cage had been kept.

"It was never fair to keep a rabbit here with Mr. Popper," she had told Billy. "You know Happy drove him crazy."

And it was true. Whenever Happy wasn't working, Mr. Popper sat on top of his cage and the rabbit would wriggle his nose excessively as if to dare the cat to try to get his claws through the wire. But God, did Nora feel alienated then. She could have shot Roger with a real .45, not the one he used in his act, which only spat out confetti and streamers. Every time she caught Billy sitting in the corner and twirling his hair, Nora wondered what had possessed her to marry Roger in the first place. She had been eighteen when they met, and he'd been so handsome just looking at him made Nora feel faint. But even back then, when they couldn't keep their hands off each other, Nora had sensed something false about Roger. She wanted to believe in him, but there seemed to be less and less of him to believe in every day. He wasn't even a good magician. His heart wasn't in it. He wasn't, for instance, the sort of magician you'd hire for a children's party, because children could see right through him. They weren't the least bit surprised when he pulled silk scarves out of his sleeve or found quarters behind their ears. They yawned and asked for M&Ms

and could tell with just one look that his magic wand was made of wood. Adults, on the other hand, found Roger charming. He may have been sloppy when he pulled the rabbit out of his hat, but he had a particular knack for killing his audience with cynical one-liners. He was a putdown artist, with definite stage presence, and yet whenever Billy tried to conjure up his father he got nothing more than an image of Roger during his blackout trick, an illusion in which Roger was a man in top hat and tails with no body, no face, and no hands.

Billy was trying to imagine his father, and failing, when they arrived at the house. The moving van was blocking the driveway, so Nora had to park on the street. When she took the silver key John McCarthy had mailed her out of her purse, the key felt hot; Nora had to hold it up and blow on it. She got out of the Volkswagen and flipped the front seat forward to scoop out the baby.

"We're home," she cooed to James.

Up in the passenger seat, Billy was stiff; he stared straight ahead, his hair a mass of honey-colored knots.

"Come on, killjoy," Nora said to him. "Out."

Billy dragged himself out and came around the car to stand beside his mother. He was slight, with thin shoulders, and in that way he resembled Roger; the perfect body for folding itself up into boxes and trunks. Nora held the baby sideways, under one crooked arm. The lawn had been unevenly mowed, and all along the driveway there were dandelion puffs.

"These weeds are nothing," Nora told Billy.

They walked up to the front door, with Billy following so close he stepped on the backs of Nora's high heels. The key didn't work, so they went through the backyard to the side door. Nora signaled to the three moving men, who were gathered around a rotting wooden picnic table, drinking coffee from their Thermoses.

"This is it," Nora said to her children, as the moving men went to lift their belongings out of the van.

The sound of traffic on the Southern State was loud enough to give you a headache if you weren't used to it, and a low plane rumbled overhead. This was clearly a house that made a better impression in the dark.

"Never mind the way it is now," Nora said. "Think about the way it's going to look."

James clapped his hands and pointed at the screen door, which swung back and forth on its hinges. But Billy just stared at his mother. Nora caught Billy studying her; she hoisted James up on her shoulder and patted his back. She bit her lip when she noticed that the painted trim on the house was peeling, and she looked so worried that Billy almost said something nice. Instead he wrinkled his nose.

"This place stinks," he said.

"Thank you very much," Nora said, even though it was true. "I knew I could depend on you to say something cheerful."

Nora unlocked the side door and stepped inside. As soon as the moving men brought in James's playpen, Nora set it up in the kitchen and popped the baby safely inside. She walked through the house to unlock the front door, then made her way past the couch and the bed frames out in the driveway and went to the car for the bag of groceries she'd brought with them. She ignored the horrible smell in the kitchen and opened a large brown box with a knife, finding her baking trays on the first try. The oven was smoky when she turned it on and there was a pot of thick, purple stuff forgotten on the rear burner, but Nora just grabbed a mixing bowl and started to tear open packages of baking soda and vanilla.

"Yum," Nora said to the baby, who was standing up, holding on to the bars of his playpen. Before she began to bake, Nora unlatched her bracelet and laid it on the counter. Roger had given it to her; she should probably get rid of it, except it seemed her whole life hung from the chain: the heart Roger had first given her, one of Billy's baby teeth, a gold-plated teddy bear Roger brought to the hospital when James was born, a tiny guitar Nora had bought for herself the day Elvis was drafted.

Nora never measured ingredients, and she wasn't much of a cook; she might even have been considered awful. But she was always lucky with her baking. Roger, the conceited bastard, was always too concerned with his looks to eat cookies or cakes. He liked the way women gravitated toward him; he always ran his fingers through his hair and pretended not to notice, but Nora was certain he noticed plenty whenever she wasn't around.

"Who's a conceited bastard?" Billy asked her.

He hadn't moved since they'd entered the house. He was still standing with his back against the screen door, twirling his hair.

"No one," Nora said. She turned to him and rattled the baking sheet in his direction. "Never say bastard."

It was a quirk of Billy's to look right through people as if they were nothing more than panes of glass. Fortunately, he never picked up a complete thought, just the frayed edges of things, and still Nora was never quite certain if she had said something out loud or if Billy's antennae had picked up what she'd been thinking in spite of any silence.

"Find something to do," Nora said. She held her nose and grabbed the pot of purple goop off the stove, then spilled the mixture into the sink.

"There's nothing *to* do," Billy said.

Nora could see that he had his eye on a box of matches Mrs. Olivera had left behind.

"Don't even think about it," Nora said. "Clean your room," she suggested.

Billy groaned, but he went into the dining room. He could hear his mother quizzing one of the moving men who had gone into the kitchen about whether or not anyone had come across her Elvis collection, which, aside from the battered velvet couch, was probably the most substantial thing they owned. The living room and dining room were really one L-shaped space. There were cobwebs hanging from the ceiling and a thin layer of white dust along the window ledges and on top of the air conditioner that had been jammed into one window.

Down the hallway were a bathroom and three small bedrooms. James's crib was a pile of wooden slats in the tiniest one, and in the largest Nora's suitcases had been tossed into a heap. In the third bedroom, the one facing the street, Billy found his cowboy boots and his globe of the world that glowed in the dark when you plugged it in. From the window he could see the identical houses opposite theirs. He could see the Volkswagen, parked sloppily, with one wheel up on the curb, and the rhododendrons Mr. Olivera had planted. Billy sat down with his back against the wall. He didn't think he was tired, but once he leaned his head forward, he instantly fell asleep. As he slept, a spider on the ceiling let out a thin, silky strand and dropped down from its web, and in no time it had climbed into Billy's shirt pocket.

Unlike most people's mothers, Billy's mother believed that spiders were good luck. She always had to close her eyes before she could force herself to take a broom, cover it with a dishcloth, and bring down a spider's web. Having had very little of it, she knew a great deal about luck. She knew that you could wrap a cut with a spider's web and stop the bleeding. Spirits would disperse when you set out a saucer of salt. Three rainy days in a row meant an arrival. And—this one Nora could testify to—a husband who talked in his sleep meant betrayal.

So it was easy for Nora to ignore the mess around her and keep on with her baking, stopping only to pry open some windows and air out the house, and then again to write a check for the moving men, who leaned against the kitchen counters watching her, made mute by the scent of vanilla and the way Nora's tongue darted out from her mouth while she signed her name. When the moving men had gone, and the first batch of cookies was out of the oven, Nora dusted the flour off her hands and lifted James out of his playpen.

"Da da," James said.

"Please," Nora said. "Don't mention his name."

The awful thing was that Nora knew she would have continued to put up with Roger if he hadn't left her. Roger would have known how to fix a roof when it leaked, he would have known there was such a thing as an oil burner. And, of course, if she was still married to him, Nora could have told herself she wasn't alone.

The baby reached for her breasts, so Nora sat at the kitchen table to nurse him. She knew she had to get him onto a bottle soon; he wanted to nurse in inconvenient places, in the grocery store or the post office, or whenever he was startled, just for comfort. Nora leaned her back against the old kitchen table and wriggled her feet out of her high heels. As the baby nursed he grew warmer, the way he always did when he began to drowse. It was a good sign when a baby fell right to sleep in a new house; that was a fact.

Nora gently eased off James's knitted yellow booties, and the baby sucked harder and curled his toes. He was ten months old, and each time he cut a new tooth Nora rubbed scotch on his gums and wept because he was less of a baby. He fell asleep with his arms outstretched and his mouth open. Nora put him down in the playpen and covered him with a warm dish towel. She put in a second batch of cookies and carefully closed the oven door.

Somewhere, Mr. Popper was mewing. Nora found him in the living room, perched on the air conditioner. The cat leapt to her shoulder and stayed there as Nora surveyed the house, stepping over the boxes, the pots and pans, the snow boots, the Elvis collection, the record player, which was in need of a new needle. The baby's room would have to be painted, the toilet gurgled, and Nora's bed seemed to have been damaged by the moving men. Nora reached up to stroke Mr. Popper. Then she went to stand in the doorway of the third bedroom, where she watched Billy sleep. His face was hidden in his arms and his hair stood away from his head, electrified by all the dust in the house. You could hear the hum of the Southern State here in Billy's bedroom, like a cricket caught in the wall.

The children were so exhausted from the move that Nora let them go on sleeping. She mopped the bathroom floor and hung her dresses and her woolen car coat in the closet. When it was nearly supper-time, Nora went out to the back patio, and she was there smoking a cigarette when the crows returned. Right away they set up a horrible racket. They cawed and shed their feathers and began to pick up stones, which they tossed down, one by one, so that stones skittered along the boards of the picnic table like hail. Nora shaded her eyes and finished her cigarette. You had to be careful about birds; they could be good luck just as easily as bad. So Nora waited, and when she was sure, she went to the side of the house where the grapevines grew. Big purple grapes were all over the ground, and Nora carefully stepped over them as she set up a rusted ladder Mr. Olivera hadn't had time to put away. She went back into the house, and while the baby stirred in his sleep and moved his thumb into his mouth, Nora took the container of salt and slipped back outside.

At this hour the traffic on the Southern State moved like a river. Nora climbed the ladder, and as she neared the roof she saw that the rain gutters were full of pine needles and dead leaves. Something would have to be done about the gutters before winter, before the sky turned yellow and new fallen leaves piled up. Nora held on to the gutter with one hand to keep herself balanced while she tossed salt upward, onto the roof. The crows huddled together on the chimney, screaming like mad.

"Go on," Nora told them, because, after all, she had her children's sleep to consider.

The crows called to her mournfully. Then, with their tails coated white, they rose up from the house and flew south, toward the parkway. They careened in a zigzag line until the salt on their tails fell onto the asphalt like snow. When Nora was satisfied that she was rid of them, she climbed back down the ladder. She tried one of Mr. Olivera's grapes and was surprised by its sweetness. She could feel her milk coming in. She could feel the pull of the new moon that would rise above her roof in only a few hours. Nora licked her fingertips, knowing as she did that if those crows had had eggs in their nest, she would never have been able to chase them off with salt.

While Billy dreamed he was playing ball in the driveway, and the baby turned, slowly waking beneath the dish towel, Nora came back into the kitchen. She wiped the table clean, then fixed a bowl of rice cereal for James. As soon as she had the chance she would buy cookbooks, she'd ask her neighbors for their favorite recipes, but tonight she took out two green bowls for Billy and herself and filled them with Frosted Flakes and milk. And later, after the children had eaten, after they'd sampled the cookies she'd baked, and the tub had been washed out and they'd both been bathed, Nora made up her mattress with clean sheets, right on the floor where it lay. She took both children into bed with her, for whose comfort she could not have honestly said, and because there were no curtains hung yet they were able to look at the stars through the bedroom window. Soon, Nora would fix her children macaroni and cheese for dinner; they would grow chrysanthemums and sunflowers in their yard. Nora would find a baby-sitter for James and a baseball mitt for Billy, and she would try to remember to fix Bosco and milk every day at three. If she had to, she would repeat the recipe for rice pudding until she knew it by heart.

2

SLEEP TIGHT

*A*CE McCarthy woke up with his body on fire and a ripping feeling in the center of his chest. He swung his feet to the floor and put his head down between his knees, and when that didn't help, he went to his closet, took a cigarette from the pack hidden on the shelf, and lit up, even though his hands shook, as if he were caught in the wind.

In the room next to his, he could hear the Saint snoring. He could hear traffic in the distance and the leaves moving in the maple tree. He blew out a stream of smoke and watched it disappear through the open window. All summer he had worked alongside his father and his brother, and there was a permanent moon of oil under each of his nails. His dark hair was longer than his father liked it to be, and his eyes were a deep, immutable green. He had always been able to get any girl he wanted, and he'd gone a lot farther with them than he'd ever told Danny Shapiro. In spite of his passion for fast cars and black leather, Ace wasn't a braggart. The Saint had taught him a sense of piety, something his brother, Jackie, who assured total strangers he planned to be a millionaire before his twenty-first birthday, had missed out on altogether.

Pride aside, this would be the year when Ace would have everything he ever wanted. He had nearly enough saved to buy the car he wanted—a candy-apple-red Bel Air one of Jackie's friends was ready to sell. This year when he walked down the hallways in the high school there wouldn't be any older guys to eclipse him. Girls' heads would turn when he pushed his metal locker shut. Teachers who wanted to get him out of their hair would stop harping at him and automatically pass him through his classes.

Today, thinking about his senior year, Ace had felt great. He and Danny had hitched to Long Beach; they'd sat under the boardwalk, drinking beer and listening to Danny's transistor radio, and then they went swimming drunk, until the waves sobered them up. They'd been best friends since the day Danny moved in and they'd had a fight on the Shapiros' lawn; they'd been more like brothers than Jackie and Ace were. And yet now, alone in his room, Ace felt nothing but resentment. After this year Danny would be going to college; even if he hadn't been smart enough to get in wherever he chose, he could have gotten an athletic scholarship; he could probably make it in the minors right now. But for Ace, this would be his last good year, and he knew it. Everything that followed would be downhill. Next year, when the boys who were seniors drove into the Texaco station and admired his Bel Air, Ace would think they were fools because he'd still be living in his parents' house, and the girls who were all so crazy for him now would be wanting something more than deep kisses and promises Ace would never be able to keep. He had already started to see the future in some girls' eyes: a house, a family, a balanced checkbook.

Ace shook out another cigarette and smoked it. When he was done he went to the kitchen and drank three glasses of water, but the water didn't put out whatever was burning inside him. It should have been easier to sleep now that the crows were gone, but it was harder. Through the kitchen window Ace could see the Shapiros' house; he could see right into Rickie's window, he could see that the shade was pulled down in Danny's room, where there was probably already a stack of college catalogues. Ace sat down at the kitchen table and lit matches. He blew each one out carefully, with a single breath. He heard the front door open and close, heard someone ease off his boots and let them fall to the floor. Jackie came into the kitchen; he opened the refrigerator and reached for the orange juice. He stank of liquor.

"Hey, buddy," Jackie said. "You're up late."

"Yeah," Ace said. "A real night owl."

Jackie pulled out his cigarettes and his silver lighter. He still ran with the same gang as he had in high school; sometimes they'd hang around the gym, checking out girls who were five years younger and didn't know any better. Jackie sat down across from Ace and smiled. He reached into the pocket of his leather jacket and pulled out a billfold.

"Get out of here," Ace said, not believing how much money his brother was waving around. He knew what Jackie made down at the station. "That's not yours," Ace said. He kept staring at the money.

"The Corvette," Jackie said.

Ace looked up at his brother.

"The one in for repairs at the station," Jackie said. "Pete stole it."

"Oh, shit," Ace said. "Don't tell me this."

"All I had to do was forget to lock the garage doors. It's like taking candy from a baby."

A bedspring creaked and the brothers looked down the hall. The Saint was turning in his sleep.

"You maniac," Ace whispered to his brother.

"I'm not pumping gas for the rest of my life," Jackie whispered back. "The guy with the 'Vette had insurance."

"Pop," Ace said.

"Pop." Jackie shrugged. "He'll never know."

Jackie peeled off two twenties and held them out.

"Nah," Ace said quickly.

"Go on," Jackie urged him, and he grabbed Ace and stuffed the bills into his palm. Ace's hand felt hot; in spite of himself, his fingers closed around the twenties. "Buy yourself a good time," Jackie said.

"Yeah," Ace said.

After Jackie had gone off to bed, Ace cleaned out the ashtray and went back to his room. He slipped the money into a dresser drawer, beneath his clean socks. He listened to the Saint breathing in the next room. How could he have thought Danny Shapiro was more like his own brother than Jackie was? Danny was nothing but a guy who happened to live next door. Ace felt a new kind of badness inside his chest, and it was cracking him apart trying to get out. Bad blood moved down his arms and legs. It was the beginning of the end of something, and Ace wasn't about to wait up for his own future. He got into bed and pulled up the sheet and told himself to stop thinking. All he wanted was to fall asleep, fast, and at eleven fifty-five he did.

And it was a good thing, too, because on Hemlock Street summer always ended at midnight on Labor Day. That was the hour when a wash of white light cut through the sky and a cold wind picked up and shook the crab apples from the trees and set the dogs circling the corners where they slept. When the wind came up, a thin trail of chalk dust whooshed from the chimneys of the school. If you looked carefully you'd see that the leaves of the poplars and willows were coated with a powdery substance, and that the letters of the alphabet formed on the leaves before disappearing into smoke. Every September had been the same. The children moved from one grade to another, their legs grew longer, they started to crack their gum and mutter to themselves when they were told to clean their closets, and eventually they'd turn right instead of left at the corner of Hemlock and Oak, and cross over to the high school. But this year, in the maple tree that stood between the McCarthys' lawn and the Shapiros', the chalk dust was so faint all it did was paint the veins of the leaves, until it seemed as if the white lines of skeletons peered through the dark.

Just before dawn, Ace woke up again. When he had fallen asleep it was summer, now he was freezing cold. The last of the season's fireflies were drawn to the warmth of his room, and they came to the screen in his window, their green light growing fainter. Ace rolled out of bed and pulled a blanket around his shoulders. He went to the window and put both hands on the screen. The fireflies congregated in the center of his palms; when they lit up, his hands looked watery and green. The last few stars were hanging over the Southern State. It was still so dark that it took a while before Ace realized that what he was looking at was the new owner of the Olivera house, perched up on her roof, cleaning the leaves out of her gutter with a broom beneath the clear, black sky.

Across the street, Joe Hennessy was standing in his driveway. It wasn't unusual for him to be out at odd hours; he hadn't been able to sleep for two weeks, not since he was promoted to detective. He could sense the outline of his gun against his chest. Even when it was in the night-table drawer, he could always feel his gun, the way they said you could feel a part of your body you had lost.

Maybe he was sick, maybe that was why he heard thunder when-

ever he put his head to his pillow. Since the promotion, all someone
had to do at the station house was jangle some loose change in his
pocket and Hennessy would reach for his gun. He had been trying to
make plainclothes for two years, but as soon as he gave up his uniform
something had gone wrong. In the past few days he had completely
lost his sense of taste; he'd stood at the refrigerator and guzzled half a
jar of black-olive water, thinking it was grape juice, until an olive slid
down his throat. Tonight at supper he realized he could eat pepper
right out of his hand and not even flinch. He was hearing things
wrong, too. The telephone would ring and he'd go to open the front
door. His daughter would beg for a piggyback ride and he'd have to
ask her to repeat herself, again and again, as if she were speaking a
foreign language.

Earlier in the evening, when the children were watching television and his wife was in the kitchen fixing coffee, Hennessy had found
himself at his own front door. He was sweating, ready to explode. He
knew that men went crazy all the time for no reason. He picked them
up outside bars on Saturday nights, and they always seemed shocked
as angels when they realized the damage they'd done. One look at
their own bloodied hands and they'd start to swoon. But Hennessy
wasn't like these men. He had always wanted to be a cop, not so
much because the law inspired him, but because he was addicted to
order. He liked to know his shirts would be hanging on the left side of
the closet; he liked to know he'd be having tunafish casserole and rice
every Friday night, although he preferred steak. He was even-tem-
pered, with the confidence of a big man who had easy good looks, and
he didn't take most things personally. He was the one they usually
sent over to the elementary school on Safety Day because he looked
like a cop. All he had to do was walk into the auditorium and the kids
would quiet down.

In a way this had complicated things for Hennessy; hotheads made
detective more easily. They were flashy; they looked for trouble. But
Hennessy, you could depend on him. He knew to drive slowly when
he received a call that teenagers were gathered behind the high
school, to give them a last chance to ditch their beer bottles when
they saw his red light. He knew to be careful when he lifted up an old
woman who had fallen down her basement steps. Lost dogs came to
him when he whistled; children put their hands in his when he

crossed them at the light on Harvey's Turnpike. He inspired confidence, and he was pleased with all he'd managed: a house of his own, two kids who knew not to talk back, a wife who still looked good to him.

But all along, even before the promotion, there was something wrong. There were times when he knew something was going to happen before it did. He'd get a spooky feeling along the base of his neck, as if he'd just walked through a spider's web, and then he'd know. He'd be sitting in his patrol car, and he'd get that feeling, and then it would happen. Not a routine call on his radio about speeders headed his way or fire alarms set off. No, it would happen when the air was heavy and still, when he was driving down a shady side street, or having a cup of coffee behind the wheel, and then, before he could even stop to think, he'd have to toss the coffee out the window so it wouldn't slosh all over him when he took off. It had happened a few days before his promotion, when a woman left her baby carriage outside the A&P. The carriage had rolled off the curb and into the parking lot; a car pulling out had just missed the damned thing as Hennessy leapt out of the patrol car so he could grab the baby, who had been sound asleep. Hennessy stood there sweating as the baby opened its eyes and stared hard into his face with complete trust. The feeling had come over him again the next afternoon down at the station house, and when Hennessy turned he saw two cops about to go at it, both of them furious over nothing more important than a screwup in the schedule.

This feeling, this premonition or expectation, or whatever the hell it was, always took Hennessy by surprise, and once in a while he'd have a false alarm. He'd reach for the back of his neck, just waiting for something to go wrong, a light bulb to explode, a fight to break out, and nothing would happen. The kids would be in bed, Ellen would be listening to the radio, and that's when the tingling would start and he'd find himself scared to death right there in his own house, on his own street. Tonight it had begun after midnight. He and Ellen had twin beds, and Hennessy was much too big for his bed, his feet always hung off the edge. Yet when he'd awakened he felt completely lost beneath the sheets. He'd wanted the promotion; he'd fought for it. Why was it, then, that getting what he wanted made him feel so hollow? Why was he standing out in his driveway at the

hour when the milkman's truck turned the corner onto Hemlock?
Now that he was a detective he was privy to things he never knew
about before. Hardly state secrets—he could have found out much of
it when he was in uniform, if he listened to gossip, if he read the news,
but he realized he had never wanted to hear about certain cases. It
wasn't ten-dollar speeding tickets and school assemblies now, it was
dirtier business, and that was why he needed to be out here while the
rest of his neighbors were in bed; he needed to believe that people
could still sleep comfortably with their doors and windows unlocked.

This week he had been called in to a domestic. His first. The patrol
officers had been waiting for him on the front stoop of a house he had
never noticed before, at the edge of the neighborhood. Two neighbors had made anonymous complaints right after supper, but when
the patrolmen arrived everyone clammed up. Hennessy stood outside the house with the officers, Sorenson and Brewer, and they all
smoked cigarettes to give the couple inside a chance to cool off.
Sorenson and Brewer had been delighted to leave; Hennessy had
always felt the same when he was in their shoes, but now he was in
plainclothes, he was the one stuck here, knocking on the door.

The guy who finally opened up when Hennessy showed his badge
through a crack in the door was a hard case. Hennessy had seen
dozens like him. But he'd never before had to insist on being taken
into one of their living rooms. The house looked fine from the outside, the shutters hung straight, the grass was cut. But inside, the
place was a disaster. Hennessy had been spoiled by Ellen's housekeeping; he never thought about dust or dirty laundry. Here, everything was neglected. The living room was unnaturally dark, as
though it had never been painted. The couch cushions were ripped
and yellow stuffing showed, and there were greasy-looking blocks
piled up on the floor. There was the stench of urine, and a mean
whiskey smell over that.

"You don't have any rights to be in my house," the guy had told
Hennessy, and he had his chest puffed out as if he were actually
proud of the stinking mess around them.

Hennessy had to calm him down, then advise him that there'd
been two complaints about the fighting that had gone on. The walls
of the house, one complainant had sworn, had been shaking.

"Oh, sure," the guy had said, satisfied in some way. "I've got great neighbors here. I'll bet not one of them had the guts to leave their name."

That was true, but a complaint was a complaint and Hennessy had to ask to look around. He asked as nicely as he could, but God, his heart had been pounding. The house made him feel trapped; the squalor grated against his bones. He found the wife in the kitchen, slapping some hamburgers into a frying pan, even though it was much too late for supper. Hennessy had to explain himself all over again, to her back, because she refused to face him. She had blond hair, and she wore a cotton dress with buttons up the back. Hennessy guessed she wasn't more than twenty-five. He went on about the neighbors' complaints while the guy stood in the doorway behind him, a little too close for Hennessy's taste. When Hennessy finished, the wife said, "I've got nothing to say," in such a flat tone Hennessy almost believed her. He was tempted to get the hell out of there right then; his throat was dry and he'd have given anything for a beer. But he began to feel something along the base of his neck. He looked down and saw that the wife's legs were purple with bruises.

Oh, shit, he thought. Goddamn it.

She had put another hamburger down into the pan and the meat sizzled and gave off a rancid odor.

"Do you mind turning around while we talk?" Hennessy said.

Hennessy had been right; she wasn't more than twenty-five, maybe younger. Her lip was split and there was a circle that would soon turn purple around her eye. But what got to Hennessy, what made him take a step backward, was the way she looked at him, with such hatred you would have thought he'd been the one who'd struck her.

"What happened to you?" Hennessy asked. He could feel her husband behind him. He half expected the woman to laugh in his face.

"Nothing," she said.

"What I'd like to know," the guy said from behind him, "is what gives you the right to waltz in here whenever you want?"

Hennessy faced the husband and pulled back his sport coat to reveal his holster. "This," he said.

The husband quickly moved back. Hennessy had known a gun would matter to a guy like this. He knew he was lucky to be six two, because in this house, force was what mattered.

"So, what happened?" Hennessy asked the wife again.

"I fell," she said. "Against the stove."

"Yeah," Hennessy said. "The stove is right at eye level."

The wife stared right through him.

"I have to look through the rest of the house," Hennessy told the husband.

"Jesus fucking Christ," the guy said. "My own goddamned house!"

Hennessy went back through the dining room and living room to the rear hallway. He knew the floor plan by heart, the house was the exact same model as his own, so no one had to tell him where the children's rooms were. He opened the door to the first bedroom and took the flashlight from his belt. A toddler was asleep, holding on to a stuffed animal. The floor was littered with toys and trash and there was a pile of dirty diapers in one corner. Hennessy quickly closed the door. He hated the idea of getting involved in a domestic; this was personal, this was between a husband and a wife.

In the living room, the guy had switched on the TV. It was a Saturday night, and in his own house Hennessy's boy, Stevie, was probably watching the same channel. *Bonanza.* Hennessy stopped in the bathroom doorway. He saw some blood on a towel draped over the shower curtain; the wife had probably washed her face when Sorenson and Brewer first arrived, and cleaned off her split lip. Hennessy told himself all he had to see was the blood, it was none of his business if the tub and toilet were filthy, he didn't need to ask himself what kind of woman would keep her house like this. But it was his job to look in their bedroom, to see the rumpled sheets on their bed and the piles of dirty laundry on the floor, in the same corner where he and Ellen had their pine bureau. Hennessy went on to the last bedroom, the one where his three-year-old, Suzanne, slept at home. It took a while before what was so different about this room registered. This room was neat, that was it. The toys were stacked in boxes, and pictures of animals, horses and golden retrievers, had been carefully cut out of magazines and thumbtacked to the walls. Hennessy moved the beam of his flashlight around the room and found a small girl of seven or eight beneath a frayed blanket.

"Jesus H. Christ," he could hear the guy in the living room say to his wife, "this jerk's going to take all night."

The little girl who kept her room so neat was doing a good job of faking sleep, certainly better than Hennessy's own kids when he checked on them. But just when he might have been fooled into believing she was asleep, Hennessy heard her quick breathing. If he hadn't had children himself he might not have recognized a child awake, but he did, and he went over to the bed and crouched down beside it.

"Did you see what happened?" he whispered.

"Nothing happened," the little girl whispered back, and that was when Hennessy knew she had seen.

"Someone was being mean," Hennessy said.

The little girl shook her head no and moved deeper into her blanket.

"You have a real pretty room," Hennessy said. "I like the pictures on the wall. My little girl is crazy about horses, too."

Hennessy could feel himself winning her over; it was so easy he could have wept. The little girl propped herself up on her elbows to get a better look at him.

"My daughter likes those yellow horses, the ones with white manes," Hennessy said.

"Palominos," the little girl said.

"Is he ever mean to you?" Hennessy whispered.

"Just her," the girl said.

Hennessy realized he had been keeping his hand inside his jacket, close to his gun.

"Does your little girl have her own horse?" the girl asked.

"Our backyard is just like yours," Hennessy said. "It's much too small. A horse would never fit."

"Oh," said the girl, disappointed. "But you could take her riding, you know. She'd love that."

The door was quickly flung open, but the little girl was quicker. She lay down flat and closed her eyes and her breathing grew heavy, like a sleeper's. The girl's mother stood in the doorway; with the light in the hall behind her you couldn't see her bruises. She looked like some pretty young woman who hadn't had time to comb her hair.

"Don't you dare wake my girl," she snarled at Hennessy.

Hennessy stood up and his knees cracked. He went over to the woman; he forced himself to sound reasonable, as if he walked into somebody's life this way every night. "You can press charges right now," he said.

The woman snorted. "Not on your life," she said.

"I could escort him from the house," Hennessy told her.

"Oh, yeah?" the woman whispered. "And then are you going to spend the rest of your life sitting on my front stoop so you can keep him from coming back? Are you going to watch out for us after tonight?"

Hennessy felt like a fool. He knew the little girl was listening. What exactly was he offering them?

"You can get a court order," he said.

"Look," the woman said. "I don't know what you're talking about."

"All right," Hennessy said. God, he said it too damned quickly. He pulled out one of his cards, which was still so new you could smell the ink on it, and handed it to the woman. "You can call me anytime if you change your mind."

The woman snorted again, as if he were crazy, and she shoved the card back at him. Hennessy followed her out of the bedroom, but before he did he slid his card under the little girl's mattress. The guy was waiting for him in the living room. He acted as if he were watching *Bonanza,* he acted as if he didn't have a care in the world, but Hennessy knew he was waiting. The guy stood up from the couch slowly. He looked at Hennessy, saw he'd found nothing, and broke into a grin.

"Tell those neighbors of mine to go fuck themselves," the guy said.

All Hennessy wanted was the front door.

"This is my house, got it?" the guy goaded him.

"I got it," Hennessy said. "But if you don't keep it down, I'll be back. You get that."

Hennessy took off and he didn't look back. He drove straight to the White Castle on Harvey's Turnpike, but he couldn't eat anything he ordered, he couldn't even swallow his coffee. He kept thinking about the house from the outside, how it looked like any other house in the neighborhood. He could have been blindfolded and still have found the oil burner in the basement. You couldn't tell a goddamned thing from the outside, and it made him wonder exactly what he'd been seeing for the past six years when he looked at the houses on his block. He felt sick. He might as well have been the one who punched that woman in the face, because he knew it had happened and, with no complaint from her, he had to walk away. And the worst of it was, he'd been relieved, and that was why, nearly a week later, he was standing in his driveway at dawn, waiting for the milkman.

He tried to think of his own children, asleep in their beds. He thought about the grocery money his wife always kept in a cream pitcher on a shelf above the stove, about the clean, wet smell of shirts as she ironed in the morning. By now he should have forgotten the pictures tacked up in the little girl's bedroom; he shouldn't even remember the shape and color of the bruise forming above her mother's eye. He could hear the hum of the milkman's truck as it shifted gears. Across the street, at Olivera's old place, the weeds had grown since Hennessy had cut the lawn; they were as tall as a man's thigh. The truck parked, and Hennessy could hear the milk bottles clink against each other as the milkman reached into the back of his truck. All Hennessy wanted was for everything to stay the same. That's all he was asking for.

The milkman came up and surprised him. "How you doing?" he said, as if Hennessy stood out here to meet the truck every day at dawn.

"Cold," Hennessy said, and he realized that he was. The weather had changed and he was wearing only a short-sleeved shirt and chinos.

"Two quarts and a cottage cheese," the milkman said.

Hennessy nodded, although he hadn't the faintest idea of what Ellen had ordered. The milkman gave Hennessy the bottles of milk and the container of cottage cheese.

"See you," the milkman said, and he took his metal carryall and headed for his truck, then pulled away slowly, since he was going only as far as the Shapiros'.

If there isn't a sign, Hennessy told himself, everything will stay the same. I'll put this milk in the refrigerator and go back to bed and be grateful that my children are safe whenever they go out in the street to play. I'll eat scrambled eggs every morning and I'll never ask for anything again. Just let me be, he thought, but it was a little too late for that. He'd wanted detective and he'd gotten it, and now he was stuck with the job and everything it forced him to know. And then he made a big mistake. He should have turned around and walked up the path to his house, but instead he looked up at the last few stars, and they filled him with yearning the way diamonds did other men. He turned his gaze east, to see if the sun was rising, and that was when he saw the woman up on Olivera's roof, cleaning out her rain gutters, oblivious to anything else on the street, and Hennessy realized that it was too late to make any deals. He had already asked for things, and what happened was what always happened whenever a desire was granted. He wanted more.

By seven thirty you could smell coffee and toast, you could hear the metal milk boxes open and shut, and the sound of cars idling as the fathers on the block got ready to commute to work. Soon the houses would be empty, except for the mothers and the youngest children, toddlers learning to walk and babies set down for their naps, because by eight fifteen bands of children headed down Hemlock Street, the boys up front, hitting each other and stopping to wrestle on the lawns in their new chinos and plaid shirts, the girls following, their hair combed into neat braids, their knee socks pulled up high.

Billy Silk watched them from the cement stoop in front of his house. He was still wearing his pajamas and his feet were bare. Inside, his mother was fast asleep. The baby had awakened at six, and Billy had given him a juice bottle, which James sucked on dreamily in his crib. Mr. Popper had followed Billy outside, and now the cat sat beside him, licking his paws and ignoring Billy. When Billy ran his hand over Mr. Popper's fur, the cat arched his back, but he didn't stop grooming himself. He didn't even blink. Billy found himself missing Happy. Early in the mornings, when everyone was asleep, Billy used to get a carrot out of the refrigerator and hold it through the wire of Happy's cage. The rabbit always seemed grateful; he would let Billy pet him through the meshing, he would drum his foot up and down with pleasure.

This morning the air felt cool. Billy Silk wished he had slippers. He was eating stale cookies for breakfast. He had already had a Yoo-Hoo, which he drained while standing in front of the open refrigerator. If he was still hungry after the cookies, he planned to eat one of the green tomatoes his mother had left to ripen on the windowsill. Lately Billy found he was eating a huge amount of food. He figured they must be running out of money, because his mother had been pretending she was on a diet, when anyone could see she didn't need it. Every day Billy swore he would eat less, but he could never keep his promise, even though all his mother ever had was black coffee, grapefruit halves sprinkled with sugar, and glasses of skim milk.

Nora would never have admitted it, but Billy knew she kept finding more and more wrong with the house. A family of squirrels was living in the garage, and the refrigerator was on the blink so that sometimes the milk went sour and other times the eggs froze in their shells. When it rained the bathroom sink filled with water, and they had found a garter snake making its way across the linoleum in the basement. Nora insisted that everything was great; or, if it wasn't exactly great, it would be soon. She had begun selling magazine subscriptions by phone, and she talked herself into a job as a manicurist at Armand's, the beauty shop next to the A&P. For the past few days, Nora had been practicing on herself, so that the house smelled like nail-polish remover, and Billy found emery boards on the kitchen counters and in between the pillows of the couch. But if it was so great, why was she drinking coffee and eating grapefruit, why had no one on the block talked to them yet?

Billy hunched over on the stoop as he watched the last of the children walk to school. They all had lunch boxes, and Billy knew that Nora had made his lunch the night before, in case she overslept, and that she had put his sandwich and his orange into a small brown paper bag. He thought of his father's blackout trick, the piece of magic in which nothing was left but his clothes, and he wondered if you could inherit a talent like that. He could almost believe he was becoming invisible; he could feel something curling up inside himself. While Billy was eating the last cookie, Ace McCarthy came outside. He was wearing a white shirt his mother had ironed while he had breakfast, and a pair of black slacks the Saint had made him promise he'd throw out because they were so tight. He stood in his driveway and shook a cigarette out of his pack of Marlboros.

"Hey." He nodded to Billy Silk across the lawn.

Billy stared at Ace and chewed his cookie. Ace was about to go get

Danny Shapiro so they could walk to school together. Instead, he crossed the lawn. There was dew on the grass and it left droplets on his black boots.

"Damn it," Ace said when he saw that his boots were wet. He went over to Billy and smoked his cigarette, keeping an eye out for his mother next door, just in case she looked out her window and caught him smoking. "You live here?" Ace asked.

Billy nodded and curled his toes.

Ace pointed his cigarette at Billy and closed one eye thoughtfully. Smoke circled around him. "Second grade," he guessed.

"Third," Billy Silk said.

"Poor guy," Ace said. He noticed that Billy was still in his pajamas. "Your father's going to let you have it."

"Nah." Billy rolled a raisin over his tongue. "He's gone."

"Gone?" Ace said, surprised. "What are you? An orphan?"

"Nah," Billy said. "He's in Las Vegas."

"No kidding," Ace said, impressed.

The front door opened and Nora stood there in her nightgown, holding James on her hip.

"You should be dressed," Nora called to Billy. "Your feet will freeze. You'll be late. Gee whillikers, buddy, let's move it."

Ace McCarthy stared at the front door after Nora had closed it.

"That's your mother?" Ace asked, and when Billy nodded, Ace shook his head. "Wow," he said.

"What's that supposed to mean?" Billy said, insulted, although he wasn't certain why.

"Nothing," Ace said, stubbing out his cigarette under his boot heel. "She just doesn't look like somebody's mother."

"Yeah," Billy Silk said, and in a way he knew what Ace meant.

"See ya," Ace said. He walked down the driveway as if he had all the time in the world to get to school. Billy sat on the stoop until Ace had called for Danny Shapiro. He watched them head down Hemlock Street, and then he felt silly being outside in his pajamas, so he went in and got dressed while Nora fed the baby his breakfast.

"Let's go, let's go," Nora kept calling, even though she wasn't ready herself. She appeared in the doorway of Billy's bedroom in a black dress and black high heels as he was examining his new blue looseleaf. Around her waist she had on a black-and-gold cinch belt with a big gold buckle.

"There's nothing to be nervous about," Nora told Billy.

Her face was flushed, and today her nails were passion-fruit pink.

"I'm not nervous," Billy said, although actually he thought he might faint.

The elementary school was only three blocks away, but because they were late, Nora drove. The Volkswagen hadn't had time to warm up; it chugged and bucked and the engine threatened to cut out completely. Nora pulled over across from the U-shaped driveway where buses were parked. There were only a few latecomers running through the doors, but the air still smelled of peanut butter and Ivory soap and gasoline. Nora took the key out of the ignition. She looked in the rearview mirror, adjusted her gold headband, and fluffed out her bangs.

"So?" Nora said to Billy.

"So I'm not going," Billy said.

"Oh, yes you are," Nora told him.

"You don't even look like somebody's mother," Billy said.

"I'll take that as a compliment," Nora said. "So thanks a million, buddy."

Nora stepped out, then went around the car, opened the rear door, and picked up the baby. She waited for Billy on the curb. Sooner or later, he had to come out of the car. Another mother was leaving the school; she was wearing Bermuda shorts and a kerchief over her hair. Nora readjusted her cinch belt. She had a pair of Bermuda shorts somewhere; she used to wear them when she washed the floors in their old apartment. She scrunched down so she could see herself in the side-view mirror. Maybe she shouldn't have worn eye makeup; maybe she shouldn't have sprayed herself with Ambush. She tapped on the window and Billy looked over at her.

"Come on," Nora mouthed through the glass.

Billy unlocked his door, then got out and followed his mother across the street. Nora's high heels made a clicking sound as they walked toward the principal's office. She had James hoisted over her shoulder, and the baby reached out his arms toward Billy and shouted, "Baba," his voice echoing down the hall. Billy hung back, so that he wouldn't be seen with them; he held his lunch bag tightly.

"What are you, a slowpoke?" Nora called over her shoulder. She should have made Billy bacon and eggs for breakfast to give him extra energy. She used to make that for Roger before he went out to perform, until she found out he was performing with his girlfriends more often than he was onstage. The morning he left her, Nora had given him a mixture of henna and onions and eggs, and that had fixed his wagon. When Roger finally called from Las Vegas he confided that he'd had diarrhea for over two thousand miles. As if she cared! As if he expected free medical advice!

"Well, great," Nora had told him. "That just proves what a shit you are."

When they reached the principal's office, Nora had to search through her pocketbook for Billy's medical files and the report from his previous school. She dumped everything out; tubes of lipstick and mentholated cigarettes rolled across the principal's desk.

"I know they're in here," Nora said brightly. She set the baby on the floor; Cheerios fell out of the pockets of his corduroy pants. Billy Silk sat in a cushioned chair and looked up at the acoustical tile in the ceiling. James pulled himself up to stand by holding on to Billy's leg, and Billy casually swung his leg back and forth until the baby collapsed on the floor.

"He's very advanced," Nora told the principal when she handed over the files.

"We'll put him in third grade today," the principal said, "but then we'll have to test him to see if he's ready."

"Go ahead, test him," Nora said. "But let me tell you he can practically read your mind before your thoughts are fully formed."

"He's had his polio shots?" the principal asked.

"Oh, yes," Nora said. Without turning to Billy, she whispered, "Your hair."

Billy stopped pulling on his hair. Nora leaned down and gathered up stray Cheerios.

"I love this school," Nora said, as the principal guided them out to the hallway. "It's so cheerful."

Billy studied the pale gray walls; he was certain they were the exact shade of gray used to paint prison cells.

"Third grade is two doors past the gym," the principal said. "Do you think you can find your way, Billy?"

Billy looked up at the principal for the first time.

"He's in Las Vegas," Billy said.

"Who's that?" the principal said, flustered.

"My father," Billy said.

The principal turned to Nora. "There wasn't any mention of your husband in Billy's files."

"Las Vegas," Nora said. "Nevada," she added as she shoved Billy in front of her and guided him toward the gym. "Stop listening in to people," Nora told him.

"I can find the room by myself," Billy said.

"I mean it," Nora said. "People don't like being eavesdropped on."

They stopped outside the door to the third-grade classroom. Billy could see an American flag hanging from a wooden pole above the windows.

"All right," Billy told his mother, although he didn't know whether or not it was in his power to keep his promise. It might be like his vow not to eat. "I'll stop."

"Good," Nora said. "Do you have everything? Looseleaf? Pencils?"

Billy nodded.

"Gee whiz," Nora said. "You're so pale."

She touched Billy's forehead to feel for a fever. They could hear the teacher inside asking someone to hand out the readers.

"It's not going to kill you, you know," Nora said. "All you have to do is relax."

"Yeah," Billy said.

"Just expect them to like you and they will," Nora said.

"You can have one when you get out to the car," Billy said.

Nora pursed her lips and gave him a little push. She waited until he had gone into the room and closed the door behind him; then she hurried out to her car, and the first thing she did once she had gotten James into the backseat, was take out her pack of cigarettes and immediately light one.

So Nora was wrong, she'd been wrong about other things before, she wasn't perfect. If she were perfect, would she be manicuring other women's nails on Saturdays while a sixteen-year-old neighbor she barely knew watched her children? If she were perfect, would she be trying to unclog the bathtub while her ex-husband was sending photographs of himself in front of the Sands Hotel, where Frank Sinatra was appearing nightly? So she couldn't fit into her red toreador pants anymore, so she'd sold only fourteen subscriptions to *Life* and three to *Ladies' Home Journal* in two weeks, so the kids in his class hated Billy, so what? Things changed, didn't they? She planned to make a huge platter of cupcakes, frosted pink and dotted with gumdrops, to take in to Billy's class at the end of the week. She'd get a class list and go right down it, inviting every goddamned child over, popping fresh popcorn for them, letting them run wild, bribing them with lemonade and cap guns. She'd start selling Tupperware, she could bring the baby with her into people's living rooms, she could have Tupperware parties right in her kitchen. And if she kept eating grapefruit, she'd fit into the toreador pants soon enough.

The stars, after all, were much brighter here than they'd ever been in the city. The evenings smelled like cherries instead of soot. Sometimes, late at night, after the children were asleep, Nora went out and walked across the lawn in her bare feet. You could feel autumn approaching here, the grass was colder, the mornings darker. Nora didn't think about anyone kissing her, she didn't think about dancing all night, or holidays spent at the seaside in a hotel room with a man whose name she didn't even know. She put one of her Elvis albums on the old record player and figured out how to hang the storm windows. She sang "Don't Be Cruel" and lined the broiler pan in her oven with tin foil. She pulled her hair back into a ponytail and put on one of Roger's old shirts. The other mothers on the street could see her, up on a stepladder with a rag in her hand. Beside the ladder, her baby played in the dirt and she didn't seem to notice that his socks were black and his hands were caked with mud. The baby put twigs and fallen leaves into his mouth, and all he wore was a light woolen sweater over thin pajamas. The mothers on the block thought they could hear her singing "A Fool Such as I" as she washed her windows. They saw the bottle of Windex in her hand and they noticed that she wore no wedding ring.

"Maybe her finger's swollen and her ring is on one of the hooks along with her coffee cups," Lynne Wineman said.

"You think so?" Ellen Hennessy said. "Then where's her husband?"

They thought that one over carefully. They were sitting in Ellen

Hennessy's living room and they had a perfect view of their new neighbor through Ellen's front window.

"Traveling salesman?" Donna Durgin said, but everyone knew Donna was extremely naïve, and they overlooked her innocence just as they did her excess weight.

"Are you thinking what I'm thinking?" Lynne Wineman asked Ellen Hennessy.

Ellen's boy, Stevie, was at school, and her little girl, Suzanne, was having a tea party in her room with Lynne Wineman's two little girls. Donna's eighteen-month-old, Melanie, was asleep on a blanket under the coffee table.

"You bet," Ellen Hennessy said. "It's the only explanation."

"What?" Donna Durgin said. "What is?"

But they couldn't answer her, they couldn't bring themselves to say the word *divorced* out loud, and yet there it was, across the street, a hand without a ring holding a Windex bottle. They were all so completely married, and they were in it together. Ellen Hennessy and Donna Durgin and Lynne Wineman saw each other nearly every day. In the summer they had picnics for their children in each other's backyards, with Hawaiian Punch and bologna sandwiches, they lent each other's children clothes theirs had outgrown, they went food shopping together, they played canasta while their children played with wooden blocks and left a carpet of graham cracker crumbs all over the floors.

The women decided to phone Marie McCarthy. And when she came over, they sat around her in a semicircle, eager to hear her opinion of their new neighbor. Marie's children were grown, and the other mothers didn't see her quite as much, but each of them knew you could always call Marie in the middle of the night when your littlest child was burning up with fever and she'd know exactly what to do. She would tell you to rub a little rum on your baby's gums when his molars were coming in and nothing the doctor had suggested would ease his crying; she had great recipes for lasagna and meatloaf with green onions and tomato sauce; she'd watch your kids if you had a dentist appointment, or if you desperately needed a new dress and didn't want to drag the kids with you to S. Klein or, if the dress was for a really special occasion, A&S. If you had a fight with your husband, one he might not have even noticed, you could sit in Marie's kitchen and she wouldn't bother you with questions. She'd just give you cookies and tea and let you sit there until you could find it in your heart to go home.

She'd been through it all, and that gave you hope, but even Marie had trouble with the idea of a divorced woman alone on their street. She should have already asked a newcomer over for coffee, she should have offered to sit for her kids. But she knew something wasn't right as soon as she saw that woman in that beat-up Volkswagen with just her two boys. Where was the man? That was what Marie asked the other mothers. "I think you've got a pretty good idea," she whispered, so that even Donna Durgin, who had never met a divorced person in her entire life, figured out Nora's situation. No one had to say it, but the word was there, it had entered their vocabularies and now hung above them, a cloud over their coffee cups, and maybe that was why they didn't speak, and why Marie passed out some of the Tootsie Rolls she had brought over for the children to their mothers instead, even though candy couldn't begin to get rid of the sour taste in their mouths.

As usual, the men on the street noticed nothing. Oh, they saw the Volkswagen and they figured it needed its tires aligned. They saw that no one had fixed the broken shutters, and they themselves would have gotten a bucket of cement and fixed the steps leading to the stoop as soon as they'd moved in. As a detective, Joe Hennessy prided himself on picking up details no one else would bother with, but later that day, when he came home and put his gun in the night table, he didn't notice that his wife had bitten her fingernails down to the quick. He changed out of his sport coat, then filled up a plastic bucket with soapy water. It was still light enough in the evenings to get some work done around the house, so Hennessy went out to wash his car. When he carried the bucket out to the driveway, water spilled over the sides and left a trail behind him. He put down the bucket, and as he reached for a sponge he had that feeling along the back of his neck. He thought about moonlight, he thought about his neighbor up on her roof in the dark, he felt as if he needed to run somewhere, as fast as he could. The white Volkswagen parked in the Oliveras' driveway shone in the last of the day's light.

Hennessy shielded his eyes and looked across the street. There was the baby, out in its playpen in the front yard. Hennessy thought the baby might be waving at him, or maybe it was just grabbing for stray blades of grass, because there was a whirlwind of grass as Nora Silk came around the side of the house, pushing Olivera's old mower. She had all her weight behind the mower, which chugged like a locomotive and threw off black smoke. Right behind her was the boy, who dragged a tall wooden rake.

Hennessy wondered what kind of man let his wife work in the yard. A flower garden was an exception, women liked that kind of thing, but a well-kept lawn was a different story. And here was the wife, working like a dog, wearing leather gloves so she wouldn't get blisters on her hands, wobbling over the weeds in her sling-back pumps. Hennessy watched Nora struggle to make a turn in the grass. The mower got stuck in the tallest of the weeds, it wouldn't go backward or forward, and although the motor would start, it kept cutting out on her. Hennessy had been Olivera's neighbor for five years, but he had been inside the house only once, near the end, when the old man's arthritis was acting up and Hennessy had gone over to bleed the radiators with a dime and check out the boiler in the basement, which, as it turned out, wasn't really necessary, since the old man had died right after Thanksgiving. Hennessy tossed his sponge into the bucket of water and walked across the street.

"Goddamn it," she was saying, right in front of the boy. Or at least that's what Hennessy thought she was saying, but it was hard to hear over the roar of the old mower. There was grass everywhere, in the folds of her cotton shirt, in the baby's hair. Hennessy could taste the grass in his throat and it made him thirsty; his neck felt worse than ever.

"It's jammed," Hennessy said—shouted, really—and Nora turned to him, startled. She wasn't quite as young as he'd thought, but her eyes were blacker than he could believe.

Hennessy reached down and turned off the mower.

"The grass is caked up," he told her, and then for some reason he felt foolish. He reached down and pulled out some of the clippings that were stuck between the blades. The boy leaned against his rake and watched; the baby pulled himself up by the rim of his playpen.

"There you go," Hennessy said. He stood up and clapped his hands together, but he couldn't get the grass off his sweaty palms. "That should do it."

"Well, gee," Nora said. She could feel her heart beating too fast. She reached up and fluffed out her bangs and wished she didn't have her hair pulled back in a ponytail. She tried to look away from Hennessy but couldn't; it was almost as if she had to look at him, as if something would break if she looked away. "Thanks a million," she said.

"You should get your husband to spring for a new mower," Hennessy said.

"A new mower," Nora said, considering.

"Who's lazy?" the boy said.

"What?" Hennessy said.

"Really, thanks a million," Nora said. "It's great to have neighbors."

"Yeah," Hennessy said.

The baby in the playpen was reaching up his arms and crowing. Nora managed to look away from Hennessy; she went over and picked James up, then balanced him on her hip. Across the street, Stevie had come outside to shout that if his father didn't come home for supper right now they'd be late for Little League.

"It's the last week of baseball," Hennessy explained. "That's my boy. First base."

"Nice boy," Nora said. She came over and put one hand on Billy's shoulder. "I'll bet you kids will really hit it off," she said hopefully.

Billy looked up at her as if she were crazy. Stevie had already begun to torment him in school; twice he'd stolen Billy's lunch and thrown it in the trash, he'd called Billy jerkface and fink and laughed hysterically when Billy couldn't climb the ropes in gym.

"That guy?" Billy said, incredulous. "You've got to be kidding."

"Kids today," Nora said as an apology to Hennessy. She gave Billy a little jab with the toe of one of her pumps. She had no idea why this neighbor of hers looked so good to her; he was tall, but he wasn't even handsome, he didn't have hypnotic eyes like Elvis, he didn't have a great smile like Roger. Roger's smile could drive you crazy, as if he knew what was inside of you. Maybe it was Hennessy's hands that got to her; they were wide and strong. She looked at his fingers and wondered what his touch would feel like on her shoulders, on her thigh.

"Little League," Nora said, thoughtfully.

The baby gave a wail and dove for Nora's breasts, leaning his head into her shirt.

Jesus, Hennessy thought.

Nora quickly shifted the baby under her arm, but Hennessy had seen a flash of her skin.

"Billy would love Little League," Nora said.

"Me?" Billy said.

I have to get out of here, Hennessy told himself.

"Sign-ups are in May," Hennessy said, as he backed away toward the sidewalk.

"That's good to know," Nora called after him. "I'd love to meet your wife sometime."

"Yeah," Hennessy agreed.

"Well, I would," Nora said to Billy when she saw the look on his face.

Hennessy waved and kept on, across the street. Nora studied his back and bit her lip. She simply refused to think about men.

"I told you people were nice here," Nora said to Billy. She jiggled James under her arm and rolled the mower back into the garage. "This is going to be great," she told Billy.

Nora went inside to fix macaroni and cheese; she always had trouble with casseroles: they came out too watery—you had to eat the noodles with a spoon—and sometimes she just threw the whole thing out and served Frosted Flakes or beef jerky on white bread. Billy picked up the rake and went to work gathering the cut grass. The rake was too tall for him, and it hurt his shoulders to use it, but Billy didn't care. A few cars passed by, and although he heard them, he didn't bother to look up. He was practicing the blackout trick, and he was getting pretty good at it; if you didn't know better, you would swear a pair of jeans and a blue sweatshirt were raking the grass all on their own. If he worked really hard, gathering the grass into neat piles, then heaping armfuls into the silver garbage cans, he could make their house look just like everyone else's. So he stayed out until dark, and while the other children on the block were finishing their dinners or playing ball or getting ready for bed, Billy Silk was still raking grass, and by then he had forgotten how much his shoulders hurt.

3

ALL SOULS

On James's first birthday Nora was pleased to find that he still didn't resemble anyone. There wasn't a trace of any family lineage when you studied his face; it was as if he'd just appeared one October day, without heritage or past, born out of labor and light rather than genes. Like all October babies, he was a good sleeper and liked the cold. He'd pull off his woolen socks and throw off his blanket at night. He'd point at the window and wail until Nora let him sleep with it open, and then he'd quiet down right away and stare at the stars that formed an arch above their house. He still smiled easily and amused himself, and although he'd taken a few steps, he was in no great hurry to walk. Whenever he stumbled into Nora's arms, she would think it wasn't possible for her to love him any more than she did, and yet each day she did; she loved him so much that she discovered that her hands and feet had grown a little larger to make room inside her for all that she felt, and because of this she had to go out and buy new boots and gloves and have her high heels stretched by the shoemaker up on the Turnpike.

Nora loved to celebrate birthdays, but because James's fell on a Saturday she didn't have time to make a cake from scratch; she didn't even have time for a mix, because Armand's was so busy she wound up staying till four when she should have been home by two thirty. The only plus about working overtime and having to pay her baby-sitter an extra dollar fifty was that she had that many more customers to whom she could pass out invitations to Tupperware parties.

"I'm not so certain I like this," Armand said when he got hold of an invitation. He had left one of his best customers teased but not combed out so he could talk to Nora privately, over by the sinks.

"Actually, it's very classy," Nora said, thankful that Armand had no idea she was also trying to sell her clients magazine subscriptions. "Salons in Manhattan have fashion shows. They give makeup demonstrations. I should bring my Tupperware right into the shop with me. I could start next week."

Armand thought this over, and finally agreed to a ten percent cut of the profits. Since he'd have no real idea of what the profits were, Nora figured she would slip him a five and that would be that. And even if he found out she was stiffing him, he wouldn't fire her. Nora was good for business. She wore her hair in a French twist and she'd let her nails grow exceptionally long and had found a new shade of polish that suited her—Roman Red—and women who'd never had manicures before asked for the same color. The customers were crazy about her; they rearranged their schedules so they could come to the shop on Saturdays. She had one client who came by bus all the way from East Meadow.

"The hand," Nora always told her clients, "is the window into the soul."

All right, she knew it was supposed to be the eyes, but what was the difference? She held her clients' hands and commented on their cuticles and their skin tones. When she realized that she got bigger tips each time she gave advice on color coordination she stopped talking cuticles. She had a gift for telling a client which colors were right for her, whether shades in the orange family or the scarlet range were best, and she often suggested whole wardrobe changes. "No gray for you," she'd advise a washed-out client. "Purple," she'd whisper to a housewife who was splurging on a manicure for the first time in ages.

On James's birthday, she left Armand's with her tip money folded into an envelope in the pocket of her black car coat. Snips of hair stuck to her sleeves and to the soles of her shoes. She took the bobby pins out of her French twist and shook out her hair as soon as she was out of sight of the beauty parlor, then ran her fingers through her loose hair as she rushed into the A&P. She quickly found what she needed for James's birthday and headed for the front of the checkout line.

"You don't mind taking me first, do you?" she asked the checker, a sweet-faced blonde named Cathy Corrigan, who was so startled by Nora's request that she began to ring her up, even though there was a discontented line stretching over to the fruit bins.

"My baby's birthday," Nora announced to the checkout line. She held up a packet of blue-and-white-striped candles. "You did a good deed," Nora told the checkout girl as she bagged the four packages of Twinkies.

Nora raced home in the Volkswagen, parked, and grabbed the grocery bag. She still loved coming home; she loved the way her high heels sank into the grass as she cut across the lawn, and the sound of crumpled leaves on the front stoop and the way her hand felt on the unlocked door just before she opened it. Rickie Shapiro had put on one of Nora's Elvis records, and even though it sounded scratchy, Nora turned up the volume when she got inside the house. As she hung up her coat, she admired the closet space. She found James in the kitchen, stacking blocks on the floor. Rickie was at the table, singing along with Elvis and painting her nails pink.

"Birthday boy!" Nora said. She picked James up and gave him a big kiss. "How were they?" she asked Rickie.

"Fine," Rickie said. "Except Billy wouldn't come out of his room."

Well, that was nothing new, so Nora put James down, and he clung to her leg while she unwrapped the Twinkies and arranged them on a plate.

"Wrong color," Nora said over her shoulder to Rickie.

"Pink is my color," Rickie said with confidence.

"Okay," Nora said. "Sure. If that's what you want to think."

Rickie blew on her nails so they would dry faster, while Nora got her purse and paid Rickie the six dollars she owed her.

"Pink looks great on me," Rickie said.

"Red," Nora told her. She went to the doorway of the kitchen. "Billy! We're having James's birthday."

"You've got to be kidding," Rickie said. "My mother wouldn't allow me to wear red. Not with my hair."

"Red is your color," Nora said. "Take it or leave it. You know, you

really should stop setting your hair. Just wash it and let it dry naturally."

"And let it frizz up!" Rickie said. "Not on your life."

"All right," Nora said. She was poking candles into the Twinkies.
"Fine. If you want to look like everyone else, instead of going with
your natural beauty, that's your choice. Did James have his bottle?"

"Yeah," Rickie said. Her nails were dry enough for her to put on
her coat. She tossed the bottle of pink nail polish into her purse, but
when she looked at her nails the color looked weaker than she'd
expected. That was what she hated about sitting for Nora Silk's kids:
she always left confused. She didn't even know why she came back;
she didn't need the money that badly. The baby was cute, but Billy
could drive you crazy. Some weeks he'd want to play Monopoly for
three hours straight and other days he wouldn't even talk to her.
He'd stay in his room, wrapped in an old blanket, eating pretzels and
potato chips and looking so mad Rickie didn't dare to speak to him.
Sometimes she thought she could hear him grinding his teeth
through the closed door.

She needed this like a hole in the head. She had always had everything she ever wanted, and, frankly, she felt awful about it sometimes. She developed a habit of giving people things, especially her
best friend, Joan Campo, who had to work Saturdays and Sundays in
her father's deli. She had a new angora sweater she now decided she
would give to Joan; it was seashell pink, and maybe Nora was right
about her coloring, maybe she was more the crimson or scarlet type.
If there was a problem that Rickie faced, it was simply that her father
made more money than most of her friends' fathers. He had a Cadillac Eldorado on order and he was always bringing home clothes from
A&S; he even thought he might be able to get Rickie a job in the
Junior Miss department next summer and she'd have her own ten-
percent employees' discount. Sometimes, especially when she was
with Joan, Rickie didn't think it was fair that good things just seemed
to happen to her family. She had already been to Florida four times.
She knew how to order room service and how to hike up her skirt to
make her crinoline show, and that, Rickie knew, drove boys crazy.
Everyone agreed that her brother was the smartest kid in the school
and the best ballplayer in the town's brief history. But they didn't
know that her mother, Gloria, spoke French, enough to order dinner

in any good restaurant, and that she always wore nylons, even when she was vacuuming.

And still, Rickie kept on sitting for the Silk kids, even though Nora had none of the things Rickie valued in a woman as old as Nora—namely a husband and a decent house. Rickie certainly didn't consider any house in the neighborhood decent; she had a split-level with a pool and a fireplace in mind. By the time she was Nora's age she planned to have not only a husband and a house in Cedarhurst or Great Neck, but also two little girls, whom she'd always imagined she would dress in identical pink outfits, although red bonnets and boots might be interesting.

"I almost forgot. Someone from the subscription company called," Rickie said as she was buttoning her coat.

"Oh, shoot," Nora said. "Did they fire me?"

"You haven't had a sale in two weeks, so they were just checking," Rickie said. "And you owe them fourteen ninety-five for your past subscribers."

"Well, they'll just have to wait," Nora said. She licked her fingers and carried the arrangement of Twinkies over to the table. "Happy birthday," she cooed to James as she stooped to pick him up again. She held him on one hip as she lit the candles. "Come on," she shouted to Billy. "The candles are burning down." She made certain to pocket the matches just in case Billy got the urge to set something aflame, and then she kissed James. "My little pumpkin," she said to him. "My sweetie pie."

Rickie didn't like Twinkies, she was on a diet anyway, but she couldn't take her eyes off Nora and the baby. He really was cute. He was a baby doll. And in the glow of the birthday candles, Nora looked so dreamy and dark with her hair hanging down, straight, like a little girl's. Tonight, Rickie and Joan Campo were double dating at eight. They were meeting two seniors from the math club to see *The Diary of Anne Frank,* which Rickie had seen twice before, so she'd make certain to bring a box of tissues. Rickie knew that whenever she cried her face flushed pink, or maybe it was an extremely pale scarlet.

"You want me next Saturday?" Rickie asked as she was leaving.

"Oh, yeah," Nora said. "I'm stuck at Armand's until my Tupperware takes off. Maybe your mom would like some. I could invite her and some of her friends over this week. Or I could go over to your house."

"I don't think so," Rickie said. "My mother thinks plastic is tacky."

"Well, she's in for a shock," Nora said. "In the future no one will use china or crystal. Just poor, uneducated people who don't know any better. Tell her that, and see if she changes her mind."

"Yeah," Rickie said. "Well, she's not really so interested in the future."

As soon as Rickie had gone, Nora took James and went to search for Billy. He had barricaded his door and it wouldn't budge.

"I'm getting mad," Nora said as she pushed against the bedroom door.

Billy sat on his bed, eating potato chips, his wool blanket around him. Nora had no tolerance for this new attachment to a blanket at his age. At night she sneaked into his room and cut off pieces of the material while he slept, so that now it was less than half its original size, less like a blanket than a cape Billy hooked over his shoulders.

"I'm getting really mad," Nora said as she hammered on his door with her fist.

Billy had managed to bring the blanket to school, but each time he did Mrs. Ellery, the third-grade teacher, had insisted he keep it on the top shelf of the coat closet. But she couldn't stop him from wearing it out in the playground, and at recess he sat on the blacktop hunched beneath it, practicing invisibility. It was working, too, better and better all the time. Now instead of harassing him, the other kids had begun to ignore him, and that's just the way Billy Silk wanted it. His mother refused to believe that. Already, she had completely humiliated him by inviting three kids he hated over to their house, one per week. Each time Nora had made cookies and played lengthy games of war with their guest, while Billy sat on a kitchen chair, watching but refusing to speak. There was no way for Billy to make Nora understand that even if these boys had liked him, which they assuredly did not, their mothers would never have let them come back for a second visit. Didn't she see the reaction when Mark Laskowsky's mother found Mark eating sugar doughnuts and drinking Coke while the record player blared "Teddy Bear" and James waved his spoon around in his highchair, where he sat covered from the neck up with chocolate pudding? Each time Nora thought she was chatting up the other boys' mothers, they were really interrogating her. The stray pieces of their thoughts Billy picked up made him blush: If she didn't know enough to wash her baby's face, she shouldn't have a baby. If she couldn't fix decent meals for her children, she shouldn't have been a mother in the first place.

By the end of October, every mother of every child in his class knew that Nora was divorced; Stevie Hennessy with his big mouth had seen to that, and that was the end of Billy's chance for any sort of social alliances. So why wouldn't she see, why didn't she wonder why Billy was never invited over to anyone's house after school, why she herself hadn't been told about the monthly PTA meetings or the Columbus Day bake sale? Nora had found out about the bake sale at the very last moment and had stayed up past midnight fixing Junket pies dotted with marshmallows and maraschino cherries, which no one bought. By the next day everyone in the third grade knew that the janitor wound up throwing Nora's pies in the trash because he couldn't give them away.

And after all this, she was still bugging Billy about Stevie Hennessy, insisting that he would be the most convenient friend in the world, since he lived right across the street.

"I've been meaning to call Mrs. Hennessy," Nora said nearly every day, a threat that hung over Billy like a cloud.

No, not a cloud—Stevie was more like a huge, formless tornado. No matter how invisible Billy made himself, Stevie found him. He found him in the boys' room, where he threw wet paper towels at him and aimed spitballs right between Billy's eyes. He assured Billy that his father killed at least one person a day, and that Billy was high on his list. He somehow had the power to make Billy into a monster, even to himself. After Stevie told Marcie Writman that Billy's parents were divorced, Marcie came over to tell Billy how sorry she was about the tragedy in his family and Billy, who had never even pushed anyone before, had hit her right in the stomach. He had felt terrible then. Marcie was smaller than he was, and a girl, and her mouth had made a strange O shape when he punched her.

Every day was torment because Billy was never certain whether or not Stevie would be waiting for him in the cafeteria. Snotboy, he would call Billy. Orphan, he would shout across the milk line.

Turdface, he'd whisper when they rushed out into the hallway to crouch along the walls for cover during an air-raid drill.

"Don't call Mrs. Hennessy," Billy advised his mother whenever she'd suggest it, and he'd wrap his wool blanket more tightly around himself and reach up to twirl his hair.

After school he'd look out his window and watch as Stevie and the other kids on the block played kickball. He'd see them get out their Hula Hoops at twilight. What could he say when his mother told him he needed fresh air? That he was afraid to walk down Hemlock Street by himself? He twirled his hair and told her nothing; he concentrated instead on the biography of Harry Houdini he'd taken out during library period. Houdini was everything Billy wished to be, everything his father, Roger, was not. Tricks meant nothing to Billy, clairvoyance was a burden. But Houdini's talent was pure and true; he could fight against real boundaries, the physical bonds of ropes and chains, and escape. He could overcome water, fire, and air. He could shine like a lamp lit from within and pass right through the hemp, the metal, the tides.

One afternoon he found some old rope Mr. Olivera had left behind in the garage, and he began practicing slip knots. He'd tie his feet together and then will his ankles to contract so he could wriggle out of the knots. He'd get under his blanket, lash his wrists together, and escape from his own net of ropes. Exhausted then, he'd lie back with a pure feeling inside him, hot as if he'd faced a battle; his eyes would sting, his mouth would be dry, but he'd tie himself up all over again.

Sometimes James would push open Billy's door and crawl into his room. He'd come over to the bed, then creep under the blanket to watch Billy practice his rope tricks. Billy always closed his eyes when he concentrated, and his neck and face would grow sweaty. While Nora fixed dinner and listened to 45s, Billy and James would lie under the blanket and just look up through the woven wool. It was quiet and dim, and Billy liked having James beside him. Picking up thoughts from James was different from the way it was with other people. Billy didn't get words; instead he picked up sensations. The scent of warm milk, the smooth brown feathers of an owl in James's favorite book, the thump of a rubber ball against a wooden floor, the softness of flannel pajamas against his skin, the way a teddy bear felt when you held him tight. No, he would never kick the baby out of his room, because James was also the perfect audience. Whenever Billy escaped from a knot, James solemnly clapped his hands and nodded his head.

"You're ruining your brother's birthday," Nora chided through the door. She figured that would make Billy feel awful, and it did. Even before Roger had left, Billy had felt responsible for the baby; it was the way James followed him around, crawling as fast as he could to catch up.

"It's about time," Nora said when Billy finally gave up and came out of his room. She forced herself not to mention the blanket as they went into the kitchen.

"Where's the cake?" Billy said when he saw the platter of Twinkies.

"This is it," Nora said. "And don't you dare let me hear you say one bad word about it."

She held James up. He puffed out his cheeks and Nora and Billy helped him blow out his birthday candles.

"Twink," James said, as Nora pulled out the candles, and it took a while for Nora and Billy to realize that the baby had said his first word.

On the day before Halloween, Stevie Hennessy started the rumor that Nora was a witch when she showed up after school dressed in black with a basket of apples over her arm. They were green apples, with shiny skins, the last few from a bent old tree that grew near Dead Man's Hill. Nora had found a recipe for deep-dish apple pie in the October issue of *Good Housekeeping*, which had expressly recommended fresh-picked apples. On the way to school she and James had stopped at the Hill and collected the apples, even though they looked misshapen, not at all what you'd find at the A&P.

Billy was shuffling down the hall toward the door when he heard Stevie Hennessy yell, "Cheez it. It's a witch." The other children screamed and scattered, and when Billy looked up, there was his mother, standing on the path in front of the school, with James right beside her.

Billy went outside and glared at his mother. "What are you doing here?" he said.

"Well, thanks a lot," Nora said. "Thanks a million. I just thought it would be nice for me to pick you up. Mothers do that sort of thing, you know. It's part of their job."

Billy rolled his eyes and walked across the street to the Volkswagen.

"Let me tell you something, buddy," Nora said when she and James had gotten into the car. "You need an attitude change."

Billy leaned his head against the window and twirled his hair.

"Are you listening to me?" Nora said. "Or am I talking to myself?"

Out of nowhere came a large stone; it fell out of the sky and landed on the hood of the Volkswagen with a thud.

"What was that?" Nora said.

"Drive home," Billy said.

Another one hit against the fender.

"Jesus Christ," Nora said.

Across the street was a group of boys, all with stones in their hands.

"Shit," Nora said. She swung her car door open.

Billy reached over and grabbed her sleeve. "Don't go out there," he said.

Nora pulled away from him and leapt out of the car.

"Mom!" Billy called, but Nora ignored him. She walked into the middle of the street.

"What do you think you're doing!" she shouted.

The boys in front of the school jeered at her and drew closer together.

"It's the witch!" one of the boys at the rear called. It was Stevie Hennessy, but Nora didn't recognize him, she didn't have time to because another rock came tearing toward her, thrown by a fifth-grader named Warren Cook. The rock missed Nora; it fell at her feet and splintered into pieces. Nora ran across the street faster than anyone's mother should have been able to, and she grabbed Warren Cook by the collar of his coat. His allies immediately took off, shrieking. Warren turned white as a ghost.

"If you ever do that again," Nora said, "I'll put a hex on you. I'll fix it so that you'll never be able to pee again. You know what that means?"

Warren opened his mouth, but nothing came out.

"That's right," Nora said. "You'll be so filled up with pee, every time you open your mouth to talk you know what will come out. We don't want that to happen, do we?"

Warren shut his mouth and carefully shook his head.

"Good," Nora said. "I'm glad we understand each other."

As soon as she let go of him, Warren Cook ran down the street. Nora went back to her car, started the engine, and threw it into gear. In the passenger seat, Billy was bent over, his head between his knees.

"Sit up straight," Nora told him. "Jesus Christ," she said.

Billy had the dry heaves; his shoulders shook and he made a thin retching noise.

"If you're going to throw up, open the door," Nora said. "I'll pull over."

When they got home neither of them made a move to get out of the car. Nora took out a cigarette and lit it; she stared through the windshield at the house. She had taped a skeleton to the front door; it had long, crinkly arms made of folded tissue paper. Billy was crying, but Nora didn't look at him.

"Not everyone is like that," Nora said.

"Oh, sure," Billy said.

"They can't all be like that," Nora insisted. "You wait and see."

On Halloween Billy refused to go out trick-or-treating, and although they could hear the whoops of goblins and gypsies, no one came to their door. But later, when the children were asleep and Nora was getting ready for bed, there was a rattling sound. Nora went into the living room and listened; she could hear footsteps in the dark. She looked through the front window. There was nothing out there but the black shapes of the rhododendrons. Still, it was worth checking on. Nora slipped her coat over her nightgown, then took a flashlight and went out onto the front stoop. There wasn't a sound on the street, not a cat, not the slightest hint of a wind, not one car passing by. Nora moved the beam of the flashlight over the lawn and the driveway. Circles of light fell across the grass and ricocheted off the lamp posts. Nora flashed the beam of light along the Volkswagen and then inside it; the car was still intact, the same crumpled cigarette packs and cookie crumbs littered the floor. But something had happened, someone had been here, there were chalky black footprints along one side of the driveway. When Nora turned back to the house she saw that the word WITCH had been scrawled across the garage door in black letters.

She turned off her flashlight and stood in the dark. She breathed in the cool air and listened to the soft hum of the parkway. Above her were Sirius and the Big Dipper. She was barely making her mortgage each month, and yesterday she had realized, after she'd halved the green apples from Dead Man's Hill, that she might never be able to make a pie crust from scratch. She could bake almost anything, but she had never had the knack of a good pie crust. It kept crumbling on her; dough stuck to her fingers and to the tabletop. It had been months since a man had kissed her, months since someone had waited for her in bed. But she refused to think about that. Instead she concentrated on the stars. She imagined her exact position in the Milky Way, a black spot, a pinpoint on the edge of the blinding white light. Inside the house, her children were sleeping, each in his very own room, and the cat was curled up on the living-room rug.

Nora went inside and filled a bucket with warm water and Lysol. She unwrapped a package of new sponges and grabbed her rubber gloves off the rim of the sink. It wasn't so bad after all, it was only charcoal, and it took her less than a half hour to clean the garage door. After that night, Nora loved her house no less and she continued to suggest that Billy invite friends home, but she always picked him up after school, and she made certain to park right behind the school buses, so Billy wouldn't have to cross the street alone.

It was bad enough to be picked up by his mother, worse because she often dragged him along when she and James went to afternoon Tupperware parties. Not on Hemlock Street. Never on their own block. Everyone Nora had contacted on Hemlock Street had been much too busy, or, like Rickie Shapiro's mother, hadn't believed in plastic, or simply didn't want anything to do with Nora. She'd been lucky enough to sell a few sets of Tupperware to some of the men on the block, a few of whom had come over to help when they'd seen her struggling with the huge cardboard boxes she toted around. Twice, Joe Hennessy had happened to be outside when Nora was unloading a new shipment and, as it turned out, he was a great believer in Tupperware.

Eventually, Nora was sure, she'd be selling Tupperware in every house on Hemlock, but for now the parties she arranged were in other towns, in Valley Stream and Floral Park, in East Meadow and Levittown. The women would always beg to hold James—he was as good as a calling card—and when they were through admiring him, it was Billy's job to keep him entertained. If you held James's hand he would walk a bit, and Billy usually took him outside and walked him up and down the sidewalk. They'd look for ants, which James would occasionally eat. They'd tear bark off small trees and pretend they were hunters who needed to start a fire and, if Billy had been clever enough to swipe a pack of matches from his mother's coat pocket, he would start a small fire, which they'd both stare at until it burned down to ash on the curb.

Sometimes Billy forgot about James. He would walk down the block without him, not remembering his little brother until he reached the house where the Tupperware party was being held. Billy would run back up the street and he'd always find James hysterical, his face snotty and streaked with tears. He'd be trying to follow Billy the best he could, scraping his knees on the cement. Billy always picked him up and carried him back. By the time they reached the house where the party was, James would have stopped crying, but he wouldn't let go of Billy. He'd grab onto Billy's neck or, if Billy managed to put him down, his pants leg. So they'd wait for Nora on the stoop, glued together. Billy would think about Harry Houdini then, how he had vowed to be the best, how he practiced night and day, how he never, ever gave away any of his secrets. He'd take the tail end of James's shirt and wipe the baby's face so Nora wouldn't know he'd been crying, then clean the blood from his knees. When Nora came out of the house, her mood completely dictated by how many sets of Tupperware she'd sold, she'd eye the boys suspiciously.

"What's going on?" she'd say when she saw the teary streaks on James's face that Billy hadn't been able to wipe away.

The baby and Billy would both look up at her, and in the yellow fall light they looked like rag dolls.

"Nothing," Billy would say.

"Well, then," Nora would say, "let's get out of here."

She'd be struggling with her big box of samples so that Billy would have to lift up the baby and carry him out to the car, and James would always reach his arms around Billy's neck and put his face against Billy's chest to listen for his heartbeat.

Hennessy had bought so much Tupperware that his wife began to complain. Since the least she could do was make good use of it, she took to sending him off with his lunch in Tupperware. Hennessy would find containers of macaroni salad and deviled eggs sprinkled with paprika and he'd instantly lose his appetite. He'd park on side streets along Harvey's Turnpike and force himself to eat bites of his lunch behind the wheel. Each time he had met Nora in her driveway as she was unloading Tupperware, it had been no accident. Once he had seen her get into her car up at the beauty shop and he'd followed her home. The next time he had looked out his front window, and when he saw her pulling boxes out of her Volkswagen, he'd left the house in such a rush he'd forgotten to shut his front door. Both times he'd been so embarrassed that he wound up buying excessive amounts of Tupperware.

The fact of it was he was casing her house. He knew that her older boy spent most of his time in his room, because his bedroom light was always on and sometimes, at twilight, Hennessy would see a small, pale face at the window. He knew that Nora stayed up late and that she had no weekly wash day, because shirts and blouses and slips would appear on the line in her backyard on no particular schedule. He knew that she left for Armand's every Saturday at a quarter to nine and was usually back by two thirty. He knew that no man, no husband, or ex-husband, or whatever he was, no boyfriend or father or uncle had visited since she had moved in. He told himself he just happened to be observant; she was a woman alone and it was his duty as a cop and a neighbor to keep an eye on the place. But of course, if that were so, he would have done something when he saw four boys in front of her house on Halloween night, and he'd done nothing at all, even though he'd recognized his own son. He'd gone to the front window when he had that creepy feeling along the base of his neck, and he'd stood by and watched as the boys ran into the shadows. Long after Stevie had climbed back through his bedroom window and Nora had scrubbed the garage door clean, Hennessy was still watching her house.

He thought about her more often than he imagined possible. He made himself sick thinking about her; it got so that he couldn't eat anything but old men's food or his stomach would turn. Cottage cheese and white bread, butterscotch pudding and rice. He was trying desperately not to think about her the first Saturday in November when he ran into Jim Wineman and Sam Romero at the hardware store. They often met here, searching the aisles for lighter fluid and snow chains. Today Hennessy had come for a new saw because Ellen wanted shelves built behind the washer and dryer.

"Putting up the shelves today?" Jim Wineman said.

Hennessy realized that Jim had probably known what he was going to do this weekend before he did. Ellen had told Lynne and Lynne had told Jim, and now here Hennessy was, buying the saw and doing just what they all knew he'd be doing. For a while they stood in the auto-parts aisle, debating what was the best side-view mirror for Sam's Studebaker, and they all stopped talking when Nora Silk walked past them with a set of screwdrivers. There was a saw, just like the one Hennessy had picked out, under her arm.

"Get a load of that," Sam Romero said.

Instead of wearing a skirt, as their wives would have, Nora had on black pants and black leather boots; her hair was pulled back into a ponytail and she wore silver earrings shaped like stars.

"I'll bet she's dying for it," Jim Wineman said.

"What?" Hennessy said.

Billy was following his mother, dragging the baby behind him. He looked at Hennessy and their eyes met, but Billy quickly looked away. He had on some kind of woolen cape that was tucked into his jacket and flapped after him like the broken wing of a bird.

"Divorced," Jim Wineman said. "You know what I mean."

Jim Wineman and Sam Romero looked after Nora sadly. "Jesus," they both said.

"I've got to work on my shelves," Hennessy told them. He left them in Auto Parts and followed Nora to the checkout counter. There was a lump in his throat.

"Oh, hi," Nora said when she saw him. She had the counter filled with screwdrivers and fuses and a dust mop. The baby was sitting on the counter pulling at the saw. "Don't touch," Nora told him.

"You don't need to buy that," Hennessy said. "I'm getting one just like it. You can borrow mine."

"Isn't that sweet," Nora said to Billy.

Billy shrugged and turned his attention to a tray of batteries.

"I keep telling him how important good neighbors are," Nora said. "In fact, I've been meaning to call your wife."

Billy and Hennessy both froze.

"My wife?" Hennessy said.

"I want to invite Stevie over. We live right across the street. They could become great friends. Maybe even best friends."

Hennessy noticed that Billy was growing fainter. It was as if he were retreating inside his clothes or as if—and this was probably just a trick of the fluorescent lighting above them—he were disappearing.

"Don't ring up that saw," Hennessy said to the cashier who was totaling Nora's bill.

Nora took out her wallet and reached for a ten-dollar bill. Her nails were amazingly red. She turned to Hennessy and looked right at him. "So what do you think?" she asked.

Hennessy stepped back, surprised.

"About the boys."

Nora took her package off the counter and handed Billy the mop. She scooted James aside so that Hennessy could be rung up.

"Well," Hennessy said carefully. "I think boys will be boys."

Nora thought this over. "I see what you mean," she said tentatively.

"I mean, they have to make their own friendships. You've got to let it happen naturally."

He swore that Billy was getting visibly more solid. The boy came to stand beside his mother, and although he didn't look up, he was obviously listening to every word.

"Good point," Nora said.

She waited for Hennessy, and as they walked out together Hennessy refused to look at Wineman and Romero. He held the door for Nora, and when they went out to the parking lot they discovered they had parked right next to each other.

"What a coincidence!" Nora said. She put James into the car, then went to open the trunk in the front of the Volkswagen.

"God, I hate this car," Nora said.

Billy was still holding the mop; he looked even paler in broad daylight.

"You ever kill anyone?" Billy asked Hennessy.

Hennessy looked down at the boy; the top of his head was knotted with clumps of unruly hair.

"I'm not usually tracking down murderers," Hennessy said.

"Yeah," Billy said. He swung the mop back and forth. "So. Did you ever kill anyone?"

"In the war," Hennessy said. "In France."

"Stevie says you kill someone nearly every day," Billy said.

"That's not exactly true," Hennessy said. He could see Nora's right arm as she reached up to shut the trunk.

"Oh, yeah?" Billy said.

"Yeah," Hennessy told him. "As a matter of fact, it's a lie."

Nora came back to them then. She was smiling and she held out her arms. For a moment Hennessy felt confused and weak in the knees. He took a step forward, and when he did Nora tilted her head.

"The saw," she said.

Hennessy stopped where he was.

"You said I could borrow it, and I need it today. If that's all right."

"Oh," Hennessy said. "Sure."

After Billy had gotten into the backseat, Hennessy helped Nora fit the saw into the passenger seat.

"Don't you kids touch this," Nora said. "Thanks a million," she told Hennessy when she got behind the wheel. "I need more shelf space."

Hennessy stood beside his car and watched her drive away, enormously pleased that Jim Wineman and Sam Romeo would be thinking he was on his way home to make the shelves that would just have to wait until Nora returned the saw.

All the next day Hennessy couldn't get Nora out of his mind. He spent the afternoon with Ellen and the kids at her sister's, and he gave the kids their Sunday baths. But he kept thinking about Nora. That night, after the moon rose, Hennessy began to dream about her. The children and Ellen were all asleep in their beds and the curtains were drawn. Hennessy was under a white sheet and a light wool blanket; he wore striped pajamas and his feet were cold and white. When he found her in his dreams he pulled her down beside him, into his single bed. Ellen never heard them, she didn't even turn in her sleep. How could she not smell the perfume Nora was wearing? How could she not hear the bedsprings creak?

He unhooked whatever Nora was wearing; he didn't care that his wife was asleep in the same room. He put his hands on Nora's breasts while Ellen pulled her blanket up, while his children slept, while the wood waiting to be cut into shelves lay on the basement floor. She was so hot his fingers burned when he touched her. He could hear the alarm clock ticking on the night table and the sound of the boiler in the basement below them. He slid one of his hands along her belly, then down between her legs. When she started to moan, he put his other hand over her mouth so Ellen wouldn't wake. But how could she not hear them? How could she not see the shape of Hennessy's mouth on Nora's skin? No, he couldn't care about that, he couldn't even think about it. He shifted and moved inside her, and stopped thinking altogether, and when he woke up he was crying.

He went into the bathroom and washed his face, but after that he was afraid to go back to sleep. He got dressed and made himself a cup of instant coffee. He couldn't drink it, so he went to check on his children, and then he returned to the bedroom, took his gun from the night table, and went out to his car.

The sky was still dark when he parked outside Louie's Candy Store. The morning newspapers were being delivered.

"Geez," Louie said when Hennessy came in, carrying a bundle of newspapers. "You're the early bird."

Hennessy sat down at the counter and had a cup of real coffee. He thought about all those people asleep in his house. He had no idea whether he even liked his wife and his children. He couldn't remember what song Ellen had been singing to herself when he came home from the hardware store, or what excuse Stevie had given when he'd been asked why his bedroom window was wide open the morning after Halloween or why, if he'd gone to sleep right after his bath, his fingers were black as coal.

Hennessy wasn't due down at the station house for a few hours and he couldn't go home, so he took a slow drive through the neighborhood. The leaves were all gone and the trees looked like black sticks against the blue sky. A black cat darted out across Harvey's Turnpike, and Hennessy wondered whether this meant the cat had crossed his path. Just to make certain, he made a left turn before he reached the spot where the cat had crossed. He kept his speed down, and at a quarter to six he found himself on the edge of the development. He pulled over and parked across from the house where he'd been called in to the domestic. He still felt as if he were in some kind of dream, because if he'd been thinking he never would have come here. His tongue was thick, and his stomach was sour, and the back of his neck felt as if someone had stuck pins into it. With the heater turned off, the car was cold, but Hennessy stayed there, parked. The men on the block came out of their houses and left for work; the children all walked to school. By eight thirty no one had yet come out of the house Hennessy was watching, so he got out of his car and walked across the street.

His bones felt bruised from sitting in the car for such a long time. He went up the steps and knocked on the door, and when no one answered he hopped off the stoop. He went to the living-room window and peered in, but even before he rubbed a circle in the dirty glass and looked in, he knew the house was empty.

A woman from the house next door had come out on her lawn and was staring at him.

"Are you the realtor?" she called.

Hennessy straightened up and walked through the bushes. "A friend of the family," he said.

"Really?" the woman said. "Well, they're not here. They moved to New Jersey."

"That explains it," Hennessy said.

"Three weeks ago," the woman told him.

Hennessy thanked her and walked across the lawn. He was late for work now, so he started his car and made a U-turn and headed for Harvey's Turnpike. But before reporting in, he stopped at a drugstore and bought a large bottle of Pepto-Bismol. He uncapped the bottle and took a long swig, then flipped open his glove compartment and threw the bottle inside. He had just been a little too late, that was all. And why that should make him feel so terribly sick, why that should make him want to step on the gas and drive as far as he could get, he had no idea.

4

THE THIEF

*T*HERE was black ice all over the streets. You couldn't see it, but it was there, waiting for you to step off the curb. Car doors froze shut, tree branches cracked and fell onto the lawns, traffic lights were so encrusted you couldn't tell red from green or stop from go. On Dead Man's Hill there was a thin coating of ice over the snow; if you set up your sled just right, perfectly in line with the ruts of the dozens of sleds before yours, you would take off like lightning. If it was evening, you would come close enough to the cars on the Southern State to make your vision blank out in the glare of the headlights; during the day the sunlight reflecting off the ice would make you so dizzy you'd just lie there after your sled over-turned, and then in a panic you'd get up as quickly as you could, terrified, convinced that if you didn't move soon the ice would freeze you into place, and that's the way they'd find you, sometime in the spring, deep within the thaw of Dead Man's Hill.

But neither the ice nor the unusually cold temperatures kept Jackie McCarthy from washing his Chevy every Friday and Simo-nizing it every other Saturday. He wore black cotton gloves with the fingertips cut off, which allowed him to hold the Q-Tips when he cleaned the dirt off his silver mag wheels. He preferred Turtle Wax and the heat of his breath and a soft cotton dish towel stolen from his mother's kitchen drawer. That was the way to get a really good shine, a shine so slick he could see his own reflection in the rear fender. He always kept the key in the ignition, the window rolled down, and the radio on. He sang "Ooh, baby" while he worked. He sang "Sweet Little Sixteen." When he caught a glimpse of himself in the side-view mirror he gave it his all, as if he were onstage. Yeah, he thought to himself. Yeah, yeah, yeah.

He felt lucky and hot; he had cash in his pockets almost all the time now. He and Pete and Dominick Amato had taken another car from the Saint's garage, Mr. Shapiro's two-week-old Cadillac. Before they took the Caddy down to Queens Boulevard, where Pete's cousin gave them cash for it, they had driven out to Jones Beach, right through the snow before the plows had cleared the parkway, and it was just about the best ride Jackie ever had. All right, it was true, in the morning he had to pay because he was the one who had to stand next to his father, the one who had to shift his weight from one foot to the other in the cold while the Saint unlocked the garage and saw that the Caddy was gone. Jackie had thought he knew what to expect, and in a way he was looking forward to seeing the Saint blow up. When the key went into the garage lock, Jackie took a deep breath. This is it, he told himself. This is when the Saint goes nuts, when he raises his voice, maybe even smacks me. But once the door was pushed aside, all the Saint did was stand there, and then he collapsed against the cold bricks, as if someone had hit him hard.

"What's the matter, Pop?" Jackie had said. He had planned to act real casual, but his voice broke. He felt as though he might be watching his father have a heart attack.

The Saint sat down in the doorway to the garage, right in the oil slicks and the pools of gasoline and the rest of the dirt that they'd never get rid of, in spite of the Saint's daily sweeping.

"Come on, Pop," Jackie said. When he knelt and helped his father up, the Saint felt like a bundle of twigs in his arms. Jackie walked his father into the office and over to a hard-backed metal chair. What Jackie really wanted was a cigarette, but he had never smoked in front of the Saint and he certainly wasn't about to start now. Before he called the police, the Saint phoned Phil Shapiro at work, and God, it made Jackie sick to hear him apologize to Shapiro, to be so fucking silent when you knew that on the other end of the line Shapiro was giving him hell. When he couldn't take it anymore, Jackie leaned over and slammed his hand down on the phone to cut off the call. His father looked up at him, confused.

"You don't have to take that crap from him," Jackie said. "Let him take his business elsewhere."

"It was my fault," the Saint said.

"Pop," Jackie said, "the car was stolen."

"I should have had an alarm system," the Saint said, echoing Shapiro's last words to him.

"Look," Jackie said, "the Jew's insured. He can afford another Caddy."

Jackie had turned to hang his leather jacket on a hook, so he didn't see the Saint get up and come at him, didn't even realize what was happening until his father grabbed him and pushed him up against the wall. This was it, this was the explosion Jackie had thought he wanted; finally he'd see the Saint act like a human being. But it wasn't the way Jackie had expected, and it brought him no satisfaction when the Saint let go of him. As the Saint backed off he looked smaller than ever; you could snap him in two with one strong hand.

An hour later, when Hennessy arrived, Jackie was in the garage rebuilding a carburetor, but the Saint was still at his desk, staring out the plate-glass window. Hennessy drove up in his unmarked black Ford, which had an attachable siren he kept under his seat. He parked beside the air pump and got out. There was no business at the station and he could hear the radio playing in the garage. "I Only Have Eyes for You." Hennessy went into the office, and when the door swung closed behind him, John McCarthy didn't even look up.

"You can't believe the roads out there," Hennessy said. "Slicker than hell." He went over to the percolator McCarthy always kept on a small pine table and poured himself a cup of coffee, then realized it was yesterday's and cold. Hennessy put the cup back down on the table and wished someone else had gotten this call.

"The car was my responsibility," McCarthy said.

"I hate to tell you," Hennessy said, "but this kind of thing happens all the time. Was the garage jimmied open?"

"He brought it in because the door squeaked. He could have taken it back to the dealer, but I offered to do it for him. It turned out the door just needed a little oil," McCarthy said. "That's all."

"Windows broken?" Hennessy asked.

John McCarthy shook his head. "I need an alarm system."

Hennessy lit a cigarette and took a look around. The floor was so clean he didn't feel right just dropping the match, so he slipped it into his coat pocket.

"Think back to last night," Hennessy said. "Did you lock the garage door?"

There was a curtain of blue smoke between them. Ice was forming inside the plate-glass window.

"I don't know," John McCarthy said. "I can't remember."

Hennessy gave McCarthy the police report to fill out and while he did, Hennessy went into the garage. It was colder here, downright freezing outside the radius of a small electric heater set up on the concrete floor.

Jackie was kneeling on the concrete, singing along with the radio he had set up on the workbench. He had seen Hennessy pull up, and now he felt the cop behind him, but he didn't stop singing.

"Maybe you're Ed Sullivan material," Hennessy said.

Jackie turned as if surprised. "Mr. Hennessy," he said, standing. "Yeah." He grinned. "Maybe I am."

Jackie watched Hennessy check the garage. No broken glass, no jimmied locks.

"It's a bitch, isn't it?" Jackie said. "Shapiro just brought it in to have the doors oiled. My dad wouldn't feel so bad if it wasn't for that Corvette a while back."

"Your father ever forget to lock the door?" Hennessy asked. He was standing beside the double doors, giving them the once-over.

"Pop?" Jackie said. "Never. He doesn't even forget to sweep the floor every day."

Hennessy looked down at the concrete; there was no place to put his cigarette out, so he let it burn down between his fingers.

"You ever forget?" Hennessy asked easily.

"Hey." Jackie grinned. He could hear his own pulse in his ears. "I may be dumb, but I'm not stupid."

"Yeah," Hennessy said. "Yeah, well, do me a favor. Just keep an eye on your father."

"What do you mean?" Jackie asked. He looked over to the office. The Saint was busy filling out the report, so Jackie figured he could sneak a quick smoke. He got out a cigarette and his silver lighter. He

leaned his head away from the lighter when the flame shot up, and he
lit his cigarette carefully.

"I don't know," Hennessy said. "He's confused. He doesn't know if
he locked the door or not."

That was when Jackie knew he had it made. Hennessy didn't sus-
pect a thing. Jackie looked over his shoulder to make sure his father
wouldn't catch him smoking, then took a deep drag of his cigarette
and tapped the ashes on the floor.

"Yeah, sure," he said to the cop. "I'll keep an eye on him."

That night, at dinner, no one said a word about the Cadillac. The
Saint ate quickly, then went out to spread salt on their sidewalk, so
children walking to school the next morning wouldn't slip and fall.
He always took care of the sidewalk all the way to the corner, past the
Olivera house. After an hour, the Saint hadn't yet gone home. He was
out there, standing on the curb, still holding the bag of rock salt.

Ace didn't hear about the Cadillac until the next morning, but he
knew who the thief was as soon as Danny walked up beside him and
said, "You're not going to fucking believe this. My dad's car was
stolen right out of your dad's garage."

"Oh, yeah?" Ace said. Not one word more; not a cough, not a shrug.
Nothing.

"My father is fit to be tied," Danny said. "Mild-mannered Phil has
gone insane."

Ace's bad blood pumped out of his heart; there was no way he'd
betray his brother to Danny.

"He'll get another Caddy and cool off," Ace said.

"Yeah, well, I'm not supposed to enter your house," Danny said.

"Come on," Ace said. "Seriously?"

"He's ripshit," Danny said. "To tell you the truth, he's been going
insane for a while. He's been leaving for work at six in the morning
and coming home at nine, and nobody even sees him anymore. But
this Cadillac pushed him right over the edge."

Ace lit a cigarette and thought about the way his brother had
leaned back in his chair at the dinner table the night before, grinning
like a millionaire when he asked for more potatoes. Ace wished he
could cut school and go back to bed. He saw Rickie Shapiro up the
street, walking with her friend Joan. Rickie was wearing leather

boots with high heels, and every now and then she slipped on the ice and grabbed Joan's arm. Something was different about her; her hair wasn't straight anymore, it was thicker and somehow wild, as if she had given up trying to control it. When she breathed, a plume of white smoke escaped and circled around her.

"You do the report on the Continental Congress?" Danny asked.

"Oh, shit," Ace said.

Danny reached into his books and took out his report. "Here," he said to Ace.

Ace stopped and looked at the paper.

"Just rip off the title page," Danny said.

"What are you going to use?" Ace asked.

"I already have an A average," Danny said. "He'll bring me down to a B if I don't have a paper. He'll flunk you."

Ace knew you weren't supposed to let some guy do this for you unless you were like brothers. He felt completely cold, mesmerized by Rickie's red hair; a victim of his own bad blood.

"Thanks," Ace said. He wedged the report on top of the books he carried home from school but never read. "I owe you one."

"Yeah," Danny said. "Just read it before you hand it in, so you can mouth off to Miller if he quizzes you on it."

Once they were inside the school, Ace went up to his locker on the second floor. He was following Rickie and her friend and thinking about his father putting salt on the sidewalk. At his locker, he quickly turned the combination, threw his jacket inside, then slammed the door shut. He went around the corner and stopped at Rickie's locker. She had hung a mirror on the inside of the door and had just taken her brush out of her purse.

"I like your hair this way," Ace said.

Rickie looked up at him, made a face, then turned back to the mirror and brushed her hair.

"Your father's really mad, huh?" Ace said.

"Oh, no," Rickie said. "He loves getting his brand-new car stolen two weeks after he bought it. He's just thrilled."

She put her brush in her pocketbook, then closed her locker. As she turned to go past Ace, she glanced down at his books.

"What's this?" she asked. She looked closer and recognized the report Danny had been working on the night before. "You're going to let him go to class without a report?"

"Big deal," Ace said. "He'll still get a B."

"You really make me sick," Rickie said.

She'd been just as nasty to him before, but this time Ace felt himself getting angrier than he should. When Rickie tried to pass by him, he didn't move.

"Oh, yeah?" he said.

"Do you mind?" Rickie said.

Ace didn't budge. Her hair was blinding; it could knock you off your feet. Rickie looked at him, disgusted. She moved to the left and so did Ace. She moved forward and Ace immediately blocked her way.

"Cut it out," Rickie said, panicky.

Ace walked toward her and backed her up against the lockers. Rickie could feel the cold metal through her sweater and her shirt and her bra. There were hot red spots on her cheeks.

" 'Cut it out,' " Ace repeated, with so much menace he surprised himself.

The hallways were less crowded now. Larry Reinhart came by and slapped Ace's back in greeting, but Ace didn't turn. He moved in even closer. He could smell something lemony, like soap or shampoo. Rickie was looking past him, down the hallway, as if something could save her. Ace felt his bad blood get hotter; he could feel himself growing hard. He would have liked to take her right there, on the linoleum floor or up against the lockers. Rickie tilted her face and stared back at him, and when she did Ace saw what he had seen many other times, when other girls looked at him. He realized that he had her.

"I make you sick, huh?" he said, real low, but he knew she could hear him.

Rickie looked so terrified that Ace finally backed off. But there was another reason he had to pull back. He realized that she had him, too. The bell rang, and Rickie still didn't move. Ace turned away and got out of there as fast as he could. He was late, so he slipped into his homeroom while the teacher's back was to the class.

Ace put his boots up on the desk in front of him. The air was heavy with chalk dust and sweat; if you took too deep a breath you might faint. In the seat in front of him, Cathy Corrigan shifted when he pressed his boots against her back. Her hair was teased up and lacquered into place; she was wearing a straight black skirt and a white blouse with ruffles at the wrists and throat. Cathy worked in the A&P after school and was well known as a slut, but she never complained when Ace put his feet up. She didn't say a word. Cathy's neck was perfectly white, and every time she tilted her head her red hoop earrings swung back and forth. Last spring two guys Ace knew had sworn that they had personally been there when Larry Reinhart's older brother had talked her into fucking his dog down in the basement, near the Ping-Pong table and the small refrigerator where Larry's father kept extra soda and beer. Ace stared at Cathy's neck while the homeroom teacher took attendance. He should have been reading Danny's report on the Continental Congress, but instead he was thinking about Rickie, and he felt himself get hot all over again. Cathy Corrigan looked over her shoulder at him; she had a soft, crumpled face and blue eyes. Ace was afraid she had read his mind and caught him wanting Rickie, but then he realized Cathy was trying to move her pocketbook, which she'd hung over her seat. Ace had put one of his boots up against the white leatherette, and now there was a black footprint on one side of the bag.

"Hey, Cathy, I'm sorry," Ace said.

"That's okay," Cathy said. She took a Kleenex out of her bag and tried to wipe away the footprint.

"Try Pine-Sol," Ace suggested. "My mother uses that all the time."

"Yeah," Cathy said. "Pine-Sol."

"Or ammonia," Ace said. "That might do it."

"McCarthy," the homeroom teacher shouted.

Ace shut up. Danny Shapiro shifted in his seat and grinned at him, and Ace realized it wasn't because the homeroom teacher had called out his name but because Danny thought he was trying to score with Cathy.

Ace leaned forward in his seat. "It's a real nice pocketbook," he whispered. "Real pretty."

Cathy turned around and gave him a big smile, as if he'd just paid her the biggest compliment in the world, as if no one had ever said two nice words to her before. That just made Ace feel worse; he wished his bad blood would take him over completely, he wished he didn't need to apologize. He sat waiting for the bell to ring, trying not to look at his own black footprint. When homeroom was finally over he waited for Danny in the hallway, then shoved the report back at him before Danny could say a word. Why not? That bastard Miller would never fail him for missing one report. If he did he'd get Ace in his class for another damned year.

All day Ace felt himself falling harder for Rickie Shapiro, and by the afternoon he was at her mercy. People couldn't go around feeling like this and exist. He couldn't stand to think of what the Saint would say if he knew what Ace had wanted to do to Rickie in the hallway. He wanted to pull up her skirt and slide his hand into her underpants; he wanted to make her gasp, to feel how wet she was, how ready she was for him, how she wanted him in spite of herself. The Saint, he knew, wouldn't say a word, it would be the disappointment in his eyes, that would tell it all, how fucking impure he would think Ace was. Jackie would have plenty to say. You jerk, that's what he'd say, not for Ace's wanting her, but because he was actually foolish enough to care. She thinks she's too good for you. All you've got to do is take her, take her and then just walk away. Walk away, man, and it would be even better if you made her crazy for you before you left. Yeah, have her call out your name as you're walking away. Have there be tears in her eyes.

Jackie once had a steady girlfriend, Jeanette, and when they were together they used to lock themselves in her bedroom, even when her parents were home. Jeanette never cared about that. But Jackie never talked to her; he made her sit in the backseat alone when they went riding around with his friends. She wound up dropping out of high school and marrying a cop over in Oceanside, and now she sent a Christmas card every year, addressed to the whole family. If Jackie was the one to bring in the mail, he always threw her card away; he didn't even remember what she looked like anymore, and when he came across her picture in friends' photographs he'd always say, "Who the hell is that?"

Jackie knew Cathy Corrigan, so did his friends Pete and Dominick, but so did plenty of other guys, and knowing her wasn't something you necessarily bragged about or even admitted. You went to Cathy Corrigan when you were desperate, or when you wanted a girl to do things no one in her right mind would do. Actually, she was pretty, even though her eyes crossed a little. The pathetic thing was she actually went for Jackie, after all the rotten things he'd done to her. She lived at the far end of Hemlock Street, and Jackie knew she came looking for him sometimes; she'd just happen to pass by when he was working on his car, she'd just happen to be wearing something she thought he'd like, a new sweater or a skirt shorter than any other girl would dare be seen in. He told her once he thought hoop earrings were sexy, and she'd worn them ever since, just because he liked them, and that only made it easier for Jackie to be cruel.

Two nights after they'd stolen the Cadillac, Jackie and his friends were still feeling like bigshots. It was a Friday night and the streets were still frozen; up on Harvey's Turnpike there were cold halos around every streetlight. The mimosas and the willow trees had limbs of ice, the chain-link fences that ran along the backyards were encased in silvery pods. Up at Louie's Candy Store sawdust had been sprinkled on the linoleum floor so that customers wouldn't slip when they came in for cigarettes or gum. It was black as midnight by seven when Jackie and his friends pulled into the parking lot. They didn't have any particular plans—pick up some smokes at Louie's, then maybe head over to the bowling alley. All three wore polished black boots, their hair was combed back and so wet that ice crystals formed by the time they had walked into the candy store.

"Take a look at that," Pete said, while Louie was getting their cigarettes.

Jackie took a pack of Juicy Fruit gum and stuck it in his pocket without paying. He saw Cathy Corrigan sitting on the last stool at the counter. She was wearing a fleecy coat that looked like a skunk and she had a smudgy white pocketbook slung over her shoulder.

"What a piece of trash," Jackie said.

"Yeah," Dominick agreed.

"You want her?" Jackie asked, and he grinned.

Dominick and Pete grinned back at him. Jackie put some change down on the counter, picked up his pack of Marlboros, and went over to the soda fountain. Cathy was still wearing her white checker's smock from the A&P under her coat. She had a hamburger special in front of her; her pack of Salems and a gold lighter were right next to the bottle of ketchup. Jackie leaned up against the stool next to her.

"Meet me outside," he said without looking at her. He lit a cigarette, and when he could feel her staring at him, he walked to the front of the store. Outside, Pete and Dominick were waiting.

"So?" Pete said.

"She'll be right out," Jackie assured him.

They stood in the cold, smoking cigarettes. Somewhere far down Harvey's Turnpike a siren sounded. The wind shook the pink neon lights of Louie's sign and rattled the letters against the bricks. Cathy Corrigan walked outside, then stopped and pushed the strap of her pocketbook over her shoulder.

"You didn't say there'd be anyone else," she said to Jackie.

"What do you care?" Jackie said.

Jackie turned and started to walk toward his parked car. Dominick and Pete grinned at each other and followed, and soon they could hear Cathy behind them, walking gingerly on the ice. They got in the car and drove over to the bowling alley, parked in the rear of the lot where it was dark, and took turns with her in the backseat. Jackie went first, and then Pete, who had had her before, and then they had some trouble with her and actually had to talk her into taking on Dominick.

"What am I, a mercy case?" Dominick said.

They told him to shut up and swore to Cathy that Dominick had never gone all the way before and that she'd be doing him a psychological favor, and when that didn't work, Jackie made it clear that he wouldn't drive her home until she said yes. Pete and Jackie stood outside and watched through the window as Dominick took his turn with her. It was freezing cold and they could hear the music from the jukebox in the bowling alley. They could see Dominick's white ass and the moons of Cathy's breasts. Neither of them had thought to undress her when it was their turn.

"Let me bring her home to meet my mother," Pete drawled.

"Yeah." Jackie laughed. "I'll chip in for the engagement ring."

Pete clapped his hands together, then blew on his fingers. "What a dog," he said.

Jackie was scanning the parking lot for Cadillacs. He had never had a smoother ride—better than his Chevy, better than a Corvette. Pete nudged him hard with his elbow.

"A dog," he said. "Get it?"

Dominick got out of the car and tucked in his shirt. Inside the car, Cathy Corrigan was folding up her checker's smock; she fumbled through her pocketbook in the dark till she found her rat-tail comb.

"You know what they're saying," Pete told Jackie. "She fucked a dog and then had its pup."

"Get out of here," Jackie said. He took a cigarette and tried to light it against the wind.

"Swear to God," Pete said. "She's got the goddamned puppy at home. I'm telling you, man, it's hers. She probably lets it suck her tits."

"You're a moron," Jackie said to him. "Anybody ever tell you that before?"

"Sure," Pete said. "Like it really bothers me."

The three friends sat up front as they drove back toward home. Dominick looked over his shoulder as they passed the only patch of woods left beside Harvey's Turnpike. "Christ," he said. "She's crying."

"I'm getting out of here," Pete said. "Drop me off at the corner."

When Jackie pulled over, Dominick and Pete both got out. "Thanks a lot," Jackie called after them. He looked into the rearview mirror. Cathy Corrigan wasn't making a sound, but in the moonlight Jackie could see tears falling down her cheeks. "For Christ's sake," he said, "don't worry. I'll drive you home." He reached for his cigarettes. When he looked in the rearview mirror again, she was still crying. "Oh, Jesus," he said. He pushed the car lighter in. "All right. You can sit up front."

Cathy got out and came around to the passenger seat. She had a circle of mascara around each eye. She looked like something you'd run over in the road.

"You could have told me about them," she said.

"So sue me," Jackie said. He ripped the car into gear; it was his game completely. Cathy looked at him, but she didn't say a word when he drove down Hemlock and went past her house. Jackie drove to the teachers' parking lot behind the school and parked. He had hated high school the whole time he was there, but now he kept coming back to it, and he didn't even wonder why.

"Take off all your clothes," he told Cathy.

"What do you mean?" Cathy said.

He knew that when her voice went up like that she was frightened. He left the car running so the heater would still work, and he turned the radio up. "I mean I'm not done," he said.

Cathy stared at him, suspicious, as if he meant to take all her clothes, kick her out, and just leave her there. That had happened to her before, in another car, with another guy.

"Oh, for Christ's sake, Cathy," Jackie said. "Trust me."

Cathy Corrigan laughed. It was a small, dry sound, as if there were something wrong with her throat. She took off her coat, started to unbutton her blouse, and gathered her nerve.

"You've never kissed me," she said.

"So?" Jackie said.

"I don't know," Cathy said. "I was just thinking about it."

If he didn't do it, she'd give him a harder time, and anyway no one would ever know. He grabbed Cathy and pulled her toward him. He kissed her lightly and was surprised to find she tasted like strawberries. She wasn't so bad. He kept kissing her and finished unbuttoning her blouse. If he hadn't been kissing her, if he hadn't had the radio turned up so loud, he might have noticed that another car had pulled into the parking lot. When Pete drove his father's Oldsmobile up and shone his headlights onto Jackie's Chevy, Jackie felt something cold go through him. He wrenched away from Cathy. Through the foggy windshield he could see Pete, and Dominick, and Jerry Tyler, but he couldn't make out any of the other guys' faces.

"Get down," Jackie told Cathy.

Cathy looked at him, puzzled, until she finally understood what he meant. He didn't want anyone to see them together; it was death to be caught kissing her.

"Get down on the floor," Jackie said.

His voice broke, and maybe that was why Cathy sat up straight and said, "No. I won't."

Jackie glared at her; he wanted to slap her, but he didn't have time for that. "Then get in the backseat," he said, and when she didn't move, he gave her a shove. "Go on."

He pushed her until she was hanging halfway into the back. The other guys had opened their windows and were calling out to him, laughing. They blinked the headlights on and off. He was trapped here with her; he had to make his move. Blinded by the headlights, he reached down and tore the car into gear. He let out the clutch so fast that Cathy was propelled back; she gave a little gasp when he floored the gas, and clung to the top of the seat with her fingernails.

At first the Chevy took off in a straight line; Jackie's foot was so heavy he couldn't have let up on the gas even if he had tried, and he didn't have time to try once they hit the ice. The Chevy made a circle and kept on going, leaning to one side so that the door scraped along the asphalt, and nothing could have stopped them when they crashed into the chain-link fence that separated the parking lot from the athletic field. They were flying on the black ice, and above them the stars pulsed with light. Cathy Corrigan held on to her pocketbook with one hand and gripped the top of the seat where she'd been perched ever since Jackie tried to push her into the back. Jackie heard her call out when they hit the fence, then all he heard was metal, as if the metal were screaming with a voice of its own. But really it was he who was screaming, as if anyone's scream could weaken the force of the accident. And that's all it was, that's how it was listed down at the station house when Joe Hennessy, who had pulled night duty, came in to file his report. He didn't have to go to the high school, but it was on his way home. The parking lot was full now; there was a car full of white-faced boys, an ambulance, three police cars, and another detective, Johnny Knight. Hennessy got out of his car and buttoned his coat. He went to stand beside Knight, and he lit a cigarette.

"The girl was dead as soon as she hit the ground," Knight said.

Out in the field there was a body covered by a gray woolen blanket.

"Kids," Knight said. "They never think anything can hurt them. She was fooling around. Sitting on top of the front seat. Right through the window on impact."

Hennessy nodded and smoked his cigarette. "Mind if I take a look?" he asked.

"Hey." Knight shrugged. "Have a party."

Hennessy went over to the fence. The Chevy was totaled; there was so much broken glass that the asphalt seemed to be covered with stars. Hennessy saw something as white as milk shimmering in the dark. Only when he reached down to pick it up did he realize he hadn't found a piece of glass. What he held in the palm of his hand was a perfect white tooth.

The flag outside the high school was at half-mast for two days, and there had been an assembly to honor Cathy's memory. Even the rudest boys, boys who had fucked Cathy Corrigan and boys who only said they had, were silent and wore dress shirts and black ties. Girls who had written that Cathy was a tramp with their hot-pink lipsticks on the mirrors in the girls' room, and who had refused to sit next to her in class, put their arms around each other and wept. There was blood on the athletic field for a week, spots that looked like rust and hushed anyone who passed by, until more snow began to fall. And now, nearly two weeks after the accident, Ace McCarthy still rose at dawn. His brother would be coming home from the hospital in only a few hours, but Ace got dressed and left the house before his parents were out of bed. By the time the sun was rising, Ace was standing beside the smashed-in fence. The snow was already deep enough to cover his ankles. He had come every day to this spot where the car had crashed, and now all he saw was snow. It was so cold that the snow turned blue and Ace had to breathe into his cupped hand for warmth. He stayed there as long as he could take it, he stayed until he could see the crash somewhere behind his eyelids. And then he turned up his collar and put his hands in his pockets.

He walked home the long way, as he did every day now, past Cathy Corrigan's house at the end of Hemlock Street. He had to make a loop around Poplar to get to her house, and by the time he reached the far end of Hemlock his boots were filled with snow. He stood outside Cathy's house and smoked a cigarette and listened to the barking, the way he did every day. Cathy's father drove a delivery truck, which was parked in the driveway; crates that held bottles of soda and seltzer were filling with snow. Ace let his cigarette drop, then walked around the truck to get a better look. He went past the low evergreen bushes to the side gate of the chain-link fence. He could see a picnic table in the backyard and a barbecue grill no one had bothered to take in at the end of the summer. He could see a thick rope, pulled tight. Ace held on to the gate and blinked snow off his eyelashes. He tried to picture Cathy the way she was six years ago, when they had all first moved in and there were kickball games every night, but he couldn't even remember much about the way she had looked the last time he'd seen her.

Cathy Corrigan's father came out the front door and got his snow shovel off the stoop. He walked around to the driveway and stopped when he saw Ace. "What the hell are you doing here?" Mr. Corrigan said.

Ace turned and blinked. Everything looked hazy and white. "I was looking to see what was back there," he said.

"Oh, yeah, sure," Mr. Corrigan said. "I'll just bet you were." He was wearing thick leather gloves. He came a little closer. "I don't want you near here. Go back where you belong."

"Okay," Ace said. His toes were freezing; he couldn't even feel them anymore. "What's back there?" he asked.

"If I see your brother," Mr. Corrigan said, "I might just kill him." He turned and started to shovel the snow around his truck.

"Want some help?" Ace asked.

"I don't want anything from you," Mr. Corrigan said, and he kept on shoveling, harder, so that his breath came out in blue clouds.

Ace walked over and watched Mr. Corrigan work.

"Didn't you hear me?" Mr. Corrigan said. He stopped shoveling. "Get out of here."

They stared at each other; behind them the barking grew more frenzied.

"I was just wondering," Ace said, "what it was you had back there."

"Cathy's dog," Mr. Corrigan said. "But it's none of your business."

"It's cold weather," Ace said, "for a dog."

"Yeah?" Mr. Corrigan said. "You're worried about a dog? What about my daughter? Anybody worry about her?"

Mr. Corrigan went back to work; he was crying as he shoveled snow.

"It's too cold," Ace said, and as he spoke his words froze, then snapped in two.

"Fuck it," Mr. Corrigan said. "Fuck it all."

The dog's barking echoed down Hemlock Street as Ace walked to his end of the block. In the snow, the houses all took on the same shape, with roofs peaked and the shrubbery blanketed and the house numbers covered up. When the snow swirled around you this way it could blind you; you could easily lose your way. Rickie Shapiro had

eaven

just navigated the drifts in her driveway so she could go baby-sit for
the Silk boys, when she saw him. He was nothing more than a black
line walking down the center of the road. Except for the sound of the
barking dog, the street was silent, although Rickie could hear Ace's
breathing as he drew closer. She could have turned and gone on to
Nora's, but she just stood on the sidewalk, wearing a wool hat she
wouldn't ordinarily be caught dead in in public, and pink-and-white-
striped mittens. Ace made his way up the curb and stopped in front
of her.

"I just happened to be here," Rickie said. "I wasn't waiting for you.
I'm going to baby-sit."

Ace's face was ashen; he had a blank look in his eyes, as if he were
seeing right through her.

Rickie felt herself flush. "I'm not waiting for you," she said, and
that's when she realized that she was, and that she had been for a
long time.

Ace walked up to her and put his arms around her, underneath her
coat.

Rickie Shapiro slid backward in the snow, but Ace pulled her to
him. If he tried anything, if he moved his hands up toward her
breasts or tried to kiss her, Rickie would have panicked; she would
have run back through the drifts and locked the door behind her. But
Ace only rested his head against hers, and then he said the one thing
that could have made her stay.

"Please," Ace said, low down, so his voice could barely be heard.

"I don't know what you're talking about," Rickie said.

But she did. She had always done exactly what she was supposed to,
and it had gotten her nothing. Maybe it was simply that she had
never truly wanted anything before.

"I can meet you tonight," Rickie said. She must be crazy; she would
never say a thing like that.

Ace backed away. There was something else he had to do tonight.

"I can leave my window unlocked," Rickie whispered, although
there was no one but Ace who could possibly have heard her.

"Yeah," Ace whispered back. "Just not tonight."

Rickie watched him walk away. She clapped her mittens together
and snow fell off and sank into the drifts. He said no, he said not
tonight, and she still wanted him. She was somebody she'd never

been before. She had no pride at all. She would have done things with him she could never have admitted to Joan Campo. Not in a million years. Her face was so hot it burned, and it kept on burning even after she was inside Nora Silk's house, after she had taken off her coat and her boots and knelt to pick up the baby. While Nora got ready to walk to Armand's, the baby reached out and touched Rickie's hot cheek with one finger. His touch made Rickie gasp, and that was when she realized she was no longer in the place where she stood. She was somewhere in the future, on the night when Ace would climb through her window, when he would drop down to the floor, soundlessly, and she would be there, waiting for him.

The Saint had shoveled the driveway and the sidewalk and was fitting chains on the wheels of his Chrysler. Marie was in the kitchen, drinking coffee. She hadn't had a bite to eat for breakfast, except two Stella D'oro cookies, which tasted like dust. All she could think of was bringing Jackie home from the hospital. He had broken his leg in two places and dislocated his shoulder and fractured two ribs, but, worst of all, he had lost all his teeth. When they crashed into the fence his mouth had hit the steering wheel, and even now as the Chevy sat in a heap in the Saint's garage, there was still white powder all over the wheel.

The night of the accident, Marie had gone to the emergency room, taken one look at her older son's bloody mouth, and fainted. They held ammonia under her nose, and when she came to she was cursing the girl who had been in the car with her boy and had led him astray. Ace had taken his brother's place down at the gas station after school and on the weekends, but he couldn't bring himself to go to the hospital. It would be weeks, maybe months, before the dentist and oral surgeon could get Jackie in shape and give him a new set of teeth; he had only just switched from intravenous feeding to milk shakes, which he drank through plastic straws.

Marie had made the Saint go out and buy a blender before the streets were plowed, but he hadn't talked to the salesgirl, just pointed to the model he wanted and then paid cash. He didn't speak when they drove home from the hospital, and he still wasn't talking when they were inside the house. Marie led Jackie to the kitchen table, helped him out of his black leather jacket, and sat him down. The way she smiled and cooed at him, you'd never have guessed she'd spent the last two weeks crying.

"A chocolate milk shake," she said.

Jackie shook his head no. He put his hands on the table, and when he shifted in his chair his ribs hurt. He had a special boot over the end of the cast on his broken leg so he could take a shower and get through the snow without soaking the plaster.

"A rich, thick one," Marie said, trying to entice him. "Lots of extra syrup."

The Saint helped himself to a cup of coffee. His throat felt raw, but the hot coffee helped.

"Just try it," Marie said to Jackie, and she grabbed the ice cream out of the freezer and reached for a quart of milk and two eggs. "This is the blender you got?" she said to the Saint. "It's not as big as Lynne Wineman's."

The Saint swallowed hard, then managed to speak. "I've got to open the station."

"Today?" Marie said. "The day your son comes home?"

"People still need gas," the Saint said. "They need antifreeze."

Marie pursed her lips and poured in the Hershey's syrup. The Saint put his coffee cup in the sink and ran the cold water to rinse it out. He could feel Jackie's presence in the room in some odd, undefined way; usually Jackie didn't stop talking, about his plans, his prowess, his luck. An accident was an accident; why was it the Saint kept feeling it had been Jackie's fault, why was the girl the one who went through the windshield? The Saint turned and faced the table; without his teeth, Jackie's face was sunken and small.

"That girl," the Saint said. "Was she your girlfriend?"

Jackie shrugged and looked straight ahead.

"What are you asking him questions for?" Marie said. "He just got home."

"You should have looked out for her," the Saint said to Jackie. "You had her in the car. What was she to you?"

Jackie looked up at his father. When he opened his mouth it still looked black and sharp, like the beak of a bird. He moved his swollen tongue. "Nothing," he said thickly.

The Saint went into the living room; he knew he was breathing too fast. He had no idea that Ace had risen early and been out already, so he called, "Let's go. We're going to work."

Because of Jackie, the family had missed Thanksgiving this year; Marie didn't have the heart to cook while her son was in the hospital. As everyone else in the neighborhood sat down to turkey dinners, the McCarthys had canned soup and grilled cheese sandwiches instead. But the following day the Saint had put up his Christmas lights. He set his ladder against the garage, hoping that the Christmas decorations would cool his anger, and knowing that they wouldn't.

The Saint sat down in the living room to wait for Ace to get dressed, but when Ace came out of his bedroom he was already wearing his coat and his gloves.

"He's home?" Ace asked.

The Saint nodded. The couch he sat on was a burnished orange; there were a mahogany coffee table and two end tables. The Saint had turned twenty-five before he made love to a woman, and then it had been with Marie, on their wedding night. Afterward he'd been so grateful, he had gone into the bathroom and wept.

"Come on, Pop," Ace said. "Let's go to work."

The Saint stood up and they both went into the kitchen. The blender was whirring and Jackie was staring at the refrigerator. Ace put his hands in his pockets. "Hey, Jackie," he said. He couldn't wait to get out of there; he slipped past his mother and went out the side door. The Saint took his key ring from the shelf above the stove; he could hear Ace cleaning fresh snow off the Chrysler's windshield.

"At least be home by six," Marie said. "Do me a favor."

The Saint reached for his pack of cigarettes and shook one out. He had always been toughest on Ace; he had to be, he loved him best. He thought of all the excuses he had made for Jackie. How many times had he looked away? When he knew the boy was stealing money from his wallet, when he realized he was smoking, and probably drinking as well, when he knew that something inside his older son was missing. "When I make my first million," Jackie usually said in the mornings before they left for work. "When I get my penthouse." "When I've got my limo waiting for me."

The Saint took out his silver lighter and flipped it open. As he was lighting his cigarette, he looked up and caught Jackie watching him. Quickly, Jackie looked away.

The Saint put his keys in his pocket; he was headed for the door, but when he reached the table he stopped and held out his cigarette. Jackie looked up at him, puzzled, but after the Saint nodded, Jackie took the cigarette and held it to his lips. He inhaled deeply, then slowly blew out the smoke.

"John," Marie said, upset when she saw he was encouraging Jackie to take up smoking.

"See you at six," the Saint said to her. He pulled his wool hat out of his pocket; it would be freezing down at the station today, even with the heater turned up high.

"Pa," Jackie said.

The Saint had reached the side door. He didn't turn around, but he didn't walk out either.

"Thanks," Jackie told him.

Ace waited until midnight, and by then the snow had stopped falling. From his window he could see that the light was on in Rickie Shapiro's bedroom. He tried not to think about her unlocked window; he put on his coat and slipped quietly through the house. Out on the street, it was dark and the streetlights were dim, their glow obscured by ice crystals. He could still hear the barking, but the snow muffled the sound, so that it seemed to be coming from a million miles away. There was no traffic on the Southern State, and maybe because he couldn't hear it Ace began to wonder about the places where the parkway led. How would it feel to look out the window of your car and see sagebrush and sand, to be in a town where nobody knew your family, or even your name? Why was it that he had never even imagined another town, another state, a place where not every house was exactly the same?

Ace walked through the snow into the blue distance of the street. His hands were split and cracked from working all day in the cold. He could be kissing Rickie Shapiro right now, but he was walking alone. There was a big moon, and Ace could hear the sound of his own boots crunching in the snow. When he reached the Corrigans' he went around to the side and quickly climbed the fence. He landed in a drift, then moved close to the house, staying in the shadows. He went past the side door and the dark, empty kitchen, past the picnic table and the barbecue. He was sweating and his sweat froze and stung his skin. He thought of all the people on the block who were sleeping: his brother, and Danny Shapiro, and Cathy Corrigan's parents. He thought about the fence down at the school, how it was folded in on itself, a broken silver chain. He kept inching forward, and he didn't stop until he saw the dog, tied to a crab apple tree.

The rope was long enough to stretch to a sheltered place, under an awning of corrugated plastic that rose above the cement patio. There were high drifts of snow along the patio, and the dog looked blue in the moonlight. It was just a puppy, a German shepherd, not more than six months old, and it had been outside since the accident. There was a large bowl of kibble beside it, and a bucket of water, which had frozen solid. The dog was still barking, but its voice was ragged. As soon as the dog saw Ace, it grew quiet. Its ears stood up, but it didn't move. Ace went over and worked on untying the rope from the metal collar; he had to blow on the rope to get it to bend. He swept the snow off the dog's frozen coat until his fingers burned with the cold, then he picked up the dog. He could feel a second heartbeat against his own; he could feel his chest go tight with cold and an agony that had no name. This time he didn't scale the fence. He went out through the gate, and even though the hinges creaked and he had to push hard to open it against the drifts, he made certain to close the gate behind him.

5

THE LOST WIFE

*D*ONNA Durgin weighed a hundred eighty-seven pounds, but she didn't plan to be fat for long. She was drinking so much Metrecal that she was fairly certain if she slit her wrists Metrecal would pour out instead of blood. You were supposed to drink one can for breakfast and another for lunch, and have nothing more than grapefruit and salad or a broiled hamburger, no ketchup, no bun, for dinner. Donna bought fourteen cans of Metrecal each week, and she kept them in the cabinet under the sink, alongside the ammonia and her supply of extra sponges.

She had a heart-shaped face and pale blond hair that curled around her neck in damp weather. Her skin was as white as snow. In the A&P people who didn't even know her told her she would be beautiful if only she would watch herself. They whispered to each other, How did she ever let herself get this way? Well, all they had to do was take one look at her shopping cart and they could figure out the answer. There were packs of Snickers and jars of Ovaltine, there were boxes of Frosted Flakes and loaves of white bread so soft you could roll a slice between your fingers and form a perfect ball of dough. What they didn't know was that, as of December first, Donna wasn't eating any of it anymore. Beneath all those sweets there were green cucumbers and lean ground meat she doled out to herself, slice by slice, one broiled meat patty a day. And on the bottom of the cart, under the chips and the noodles, were cans of Metrecal in assorted flavors.

Donna had been fat for seven years, so her neighbors on Hemlock Street had never known her any other way. She'd gained sixty pounds with her first child, and although she'd lost some of that weight before her second, by the time her last was born, she'd given up. Her feet were still size five; they were so small that when she looked down at them she felt like crying. But most of the time she didn't look at herself, she didn't even think about herself, or, if she did, she imagined herself as a cloud, as if the center of herself had drifted away in strands of cotton netting. And then on the last day of November her heart had broken, and that was how Donna discovered that she still had a body.

She had a load of laundry going in the basement when it happened, and her two boys, Bobby and Scott, were settled in front of the TV. Her littlest, Melanie, had fallen asleep on the living-room floor with a bottle of chocolate milk in her mouth. There was a tunafish casserole in the oven at 350 degrees and a package of frozen green beans out on the counter. Donna's husband, Robert, arrived home at five thirty, the way he always did. He worked as a printer, and the cuffs of his shirts were black with ink; the first thing he did was go into the bathroom and scrub his hands with Lava soap. When he had washed up, he changed into clean clothes; then he made his way past the limp bodies in front of the TV and came into the kitchen to get himself a beer. He had seen the Sears truck parked out front and he could hear the serviceman banging away at the pipes.

"What's broken now?" Robert asked.

He was a thin, dark man who wore a watch on a metal wristband that left a pattern on his skin. He opened his beer over the sink, in case foam sprayed out.

"It's under warranty," Donna assured him. "The washing machine just stopped working."

"So they come at suppertime?" Robert said. He was easily annoyed, and Donna noticed that when he was, a vein in his neck moved up and down, pulsing like a moth. "Couldn't they have sent someone over earlier to fix it?"

"I called at eight this morning," Donna said.

Robert made a sour face; then he went into the living room to sprawl out on the couch, which was covered with a bedspread to protect it from stains. Luckily for the kids, he didn't mind how much TV they watched, as long as they watched the programs he liked. Donna pulled the casserole out of the oven, and while it cooled she scooped three Hershey's Kisses out of a canister and popped them into her mouth.

"Now we're getting somewhere," the serviceman called up from the basement. "It's sticking on the spin cycle."

Donna Durgin went to the top of the basement stairs. "Oh, no," she said. She went down to the laundry room, wishing she'd made that five Hershey's Kisses. The serviceman had been working since seven thirty that morning and he was tired. He had blue eyes and was so tall he had to duck under the pipes that ran along the ceiling.

"There's been a strain on the belt," he said in an excited kind of way, as if he'd just solved some major equation.

The serviceman nodded for Donna to come closer, and she did. Out-of-season clothes were kept down here in the laundry room, safe in plastic clothes carriers, which hung on a metal pole. There were bathing suits and beach towels in a large brown box, and in another, smaller box Donna stored the neatly washed and folded baby clothes she couldn't bring herself to throw out. The serviceman held up his hand; he had one of Bobby's toy cars.

"This is what's been slowing down the motor," he said.

Usually Donna checked everyone's pockets before she did a wash, but somehow this small red Corvette had gotten past her. For months it had been grinding against the gears.

"I'll tell you what," the serviceman said. "Let's pretend it never existed."

A bare bulb hung above the utility sink; the light it gave off hurt your eyes, and Donna had to blink. The serviceman reached out and took her hand in his, and when he did Donna was so surprised she took a step backward and her tiny feet slid out of her sling-back shoes. The serviceman placed the toy Corvette in the palm of her hand, then closed her fingers over the car.

"Otherwise it won't be on warranty," he said.

Donna nodded and held her breath.

"I can tell you work hard," the serviceman said. "You wouldn't believe some of the laundry rooms I've seen. You're somebody who really cares."

The serviceman turned and went back to the washing machine, but Donna Durgin didn't move. She'd been wounded by his kindness; all it took was a few words from a stranger and something inside her snapped. When she went upstairs she felt dizzy, as if her lungs weren't getting enough air. The casserole was cooling on the stove, the TV was still on in the living room, Melanie was whimpering the way she always did when she woke from a late nap. Donna went out through the side door without bothering to put on her coat. She stood at the fence, clinging to the metal because the sky was coming down at her, hard. She had eaten a bowl of leftover lasagna for lunch, and she'd had some Twinkies with the children after school, but she felt as if she had swallowed bowls and bowls of white rocks. She went across the street, to the Hennessys', and made her way around to the side door. She knocked sharply, and when Ellen opened the door she was surprised to see Donna; they never visited each other at suppertime. Donna could smell dinner cooking on the stove; minute steak and onions and scalloped potatoes.

"Are you all right?" Ellen said.

"I don't know," Donna said. She had a very little voice, which everyone agreed belonged to a thinner person.

"Do you need something?" Ellen asked. "Some butter? I've got extra milk."

"Oh, God," Donna said.

"What?" Ellen said, frightened.

Donna Durgin leaned against the storm door. "I can't breathe," she said.

"Have you called a doctor?" Ellen asked. "Joe can drive you over to the hospital. He can turn on his siren and have you there in five minutes."

"No," Donna said. "It's not like that." She leaned in close and then she whispered, "It's like I've eaten stones."

Ellen smiled. She had to bite her tongue so she wouldn't say, Are you sure it wasn't Milky Ways?

"How about Pepto-Bismol? Joe's a Pepto-Bismol fanatic these days."

Donna Durgin stared at Ellen; she couldn't seem to focus. "I have that at home," she said finally. "I think I'm okay now."

"Are you sure?" Ellen said. Her onions were burning on the stove and she looked over her shoulder when she heard them sizzle.

"Oh, yeah," Donna told her. "Positive."

Donna Durgin crossed the street and stood in the dark while the stones rattled around inside her. She had been married for eight years. On her wedding day it had been raining, and when they left the church Robert had carried her to the black limousine, but the hem of her dress got soaking wet anyway. Some of the paste pearls fell off the bodice and the sleeves, and Donna's nephews and nieces scattered to grab up the pearls as though they were pirates' treasure. Now, after three children, Donna Durgin hadn't the faintest idea of who Robert was or why she had married him. When she looked down at her hand in the dark, she saw red marks on her fingers where the serviceman had touched her. From her yard, Donna could see the Christmas lights John McCarthy always strung across his garage the day after Thanksgiving. Who had smiled at Donna in the past few months? Who had asked her what she thought or what was inside her or noticed that the cuffs of Robert's inky shirts were always white after Donna had washed them and ironed them and folded them into the bureau drawer?

That night Donna reheated the casserole, but she didn't eat any supper. In the morning, she made the boys their lunches and walked them to school, then she went up to the A&P and bought her first cans of Metrecal. She didn't have a bite to eat all morning, didn't even pour her first Metrecal until Melanie had gone down for her nap. Later in the week, she began to make Christmas cookies. There were crescents coated with confectioners' sugar, chocolate peanut-butter balls, ginger cookies in the shapes of reindeer and elves, but Donna hadn't even tested the batter. She lined her tins with waxed paper, filled them with cookies, and stored them above the refrigerator.

After fourteen days of dieting, Donna had lost eleven pounds and her clothes began to feel looser, but she still wasn't there; when she looked in the mirror she couldn't see herself. And clearly, other people didn't see her either, because no one, not even Ellen Hennessy, noticed that she was thinner. Donna stopped weighing herself and kept to her diet solely for the sake of being true to her regime. She put the diet out of her mind completely, and then one day, when she was looking for a roast that would be big enough for Christmas dinner, her pants fell down around her ankles in the meat section of the A&P. Donna calmly pulled them back up, but she was thrilled because she hadn't realized till now that the elasticized waistband was inches too big. That night she seasoned the roast, and after she had pretended to eat supper and had put the kids to bed and Robert had switched on the news, Donna went into the kitchen and devoured three pink grapefruits. When she was done, she wiped her hands on a red-and-white-checked dishcloth; she still felt light as air. She went to the sink, where the dishes were soaking, and when she cleared away the bubbles Donna could see her reflection in the dish water.

Robert's whole family came for Christmas, and they had to borrow extra chairs from the Winemans and the McCarthys so all the Durgins could squeeze around the table. They served the roast and small pink potatoes and peas and onions and three kinds of pies. By the time Donna put out the coffee and mints, the kids were so wild that Bobby's new punching bag tore and exploded with a gush of air and Melanie was so overexcited she had to be put right to bed, although she refused to let go of her new stuffed animal, a cat that mewed when you shook it. The cousins gave Donna a box of nougat. Robert gave her a new G.E. blender and a set of Tupperware he had bought from Nora Silk, and his parents presented her with an angora sweater Donna's mother-in-law had bought at a big-ladies shop in Hempstead. Donna let the children stuff themselves with the nougat. She put the blender on the counter, the Tupperware into a cabinet, and the sweater, still folded in its cardboard box, up on the top shelf of her closet.

The day after Christmas, Donna was still picking up stray bits of wrapping paper and ribbon. That afternoon she had Ellen and Lynne Wineman and all their kids over and she fed them hot chocolate and Oreo cookies, but after they'd gone she realized she hadn't said a word to her friends. She knew she'd have to try harder. She took the kids sledding over at Dead Man's Hill with Ellen; she helped plan a New Year's Eve party with Lynne; she went house to house with Bobby, dragging the other children behind, selling raffle tickets to raise money for new Little League uniforms. But none of it worked, none of it mattered. And then one night when the snow was coming down hard, Donna's engagement ring fell off while she was bathing Melanie. She had had the ring enlarged when she gained all her weight, but now she had to wrap tape around the band so it wouldn't slip off. Every night she wound another piece of tape around the gold band, and she forced her finger inside, even when it hurt.

After she had lost eighteen pounds, Robert noticed. But instead of telling her he was proud of her, he complained about the price of Metrecal. He started to pick up Carvel on his way home from work—Donna's favorite, chocolate marshmallow sundaes. He left Mounds bars on the dashboard to tempt her, and when Donna didn't give in he started to harangue her that the house wasn't as clean as it used to be. His shirts weren't as white, even sex wasn't as good: Donna seemed so jumpy he half expected her to bounce right off the bed. Donna Durgin said nothing and continued to drink Metrecal and eat her grapefruit. She started to wear one of Robert's old leather belts knotted around her waist so her clothes wouldn't fall down. Sometimes when she took the children sledding she'd see Nora Silk wearing a woolly green jacket and black stretch pants, going full speed down the hill on a wooden sled with her older son behind her, his arms around her waist, and her baby up front, squealing and clapping his hands as their sled careened toward the parkway. She'd see Nora in the supermarket, thoughtfully reading recipes on the back of cereal boxes while her older boy stole sourballs from an open bag of candy on the shelf. One evening at dusk when Donna went out to retrieve a toy from the backyard, she looked through the grid of fences and saw Nora out in her backyard, lying in the snow and moving her arms up and down to form angel's wings. There was snow in Nora's hair and her cheeks were red and she let the baby crawl around without a hat while he stuffed handfuls of snow into his mouth.

Donna stood there staring, even though any other mother on the block would have looked away. On Dead Man's Hill, Lynne Wineman and Ellen Hennessy clucked their tongues when they saw Nora's baby on the sled and when they noticed that Billy Silk's winter jacket had a hole in the elbow. Ellen occasionally let loose with some of the information she'd gotten from her boy, Stevie, who sat two desks away from Billy Silk, so they all knew that Billy had once brought a sandwich for lunch that consisted of nothing more than a chocolate bar inserted between two slices of Wonder Bread. They knew his mother didn't allow him to climb the ropes during gym and that he often came to school sick and that he had vomited in the library corner. Donna Durgin listened to all this information, but really she was more interested in the jangling charm bracelet Nora wore, and the beat of the radio she heard when she walked with Melanie past the old Olivera house, and those black stretch pants, which were so tight you couldn't be more than a hundred fifteen pounds and get away with wearing them.

The truth was, Donna had begun to dream about clothes. Cinch belts and gold lamé dresses and little fur jackets made out of rabbit skins. She dreamed she was behind a counter of silk blouses and lace lingerie. She could feel the fabric when she woke up, and she felt as though she had somehow been unfaithful. She stayed away from silk and chiffon. She was still wearing her fat clothes, held up with Robert's belt and several safety pins. On the day she met Nora on line at the A&P she had on a smocked blouse she'd bought during her first pregnancy. Because it was school vacation, Nora and Donna both had their kids with them, and if Donna hadn't been so distracted by her boys' fighting she might not have pulled her cart up behind Nora's.

"Billy," Nora said sharply.

She was loading her groceries onto the checkout counter and holding the baby at the same time. Billy was standing beside the rack of candy and gum; he had begun to slide a pack of Black Jack into his coat pocket. He looked up, cool as a cucumber, when Nora called his name, but Donna could see that he had dropped the gum into his pocket. Nora came around her cart, dug into Billy's pocket, pulled out the gum, and replaced it in the rack. She gave Billy a little shove, but then she noticed Donna Durgin staring at her and she ran her fingers through her hair and smiled.

"Kids," Nora said. "They think it's their job to drive us crazy."

Donna nodded and lifted Melanie out of the kiddie seat of her shopping cart.

"Holy moly," Nora said appraisingly. "You sure look a whole lot thinner than you did in the summer."

Nora was wearing a black car coat and a straight black skirt. She had a red scarf around her neck. Chiffon.

"How'd you like the Tupperware?" Nora asked. "To tell you the truth, I would have killed my husband if he ever gave me Tupperware for Christmas, but I needed the sale so I couldn't tell him any wife would prefer a gold necklace. I did talk him into the three-quart container, because the four-quart is worthless unless you're cooking for an army."

Donna Durgin was smiling at her, but Nora could feel her slipping away, and Nora didn't want to lose her; she was, after all, the first mother on the block who had stayed put long enough for Nora to get in two words. Fortunately, the checker who had replaced Cathy Corrigan was so slow they were trapped there together on line.

"Your husband happened to drive up when I was unloading mixing bowls. He told me you were a great cook, and I can't find a decent recipe for macaroni and cheese. People think it's so basic, but as far as I'm concerned, fixing good macaroni and cheese is a real talent."

Donna Durgin was staring at the gold heart on Nora's charm bracelet. She didn't notice that Melanie and Scott had begun taking all the Almond Joys down off the candy rack.

"Do you use cheddar?" Nora asked.

"Velveeta," Donna Durgin said.

"Aha," Nora said. "That's the secret. I really appreciate this. My kids turn up their noses at everything I cook. They're very particular."

Donna Durgin opened her mouth but nothing came out.

Nora grabbed a bag of potato chips and tossed it onto the checkout counter.

"You should come over to Armand's sometime. I could do your nails for half price and Armand would never know. He's a financial moron."

Two huge tears slipped out of Donna Durgin's eyes.

"Oh," Nora said when she saw Donna's tears. She put down the iceberg lettuce.

Donna Durgin still wasn't talking, but she had begun to cry in earnest. Her tears filled up the top of a sour cream container, then sloshed over onto the floor.

Nora hoisted her baby up and grabbed Billy. "Put up the rest of the groceries," she told Billy.

"Me?" Billy said.

"You," Nora told him. She put an arm around Donna and led her over to the empty carts.

"What is it?" Nora asked. "The Tupperware?" James struggled to get out of her arms, until she let him play with her bracelet.

Donna shook her head and kept crying.

"Everything?" Nora suggested.

Donna Durgin nodded and took a tissue from her coat pocket.

"Those black stretch pants you have," Donna said finally. "Where did you buy them?"

"Lord and Taylor," Nora admitted. "Not that I'm one of their regular customers, but sometimes you've got to splurge. Good clothes last forever." Nora looked over at Billy and made a face at him so he would hurry up with the groceries. Between his taking his time and the checker's amazing lassitude, the line that had formed behind them was backing up past the fruit aisle and into poultry. "You'd look great in black," Nora told Donna Durgin.

"You think so?" Donna asked.

"Trust me," Nora said. "Black is classic."

Donna blew her nose. She noticed that her children had taken most of the candy off the shelves.

"I'm okay now," Donna said.

"You think so?" Nora said doubtfully.

"Oh, yeah," Donna said. "Really. Thanks."

They walked back to the checkout counter, and Nora paid for her groceries, then searched Billy's pockets for stolen gum while she waited for the checker to make change.

"Mom!" Billy shouted.

"Mr. Innocent," Nora said to Donna Durgin. Nora grabbed her grocery cart and popped James inside to stand among the paper bags. "We should talk again," she told Donna.

Donna smiled, even though she seemed to be looking past Nora. "Definitely," she said. "I'd like that."

Out in the parking lot, Billy leaned against the cart and watched as Nora loaded the car.

"You could help," Nora told him. "It's a great way to build up your muscles."

Billy grabbed a bag and set it in the front seat.

"I knew this would work out if we just gave people a chance," Nora said. "People are basically shy, they have to warm up to you, they have to be won over. That's what you should be thinking about in school."

"Mrs. Durgin's going somewhere," Billy said.

"What?" Nora said, frightened that her one new friend planned to leave her in the lurch. She forgot to yell at Billy for listening in on Donna and grabbed him by his collar. "Where is she going?"

"For a walk," Billy said.

"Oh, well," Nora said, relieved. She let go of Billy and settled James into the backseat. "We should all do more of that."

Donna Durgin went for her walk on December 29, after her children had been tucked into bed and her husband had fallen asleep in front of the TV. She dragged out her old black winter coat, which fit her for the first time in years, and put on some lipstick. She slipped into her snow boots; then, right before she left, she made the children's lunch for the following day and set the tunafish sandwiches and carrot sticks wrapped in foil on the bottom shelf of the refrigerator. At a little after eleven she put her car keys on the kitchen table and went outside. There was some fresh powdery snow covering the ice and a pink moon in the center of the sky. Once she passed the line of poplar trees along her driveway, it was easy to just keep going, and by the time Robert woke up in the morning and realized she was missing, her footprints had all disappeared.

"Look," Joe Hennessy said, "women do things we can't understand every day of their lives. They think in a completely different way, so if you're trying to figure out what she was thinking, forget it; that's not going to help you now."

"You've got it all wrong," Robert Durgin said to him.

They were sitting in the living room while Johnny Knight talked to the children in the kitchen over oatmeal cookies and milk. Ordinarily, Hennessy would have been the one to question the children, but Robert was his neighbor, so Hennessy owed him. And, actually, Johnny Knight wasn't as bad with the children as Hennessy would have guessed. He had overheard Knight ask the children a few questions about their mother—if she had a favorite place to go, if she had any secret money or bankbooks hidden in a bureau drawer or in the bread box—then he had sat down with them, enjoying the milk and cookies as much as they did. Sometimes being childish paid off.

"Donna wouldn't just take off," Robert Durgin told Hennessy. He had smoked a cigarette down to the filter, but he was still holding on to it. "She's devoted to the kids. She wouldn't walk out of here. Not alone."

Hennessy hadn't taken off his coat, and he leaned back carefully on the bedspread that covered the couch. Donna Durgin had been gone for nearly twenty-four hours, but even though the kids had left their toys around, Hennessy could see she had taken good care of the house. There wasn't a bit of dust on the venetian blinds; a lace doily was neatly centered on the coffee table.

"Meaning?" Hennessy said.

"Somebody forced her," Robert said.

"You were right here on the couch," Hennessy said. "You slept here all night. You would have heard someone come in."

"They snuck in," Robert guessed. "Or they threatened the kids earlier in the day, so she was forced to go meet them in their car."

"All right," Hennessy said. "Let me think it over."

Both men sat back and tried to imagine a madman loose in the neighborhood.

"It doesn't wash," Hennessy said.

"I'm telling you," Robert said. "She wouldn't leave here of her own free will. Just consider it might not be the way it looks."

That meant Hennessy had to consider the man beside him. He might have a girlfriend hidden away somewhere, he might have taken out a big life insurance policy. Maybe he was chain-smoking not because Donna was gone but because he feared for his own skin.

"We'll look into all the possibilities," Hennessy said.

When they were done in the house, it was too cold to do much talking on the street, so Johnny Knight came to sit with Hennessy in his car. Knight blew on his hands and rubbed them together. "The kids don't know a thing," he said. "What about the husband?"

"Robert," Hennessy said. He reached across and flipped open his glove compartment, took out his Pepto-Bismol, and uncapped the bottle.

"Robert," Johnny Knight said. "Whoever. Think he's involved?"

"He's a printer," Hennessy said. He took a swig of Pepto-Bismol and replaced the bottle in the glove compartment for later. "He's never cooked a meal or made a bed in his life, and now he's got three kids to take care of."

Johnny Knight shrugged. "She's gone. He's still there."

"Shit," Hennessy said.

"Yup," Johnny Knight agreed.

There had never been a murder in town, assault was the absolute limit, but Hennessy had to begin his investigation as if there'd been one. He checked for life insurance policies and found there was one taken out on Robert and nothing on Donna. He drove to Queens and questioned Donna's mother and sister; he went to the bank where they had their savings account. He found no boyfriends, no bad debts, no leads at all. He stayed out till midnight, searching the neighborhood, talking to neighbors, and when he came home Ellen was waiting up for him in the kitchen.

"Nothing," Hennessy said.

Ellen had made him a cup of tea and set a plate of cookies on the table. She was wearing a flannel nightgown and her face was drawn.

"It's as if she was swallowed up by the ground." Hennessy shook his head.

"I can't believe it," Ellen said. While Hennessy was out, she had gone around the house locking the windows; she even latched the storm doors. "Donna and I talked all the time. I would have known if anything was wrong."

Hennessy took a graham cracker from the plate and broke it in half. "Would you have?" he asked.

"Of course I would. She was my friend. Oh, God." Ellen put down her teacup. "Was."

They stared at each other across the table.

"Nothing to show that she's dead," Hennessy said.

"Joe!" Ellen said. "Don't even say that." She took a cookie and broke it in half. "What did Robert tell the kids?"

"She's on a trip, a vacation."

Ellen stood up and rinsed out the teacups, then put them in the drain rack.

"She wasn't feeling so well," Ellen said.

"What?" Hennessy said.

"She came over here a few weeks ago and started talking about eating rocks or something. I thought it was indigestion."

"What exactly did she say?" Hennessy asked sharply.

"Joe!" Ellen said. "I'm not a witness. Don't talk to me as if I'm a criminal."

"All right." Hennessy began again, calmly, just as he would with any witness who was starting to balk. "Just think it over. Any little hint that something was wrong?"

Ellen shook her head.

"Rocks," Hennessy said.

"I have to go to bed," Ellen told him. "I can't stand this."

Hennessy went into the bedroom with her, still thinking about rocks. The only way to eat them would be to swallow them whole, otherwise you'd crack your teeth to bits, you'd wind up choking on the small, hard pieces. No, you'd have to pick them up, one by one, and open your mouth. You'd have to close your eyes and swallow, and after that you'd have to just accept the consequences of your choice.

The dog slept beside the bed, on a small blue rug, and at night he ran through his dreams. He ran through the grass and through the rain and in between stars set into the black night.

"Whoa, boy," Ace would say sometimes, and from where he lay in bed he would stretch out and pat the dog's head. But the dog never woke from his dreams. He only whimpered and turned on his side, and then began running once more. Someone had once cared for this dog, so it did not come as a complete shock to find that someone cared for him again, and he gave himself completely to Ace. All Ace had to do was purse his lips and the dog would run to him before he whistled. The dog spent a good deal of his time waiting for Ace, in the bedroom—where Marie grudgingly allowed him to stay, although she would have preferred the basement or, better yet, the yard—or in the schoolyard, near the door Ace always came through when the bell rang at two forty-five. Someone had once cared for him, that's all he knew. Someone had bought him a leather collar with a silver tag that read: *My name is Rudy. I belong to Cathy and I live at 75 Hemlock Street.* Ace had slipped the name tag off the dog's collar, but he couldn't throw it out. He kept it in the inside pocket of his leather jacket, and already the name tag had etched its shape into the pocket, leaving a permanent ridge.

"Rudy," Ace would whisper as the dog slept beside him. "Go, Rudy," he would call as he threw a stick across the playing field after school. He had waited for somebody to ask where in hell he had gotten a purebred German shepherd overnight, but nobody did. For the first few days he had kept the dog hidden in his bedroom. He had smuggled in hamburger meat and bowls of milk. He set down newspapers for the dog to pee on. During the first week Ace let the dog on his bed at night, where he curled up beneath the covers, exhausted from the treatment Cathy Corrigan's father had doled out. The dog's paws were cold as ice and there was still blood between his pads, which left faint red streaks on the floor.

When Marie discovered the pee-stained newspapers in the garbage, she tracked down the dog. She had a nose for anything unclean, and, as far as she was concerned, dogs were worthless creatures. Ace expected her to give him the third degree and scream for the dog to be taken to the pound. But all Marie did was announce that she wouldn't have the dog up on her furniture, and she wouldn't have him begging at the dinner table, and she expected Ace to walk him three times a day. That evening, as soon as the Saint came in from work, Marie said, "Go see what your son brought home." The Saint knocked on Ace's door, and when he went into the room and saw the dog he crouched down and clapped his hands.

"Come on, boy," the Saint said, but Rudy was afraid of him and ran under the bed. The Saint stood up and whistled, but the dog wouldn't come. "I could use a dog like that down at the station," he told Ace.

"Sorry, Pop," Ace said. "He doesn't like to let me out of his sight."

That night when they were sitting down for supper, the dog yelped and scratched to be let out of Ace's bedroom.

"That your dog?" Jackie asked.

Ace concentrated on his meatloaf. He'd been avoiding Jackie ever since the accident; he hadn't even gone for a ride in Jackie's new Bel Air, the one Ace had been saving for and hoping to buy. "That's right."

"Well, keep that woofer quiet at night," Jackie said.

Ace stared at his brother. With his new teeth and his rebuilt jaw, Jackie looked more substantial, more solid. And yet when the dog yelped Jackie seemed nervous. That was how Ace realized that his brother knew it was Cathy's dog, and that his parents also somehow knew, but they didn't let on any more than Mr. Corrigan had. Ace had worried about Mr. Corrigan; he'd figured there'd be some kind of a scene. Mr. Corrigan would call him a thief, he'd say it ran in the family, then he'd grab the dog or call the police. Or worse, he'd punch Ace, hard, and Ace wouldn't be able to fight back. But that wouldn't stop Mr. Corrigan; he'd smack Ace on the side of the head and leave him lying there on the lawn, in a heap.

Yet the day they finally crossed paths, Mr. Corrigan acted as if he'd never seen Ace or the dog before in his life. You would have thought that fitting the covers onto his silver trash cans took all his concentration. But the dog recognized Mr. Corrigan. The hair on his neck and his ears went straight up, and he made a low growling noise in the back of his throat. Ace stood paralyzed, waiting for Mr. Corrigan to attack him, but all he did was turn and drag his trash cans up to the house.

So Ace wasn't surprised when no one at school asked where the dog had come from. The guys on the corner, out for a smoke before the homeroom bell, didn't say a word, although they all backed away when they saw the dog. Rudy followed Ace everywhere. He stretched out on the tile floor in the bathroom while Ace took a shower; he trotted at Ace's heels on nights when Ace met Rickie Shapiro at the fence along the Southern State, where they kissed until their mouths were bruised. But, like the guys on the corner, Rickie was afraid of the dog. Even Danny Shapiro seemed uncomfortable when he realized the dog would be walking home from school with them every day.

"Does he bite?" Danny asked.

"He's a goddamned puppy," Ace said. "He's got baby teeth." Ace threw a tennis ball over the snow on the Winemans' lawn, and Rudy went after it.

"Yeah," Danny said uneasily as the dog raced back toward them. "Baby fangs."

"Drop it," Ace said, and the dog laid the ball at his feet.

"He understands you," Danny said. "I swear to God."

Ace knelt down. "Speak," he said to the dog. Without Danny's noticing, he signaled to Rudy by opening and closing his hand. The dog barked on cue, just as Ace had taught him to do.

Danny Shapiro stepped off the sidewalk and into the street. "That dog's too weird for me," he said.

Ace was still facing Rudy; the dog stared up at him, his gaze unblinking, his tongue hanging out. "Good boy," Ace said. Rudy leaned over and sniffed Ace's hand, then slowly licked it. Ace gave the dog a pat, then he stood up and started down Hemlock. When he passed the Durgins', he realized that Danny was no longer beside him.

"What's the matter?" Ace called.

Danny just shrugged. Ace walked back to him, the dog behind him.

"I don't like the idea of that dog around my sister," Danny said.

"Oh?" Ace said.

"To tell you the truth, I don't know if I like the idea of you around her."

"You're kidding," Ace said.

"She's sixteen," Danny said. "She's my sister."

"So what?" Ace said.

"So she asks me questions about you all the goddamned time," Danny said. "I know what's going on. Man, you're not even allowed in our house because of the Cadillac."

"I had nothing to do with that Cadillac," Ace said. "And anyway, he got a new one."

"Yeah. Well," Danny said.

"Yeah, well, maybe you're an asshole," Ace said.

"Maybe I am," Danny said thoughtfully.

Ace turned without a word and walked home with his dog. Danny stayed where he was and pitched snowballs at a poplar tree on the Winemans' lawn. He had a decent fastball, but he wasn't a pitcher. He was a hitter. He had spent years practicing with Ace; Ace couldn't hit, but he sure could tell someone else how to, and he didn't mind spending hours in the deserted athletic field when the temperature hit ninety-five degrees in the shade. He was the only one willing to pitch balls to Danny until dark, or until one of their mothers came looking for them.

They weren't friends anymore, that was all there was to it. Danny didn't know it could happen this way, but it had. Maybe something was wrong with him, maybe something was missing; he should have been thinking about girls, or his college applications, which were sitting in the admissions offices at Cornell and Columbia right now. He should have been thinking about his senior prom in June or the fact that his best friend was walking away from him without a word. But he wasn't. He was thinking about baseball and July afternoons and the way the bat reverberated in his hands when he hit a curveball.

When he stopped throwing snowballs he had no choice but to go home. He went in through the side door so he wouldn't track snow onto the living-room rug. He kissed his mother and told her the rolls she had just put into the oven smelled great. She didn't bother to ask Danny how his day had gone or if he had homework; his days were always great and he always did his homework. He was trustworthy, everyone knew that. He'd be the class valedictorian in June, and he would easily earn admission to either college he'd applied to on the basis of his advanced science projects. He'd been working as a research assistant for Dr. Merrick at the state university every Saturday, studying the effect of vitamin C and cannabis on growth and aggression. He still took the bus up on Harvey's Turnpike over to the biology department every Saturday, but he no longer bothered to feed marijuana to the hamsters. Instead, he fed them oregano brought from home, falsified his data, and pocketed the marijuana.

He would never have thought of smoking it and would have dutifully fed the hamsters all semester, if he hadn't overheard two graduate students joking about how some people would give their eyeteeth to smoke what the damned hamsters were being given for free. Danny stole a cigarette from one of the graduate students, and in the bathroom next to the lab he rubbed the cigarette between his fingers until all the tobacco fell out. Before he left for the day, he replaced the tobacco with marijuana and smoked it on the corner while he waited for the bus. He never wasted the marijuana on the hamsters again.

After he'd greeted his mother and hung up his coat, Danny grabbed a bag of chocolate chip cookies and went into his bedroom. He was fairly certain that no one on Hemlock Street even knew what marijuana was, but he opened his window a crack just in case his mother came in unexpectedly; she'd assume he was smoking cigarettes, and she'd be crushed.

Danny lit up and lay back on his bed and thought some more about baseball. His mind was clear and cool. He listened to the sounds in the house. His mother making dinner in the kitchen, a dinner his father would, as usual, be home too late to share in. His sister in the bathroom, washing her hair in the sink. People thought they knew you, but what did they really know? Danny stubbed out what was left of the marijuana-filled cigarette and put it in an ashtray he kept hidden in his closet. He flipped on his clock radio and watched the dial glow. He had absolutely nothing in common with anyone anymore, and he didn't know why. He loved Ace, but every time Ace started to talk Danny felt like punching him in the mouth.

The music gave him a headache, so Danny turned the radio off and listened to the sound of the parkway. He hated the feeling that everyone was passing him by, but he couldn't stop listening to the Southern State. He fell asleep to it, and woke to it, and, if he wasn't careful, he was about to go nuts to it. He forced himself to get off his bed and change into a clean shirt, then went into the bathroom to wash up for supper. Rickie was still in there; she sat on the rim of the tub reading a magazine. There was a plastic bag over her hair.

"Yikes," Danny said.

"Do you mind?" Rickie said haughtily. "I'm conditioning my hair."

Danny ignored her and went to the sink to wash his hands and face. The water that came out of the tap stung him, as if there were tiny bees in the droplets.

"Notice anything strange around here?" Danny said as he reached for a towel.

"Like?" Rickie said.

Danny closed the bathroom door, then hoisted himself up to sit on the counter.

"Like Dad is never here."

"He's getting ready for April fifteenth," Rickie said.

Danny wondered if Rickie was truly an idiot or if she had to work hard to be so thick.

"All right," Danny said. "How about this one: Ace McCarthy."

Rickie took the plastic bag off her head and ran her fingers through the goopy conditioner. She caught a glimpse of herself in the mirror and stood up to get a better look. She might have a chance to be really pretty if she could only get rid of her freckles. Sometimes she just about went crazy covering each freckle with pancake makeup until her face seemed to be dissolving in the mirror.

"I don't know what you're talking about," Rickie told her brother.

She and Ace had been meeting every night when he went out to walk the dog. He would never have anything she wanted, but she couldn't stay away from him. She was frightened by Ace's silence and the way her pulse seemed so hot and fast when she was with him. But more than anything, the dog frightened her. It followed too closely as they walked along the fence beside the parkway; it nipped at the backs of Rickie's legs and made peculiar sounds, so that Rickie was never quite certain if it was growling or trying to speak. Ace never said much, but when they were far enough from home he always put his arms around her and kissed her for such a long time Rickie didn't know if they'd ever be able to stop. Each time Ace was the one who kept them from going too far; he'd pull away and whistle for the dog, and on the way home he'd walk so far ahead of Rickie she'd have to run to keep up.

"Who do you think you're talking to?" Danny said. "I've seen you."

Rickie ran the water in the sink and reached for her shampoo.

"Mind your own business," she said.

"Dinner," their mother called from the kitchen.

"All right, stupido," Danny said to Rickie. "But you're making a big mistake. Ace is definitely not for you. You're the cashmere type, so you might as well face up to it."

Rickie let the water run in the sink; she looked over at her brother. "I thought he was your best friend."

"Was," Danny said softly. "That's the operative word."

In his clean white shirt and blue jeans Danny looked the same as he had when he was ten years old. He never had to be told to take the garbage out on trash nights. You could trust him with your life, but

you couldn't talk to him; you had the feeling that if you even tried
he'd dart away from you, he'd disappear under layers of glass. Rickie
put her head under the water and lathered up some shampoo. She
didn't ask her brother what had happened between him and Ace
because she didn't want him to question her.

Danny was used to being smart, but he didn't know everything. He
didn't know, for instance, that on New Year's Eve Rickie and Ace
planned to do a lot more than kiss, or that Rickie had been the one to
suggest, once again, that she leave her bedroom window unlocked.
He might know biology and he might know calculus, but he certainly
didn't know that Rickie had already planned to be wearing pink satin
baby doll pajamas that would drive Ace crazy when he finally came
in through her unlocked window. He had no idea that, sitting there
on the bathroom counter, he looked so lonely you had to wonder how
he could stand it. You had to wonder if loneliness like his was catching
and if, in spite of everything you were feeling, you'd better just steer
clear.

They were having a party over at the Winemans' just the way
they'd planned, in spite of Donna's disappearance. They decided
they had to, and not just because Marie McCarthy had already baked
two banana cream pies and Ellen Hennessy had fixed a cheesecake
and Lynne Wineman had learned how to make sloe gin fizzes. They
went on with it because it was the last night of the decade and it
would never be the first minute of 1960 again. They did it because
they needed to put on earrings and high heels. They needed to see
that their husbands still looked handsome when they put on their
suits and ties, that their arms still felt strong when they danced to the
slow songs down in the Winemans' finished basement.

Nora Silk was trying her best to have a party of her own. She was
wearing a black cocktail dress and she'd made pigs in blankets and
cheddar cheese balls, which she set out on a silver tray. She fixed a
highball for herself and a Shirley Temple for Billy, but after eleven
she couldn't get him to stay awake and watch Guy Lombardo with
her on their new TV. He fell asleep on the couch, clutching his
blanket, while Nora went into the kitchen to freshen up her drink.

It was a cold, starry night. It was the kind of night when, if you left
your two sons sleeping and went to stand on the front stoop, you

could hear the music from a house halfway down the block. Nora had taken her highball out with her, and she took little sips as she watched the stars. Ten years earlier, when it was almost 1950, she'd gone dancing with Roger, and later in the night he'd gotten so drunk he'd thrown up on Eighth Avenue. She had been completely in love with him. She'd taken him back to their apartment and put a damp washcloth on his forehead and fixed him coffee that was so strong it made him gasp. Then they'd gotten into bed, just a mattress made up on the floor, and made love until it was light. So maybe he was a better magician than Nora had ever admitted, because for years he'd made it seem as if what they had was enough. Washing diapers in the kitchen sink, walking up four flights of stairs with her groceries—it was enough when he kissed her, when he brought home the gold charm bracelet, when he put on his tuxedo and combed his hair back with water. If they had never had children, they might be together still, in Las Vegas, where the light was thin and purple and New Year's Eve was a drunk and sweaty night, celebrated as it should be.

It caused Nora great pain to hear the music from the Winemans', physical pain, as if she'd drunk sour milk that was turning her stomach. Who were these people who danced in the dark, whose children taunted Billy and threw rocks? Good people, she had to believe that, people who tucked their children in at night, who packed school lunches with tender care, who made the same sacrifices she did, maybe even more, so that their children could play in the grass and sleep tight and walk to school holding hands, safe on the sidewalk, safe in the streets, safe the whole night through. And it was not their fault, or anyone else's, that tonight Nora felt as if she were the only person on the planet who was all alone.

But two houses down, at a quarter to midnight, Rickie Shapiro would have given anything to be alone. She had just decided that she had made a terrible mistake, and, if she wasn't careful, she might never recover. Something as simple as this could ruin her whole life. She had never let anyone touch her before, and he had somehow gotten his hand under the elastic waistband of her pajamas and was moving his fingers in and out of her. Her lips were swollen from all their kisses, and her skin was hot and flushed. There were marks on her breasts, as if his touch had burned her. If she wasn't careful, he would reach up and pull off her pajama bottoms and then it would be too late. But nobody could make her do this if she didn't want to. He looked like a complete stranger, like somebody on fire and far away. And what would she get from him, what did he really have to offer her? Nothing. Her mother's heart would break, and her father would weep and tear out his hair, and her brother would tell her, You're so stupid, I told you not to. She had twelve sweaters folded in her bottom bureau drawer; she had college to think about after her senior year; she had boys dying to go steady with her, boys who were in the chemistry club and on the football team both, who'd be too shy to put their tongues in her mouth when they kissed her.

She'd have these marks on her breasts for days. She knew that. She would open her blouse and unhook her bra and run her fingers over the marks, and her eyes would fill with tears. Girls like her didn't do this, and that was why Rickie Shapiro was changing her mind. Because if she didn't stop him now, she never would.

"Wait a second," Ace said, when she pushed him away. "This was your idea."

Her parents were out at their favorite restaurant, a French place in Freeport, and Danny had left the rest of the math club at the bowling alley and was down at the creek behind the high school smoking marijuana and listening to his transistor radio. She would never get caught, but she just might get trapped.

"I can't do this," she said.

She had let him in her window nearly an hour ago. She made him leave his dog outside, in the yard, and every once in a while they'd hear a faint yelp, but they had gone on kissing, they had gone crazy. Now the sound of the dog got through to Rickie and made her panic. She thought about Cathy Corrigan and the other girls like her, the ones who used too much hairspray, and put on eyeliner so thickly they looked beaten up, who sometimes disappeared weeks before graduation, mysteriously removed to an aunt and uncle's in upstate New York, to return the next fall subdued and sullen and treated like poison.

Rickie wrenched away from Ace. She was shaking when she stood up.

"All right," Ace said. He had his shirt off, and now he reached up and put it on and began to button it. "Don't get upset."

Rickie was breathing too fast. It seemed to Ace that she just might hit him if he moved too quickly.

"I made a mistake," Rickie said. She went to her closet for her bathrobe and put it on. "I could never be with you." She reached toward her bureau and grabbed her brush, the expensive kind, made in France, with a real tortoiseshell handle. She brushed her hair with hard, even strokes. "You can't even write your own term papers."

Rickie put the brush down; she felt like crying. Ace looked up at her blankly. "You don't even know when you've been insulted," Rickie said.

Ace stood up and tucked his shirttails in and grabbed his jacket off the wicker chair.

"You can't tell anybody about this," Rickie said. "You wouldn't do that to me."

Ace went to the window and opened it. He stepped on the wicker chair to hoist himself up.

"Look, I'm sorry," Rickie said. "I didn't want to hurt you."

"What makes you think you did?" Ace said.

At the very least he wouldn't give her that. He wouldn't turn to glass and let her see into his soul. He went through the window and dropped to the ground. In the dark, the dog was waiting; he rose to his feet and shook himself, then stood close to Ace, leaning against his legs.

"Good boy," Ace whispered.

He was so empty that he didn't question Rickie's change of heart. He'd never believed he deserved very much, and now he could see he would get even less than he'd imagined. The air was sharp and clear; it hurt to breathe. He went through the Shapiros' yard, the dog at his heels. He could have cried, if he'd had anything left inside him. He stopped in the Shapiros' driveway and took out a cigarette, but before he lit it he held his hand over the match, and when the flame touched his skin, he didn't feel a thing.

He had nowhere to go, and maybe he never had. But he started walking anyway; if he didn't move he'd turn to stone. It was getting cold fast, dropping one degree every second. As Ace passed the Winemans' he could hear music from inside. The sound was muffled because a dense white fog had begun to rise from the lawns. He kept walking, even though he was afraid, and the hair on his arms rose up, as if he'd been charged with internal static electricity. But it was the air that was electric. The crab apples and the poplars crackled and their branches turned blue. The sidewalk was the color of bones, the stars formed a constellation no one had ever seen before, like the spine of a dinosaur arching above the rooftops, brilliant and terrifying. And it was no use to walk any farther, because at the far end of Hemlock Street Cathy Corrigan's ghost had appeared on her father's front lawn.

She stood between the azaleas and the ivy and her feet were bare. He knew it was Cathy because she was wearing white, because her earrings were bitter globes and there were rings on all her fingers. He knew it because no other ghost could fill him with such despair or make him bleed from a wound that wasn't even there. What was the blue light that surrounded her, like a moon of the wrong color or a thumbprint of sorrow? The dog had stopped beside Ace on the sidewalk. He didn't bark or growl, but he cocked his head, then took a few steps forward, as if he'd been called. Ace reached out and grabbed the dog's collar.

"Stay," Ace whispered.

The dog didn't pull, but he made a soft whining sound. Cathy Corrigan's ghost was disappearing as they watched, molecule by molecule, as if it were made up of fireflies. Soon there was a blanket of light over the lawn, and the light went deeper and deeper, through the ice and into the grass, and finally between the blades of grass and into the earth.

Ace McCarthy lowered his head and wept; not knowing if he'd been blessed or cursed, he was completely lost. Now more than ever, there was no place for him to go, but he couldn't stay where he was. He took off as fast as he could. The dog ran beside him, along the sidewalk and across the lawns, but the air was so white they might have been running through stars. They ran with all their might, side by side, every breath tearing at their ribs. They weren't about to stop, and they might have gone on running this way forever, headlong into the oncoming traffic on the Southern State, if Ace hadn't found himself in Nora Silk's arms, where he cried for as long as he needed, before she took him home.

1960

6

THE SIGN OF THE WOLF

*T*HE air was white and full of whispers, clair-voyant air, as if there were ghosts on the chimney tops and under the beds and in your own freezer, between the ice cube trays and the Eskimo Pies. As soon as twilight fell, a trellis of ghosts would appear in the white air and the children would stop throwing snowballs and race inside their houses. Late at night there would be the sound of something tapping at your window and not even the TV or the radio could get rid of the voices telling you things you shouldn't know. People began to long for color, for a line of crimson over the parkway at sunset, or a blue sky; but day after day there was nothing but snow and fog, and in the stillness you could find yourself overcome with desire, a desire that made everything ache, fingers and elbows and toes.

On Hemlock Street desire did not come alone but was twisted around a core of dissatisfaction. You might find it when you slipped your hand into a rubber glove to scour the kitchen sink, or in the wedges of pear sliced onto a plate for a baby's lunch. It was in the bottom of lunch pails brought to work, in the sleeves of black leather jackets thrown on after the last bell rang at the high school. And in the morning, when the fog was at its thickest, people stared at each other from their driveways and wondered what they were doing on this street, and the ghosts whispered in their ears, egging them on,

and things began to happen for no reason at all. Things no one had
imagined or ever expected and certainly had never wanted. Some of
the men on the block forgot to pay the bills on time, and you'd know
it when the lights in the house next door began to flicker. There were
evenings when the women didn't even bother to cook but slipped TV
dinners into their ovens and let their children eat right in front of the
set. On Friday nights it was almost impossible to get a baby-sitter
because most of the teenage girls had decided they had better things
to do. They had given up wearing panty girdles and stockings and a
few of the wilder ones had stopped wearing underwear and you
could see their flesh through their blue jeans and their pleated skirts.
Looking at them, the boys went crazy all at once and turned up their
transistor radios so loud you'd have thought they'd go deaf, and they
got so hot the air around them sizzled and they smelled like fire even
when they stepped out of the shower, clean and soaking wet.

Everyone was edgy and ready to snap, but the ghosts kept up their
whispering, a jumble you couldn't quite make out, and yet you knew
it had something to do with the way you lived your life, and that just
made you more furious when dinner wasn't on the table at six o'clock
or when your daughter mouthed off to you. It was the weather, the
dampness, the January blues, the mothers told themselves when the
laundry piled up and they just didn't care. It was this and nothing
more that made the children pull cats' tails and the neighborhood
dogs tip over trash cans and scatter garbage over the lawns. But it
kept getting worse, and toward the middle of the month some people
started to believe that it was Donna Durgin's disappearance that had
started to make things go wrong. People began to turn away when
they saw her husband walking the two boys to school, with the little
girl running after them, all their clothes wrinkled as could be and
Melanie's braids fixed so poorly you could tell no one had bothered to
comb them out the night before. They tried not to run into Robert
Durgin at the supermarket, where he took boxes of cereal and jars of
mayonnaise off the shelves while the children, who were all piled
into the cart, grabbed at bags of potato chips and bottles of Pepsi.
They stopped taking casseroles over to the Durgins' house and they
stopped offering to baby-sit, and after a while they even stopped
feeling bad about it because Robert hired a woman from Hempstead
to sit for Melanie during the day and pick up the boys after school,

and from a distance she could almost pass for the children's grand-mother, although she never bothered to pull up their socks or tuck their pants into their snow boots. But even though people in the neighborhood avoided Robert Durgin, it seemed what was happen-ing was contagious. Ellen Hennessy noticed that the braids in her own daughter's hair kept slipping out of their rubber bands and Suzanne, who usually looked like a little angel, seemed messy no matter what, and that her son, Stevie, refused to mind her and talked back in a way she would never have dreamed of when she was his age, and that she herself forgot to defrost chops and steaks for dinner so night after night they had fish sticks and baked beans and, al-though Joe never said a word, the children were beginning to com-plain.

Ellen still had a double boiler she had borrowed from Donna, and maybe that was why she couldn't cook. She had a breathless feeling sometimes, too, and even breathing slowly into a brown paper bag did no good. When she and Joe were alone she got all shaky, and Joe had actually asked her if there was another man and she'd laughed and said, Who on earth could there possibly be? He'd let it drop at that, he didn't go as far as her sister Jeannie's husband, who had made her take down a photograph of John Kennedy she'd tacked to the wall because he was too damn good-looking. It wasn't another man Ellen Hennessy wanted, and although Kennedy made her feel some-thing, too, it was Jacqueline Kennedy she couldn't get enough of; she'd search the newspapers for her photograph, she'd read what-ever she could find about what designer Jackie liked best, what books she had read, anything to give her a clue to how this woman could be so perfect and so completely filled with promise. Jacqueline Kennedy was the future, Ellen could see that, and as soon as she did she had to consider her own future as well. When Stevie was in school and Suzanne was down for her nap, Ellen would stand by the back door and look at Donna Durgin's house and she'd feel something she didn't want and didn't understand surface within her. It was the desire, and it hit her hard, and she was so furious about all those years when she had never wanted anything that she grew colder each day, until she was a perfect piece of ice and Joe Hennessy couldn't touch her, he couldn't even be in the same room with her.

Hennessy would have wept if he'd allowed himself to, he would have banged his head against the wall, but instead he downed ten cups of black coffee each day and half a bottle of Pepto-Bismol. He was still on the Durgin case, and it was a relief to think about Donna instead of feeling sorry for himself. Hennessy was the only one on the block who still went to the Durgins'. It got so that he'd make up excuses to go over and look for clues. He'd search Donna's closet and look through her cookbooks for secret messages. He telephoned her relatives in Queens twice a week to make certain no one had heard from her. Robert didn't talk about her disappearance much, not even when Hennessy pressed him. Oh, sure, if Hennessy pushed hard enough Robert would come up with the name of Donna's favorite restaurant when they were dating and living near Queens Boulevard, although when Hennessy went to look at the place, he found it had been demolished and an apartment building was going up on the lot. And even when there were no clues to look for, Hennessy would find himself heading to the Durgins'. He'd run errands for Robert on the weekends; he'd pick up one of the kids' prescriptions at the drugstore or some takeout Chinese food and then stay to watch wrestling on TV after the kids were all tucked into their beds. It wasn't as if Robert was a friend—they didn't talk much and could watch television for hours without speaking, other than to comment on the refs' lousy calls—it was more a feeling that somehow, for whatever reasons, both their wives had left them, even though Ellen was right across the street and hadn't gone anywhere at all. And it was something more. When Hennessy was at the Durgins' he could almost erase the desire that had been getting worse every day. He'd do almost anything to avoid going home. When it was too late to go to Robert's and there wasn't any extra duty down at the station, Hennessy would be trapped in his house, and after a dinner of fish sticks and beans and twelve hours of black coffee, he'd be so stricken with desire that he would have given it all away, his house, his family, his job, for one night with Nora Silk.

He wasn't lying to himself anymore, he wanted her that much, and before he knew what he was doing he had opened a savings account in Floral Park at a bank he'd never been to before. Each week he added to the account, and he kept the bankbook hidden in the garage and wasn't even sure why. He started looking through the real-estate section of the paper for garden apartments farther out on the island

and up in Albany. He got in touch with the PBA to find out if he could transfer to upstate New York. He found reasons to hang around the courthouse in Mineola, and after a while everyone knew his special interest was divorce cases. The lawyers got to know him by name, and over lunch at Reggie's Bar around the corner from the courthouse they each had a divorce story to end all divorce stories: about a woman who burned down her house in Levittown rather than split the proceeds with her husband, or a man who had shot off his toes so he wouldn't have to work and support his ex, or a sportswriter who had taken his ex's photo out to the dunes at Jones Beach and shot at it, and missed by a mile, accidentally wounding an old hermit who lived in a hut made of beach grass and who pressed charges and collected a quarter of a million.

Hennessy ate up these divorce stories; he couldn't get enough of them, the nastier the better. The chiselers who fled to Florida so they wouldn't have to pay child support, the wives who hired private detectives at twenty dollars a day so they could get close-ups of their husband's infidelity. Each story gave him hope and fueled his desire. The truth was it could be done and had been done before. In his family, in his universe, there had been no such possibility, people got married and were married forever, and that was the way it still was, except for down at the courthouse, where people were breaking up with each other right and left, tearing their families apart and shooting off their toes, and not one of them had half the reason Hennessy did, because Hennessy was in love. It truly tore his heart out just to see her. He wouldn't shovel after a heavy snowfall if Nora was out there first, because if he did he might just pick her up and carry her to his car. He didn't care if she wanted to bring her kids with her, they could all take off; and it didn't matter one damned bit if the department couldn't transfer him and he lost his pension; and he didn't give a damn about who would finish the shelves for the laundry room or even what his kids would think.

Whenever he thought of her he'd get that feeling along the base of his neck, and it drove him crazy. He started watching her house every chance he got. He found his old binoculars in the basement and cleaned them up and then locked himself in the bathroom. At night she kept the living-room blinds down, but not completely closed. He could see the lights turned on at dusk, he could see her in her bathroom, sitting on the counter so she could put on her mascara and shaking her hair in front of the mirror. Twice he had seen her lift the baby up and dance in a circle with him, and when Hennessy saw that he got shivers down his spine and he had to wash his face with cold water, and by the time he was through she was gone.

Down at the station house no one noticed that Hennessy was more withdrawn than ever. There was a red scare now that Castro had taken Havana, and Johnny Knight, who had been to Cuba on vacation once to go deep-sea fishing, was particularly upset. The other detectives said Castro wouldn't last much longer, but Johnny Knight, who already had plans to build a bomb shelter in his basement, suggested they all go to Miami this winter because by next year Florida would be red all the way up to St. Petersburg.

"You don't give a crap about Castro, do you?" he'd said to Hennessy when they went out to their cars.

Hennessy had turned on him savagely. His hands were blue with the cold. "You don't know what I think," Hennessy had told him. "You don't know what I feel."

"All right," Knight had said, backing down. "Jesus."

Hennessy had walked to his car and slammed the door shut, but he would have done anything to be in Cuba right then, red or not, he didn't give a damn. That was when he realized how far gone he was and he knew that he had to make his move. He waited for a Saturday, when Ellen took the kids to her sister's, and if he should have felt that he was betraying her, he didn't. Why should he? Ellen didn't want him any more than he wanted her, that was clear; she never would have thought of another possibility, the desire just wasn't in her. Hennessy shaved and dressed and went out to shovel snow, and when he'd cleared his sidewalk, and part of the lawn as well, Rickie Shapiro finally came out of her house and went over to baby-sit. Then minutes later, while Hennessy was working on the Winemans' sidewalk, Nora came out and began to scrape the ice off the Volkswagen's windshield. Hennessy leaned his shovel against a crab apple tree and went across the street, his neck all crazy and his pulse crazy, too. Nora was wearing sunglasses because of the snow's glare and her charm bracelet jangled against the windshield as she worked. She stopped and waved at Hennessy when she saw him, and Hennessy wished he could see her eyes.

"Armand always has a fit when I'm late, and I'm always late," Nora said.

"I'll do that for you," Hennessy said. He took the scraper from her and set to work on the driver's side of the windshield.

"You're the greatest," Nora said.

When Hennessy looked at her she was adjusting her bracelet.

"Maybe someday you won't have to work," Hennessy said. He felt choked up, as if each word he said were a sharp, dangerous object.

"Oh, no," Nora said. "I'm not kidding myself about that."

"If you got remarried," Hennessy said. He actually had the nerve to say such a thing.

"Even if I didn't have to work, I'd still work just in case I ever had to again," Nora said. "If you know what I mean. I learned my lesson."

Hennessy went around to the passenger's side and kept scraping. Nora reached into her purse, then bent down to look into the side-view mirror and put on her lipstick. Hennessy took the ice off the scraper with his fingers.

"Not that I'm planning to get married again anytime soon," Nora said.

He could see he would have to give her time. He finished the windshield and came around to hand her the scraper.

"Well, that's a loss for any man," Hennessy said before he could stop himself.

"Oh, yeah, sure." Nora laughed. Up close she smelled like honeysuckle and lipstick. She grabbed his arm, just for an instant, but that was long enough. "You're a certified doll," she said.

Hennessy stood in her driveway as she got into the car and started it up. He would save as much money as he could, for the time when she changed her mind. He'd have everything ready, maybe even the apartment, and then he'd question her and find out what kind of furniture she liked best and he'd have it all there, waiting for her. When she put the car in gear and backed down the driveway, Hennessy realized he didn't have that sick feeling in the pit of his stomach. He felt great; he could wait if he had to, he would act as if everything were the same when in fact nothing, not a goddamned thing, was. That night and the next he ate the dinners Ellen fixed as though he were really hungry. And the next day at lunch he listened to Johnny Knight curse Castro over hamburgers from White Castle.

He took Suzanne to her first ballet lesson and he spanked Stevie for saying "bitch" in front of his teacher. He couldn't have done any of it if he hadn't had hope, if it all weren't just temporary. But the waiting made him edgy and at night he couldn't sleep. He'd get into bed at eleven, and when he was certain Ellen was asleep he'd get up and fix himself some coffee and he'd wait. Sometimes Nora's cat would be out on the front stoop and sometimes her kitchen light would still be on at midnight, when the moon was in the center of the sky. When she forgot to close her venetian blinds, Hennessy liked to guess what he was looking at in the darkened living room before he got out his binoculars to check. A baby blanket on the couch, a pile of 45s forgotten on a chair, a rubber tree plant with the leaves wrinkled and turned up at the tips.

And then one night, when the air was particularly cold and still and the moon looked blue, Hennessy saw something moving in a corner of her living room. It wasn't the cat, who was out on the stoop. Perhaps the baby had climbed out of his crib, or a bundle of clothes had fallen? Hennessy put down his coffee and got his binoculars; the back of his neck was so tight he could barely turn his head. The thing stood up slowly, and only when it walked halfway across the room could Hennessy see its shadow on the wall. It was, without a doubt, the shadow of a wolf.

Hennessy went to his bedroom, opened his night table drawer, and got out his gun. His hands were shaking as he cocked the gun open and slipped in the bullets. His breathing was so raspy and loud it was hard to believe Ellen didn't wake. But she slept on, unaware that Hennessy had run out of their house with the gun in his hand. He went across the dark street, with the sound of his own breathing filling his head. When he reached the bushes beside the stoop he forced himself to slow down. He made his way to the window carefully, crouching low. The wolf was under the dining-room table. Hennessy might have been fooled into believing it was asleep, but its ears stood straight up, listening. This was fate, it was almost a miracle, because the waiting was about to be over. It didn't matter how the beast had gotten into Nora's house, or even if it took a chunk out of Hennessy's leg when they faced each other; he was about to save Nora, and when he did she would know he was the man she needed. Certain of this, Hennessy felt his fear drop away. He stood up to his full height, but as he did he knocked against the window and the wolf saw him. And then Hennessy was not quite so certain.

The wolf got up on all fours and came out from under the dining-room table. It was huge. Its paws were as big as a man's fist. It came forward, sniffing the air, and Hennessy had a clear shot, right through the window, but he couldn't stop staring at the wolf. It had him hypnotized, as though he were a rabbit. The wolf put its head back and howled; the sound was so powerful and so lonely that Hennessy lost his footing on the patch of English ivy where he stood. He would have shot the wolf right through the plate glass, but when the wolf began to howl Nora ran into the living room. He should have shot it, but he didn't. He stood there while Nora approached the wolf. She was wearing a white nightgown and her feet were bare. She went right over to the wolf and slapped it on the nose. Then she bent down and put her arms around it; she scratched its chest and called it a bad boy. Hennessy held on to the window ledge to steady himself; he was up to his ankles in ivy and his gun was still drawn when he realized the wolf was Ace McCarthy's dog.

Hennessy went back across the street. He closed the door behind him and locked it, and then he went down to the basement and got out all the newspapers, the ones he'd kept because he'd circled apartments in the real-estate sections. He carried the whole load upstairs and out to the garage, where he threw it into a trash can. And because he no longer had to wait, he lay down on his bed fully dressed and slept, a long dreamless sleep. In the morning he drove to the bank in Floral Park and withdrew all the savings from his account, and he stood there at the teller's window as his bankbook was torn in half.

The first night Nora took him into her bed they didn't speak at all, not just because the children might wake, but because what they were about to do was a long way beyond words. She led him into the house and closed the door behind him and that was when she pricked her finger, on the hinge of the storm door. But she hadn't even known she was bleeding; she didn't know she'd been cut until the next morning, when the baby grabbed her finger and said, "Booboo." She had thought she would go to the kitchen and get him a glass of cool tap water, but once he was inside the house she knew she wasn't going for water. He was trembling in her doorway when she put her arms around him, so she kissed him, thinking the kiss would be gentle. But it wasn't.

They went through the dark, into her bedroom, and they let the dog follow to make certain he wouldn't scratch at the locked door. As they went on kissing each other, they could hear the dog breathing in the corner, where he lay curled up on a nightgown that had slipped from the hook. They didn't want to stop touching, and in the end there wasn't time for Nora to finish getting undressed. Ace pulled her underpants down to her knees and Nora pulled them off the rest of the way. Nora and Ace got down on the floor, with pillows beneath them, and held on to the metal bed frame, and when they spoke it was only to ask each other for more. The dog slept in his corner without dreaming, the baby didn't call for his bottle, Billy didn't wake to go to the bathroom; they could go on and on, covering each other's mouths with their hands so they wouldn't cry out. At five in the morning, when the sky became milky and the stars disappeared and the sheet they had wrapped themselves in was shredded beyond repair, they both knew it was the end of the night, but not the end of them.

They never spoke about being together again, they didn't need to. Ever since that night, Ace would get up early for school, he'd have breakfast and sit through homeroom and all his morning classes; but when the lunch bell rang, he knew Nora would make certain to put the baby down for his nap. Then Ace would cut out of school and run down Poplar Street, zigzagging through the Amatos' backyard and scaling Nora's fence, and he'd go right to the side door, which she always left open for him. He didn't stop to consider what was happening to him, but he knew that whatever it was, it was getting worse. He couldn't wait to get her into the bedroom, and sometimes he didn't. They made love on the living-room couch and they didn't stop until the baby woke from his nap and called out. Then Ace would pull on his clothes while Nora fixed a bottle, and he would leave through the side door and run back to school in time for eighth period.

Weekends were bad, because he couldn't see her at all. He'd work at the station, pumping gas while Jackie and the Saint rebuilt engines, and if he even thought about her he'd get so hot he was afraid he'd explode. Nights were the worst, nights drove him crazy. Nora would risk some nights, but on other nights Ace would get to the side door and find it locked; then he'd know that Billy was having nightmares or the baby was teething again. Whenever he found the door locked Ace couldn't sleep at all. He started losing weight because he just couldn't be bothered with lunch, and he couldn't eat dinner with his family, not even when Marie made his favorite meals. Whenever Ace found Nora's door locked he took the dog for long walks, all over the neighborhood, but no matter what direction he started off in, he always found himself in front of the Corrigans'. He'd stop when he got to the edge of the driveway, but he'd tell himself only a coward would turn and run; he'd make himself go closer and closer to the circle of pale grass on the lawn where Cathy's ghost had appeared. This was one place Rudy would not follow him. The dog refused to go past the driveway; he'd sit and whine as Ace went across the lawn. No matter how hard he tried, Ace couldn't force himself to go any farther than the edge of that circle of grass. And then one night he actually began to do it; he reached his hand into the circle, but as soon as he felt the warm air within it, a car horn honked. Ace quickly pulled his hand back and when he turned to the street he saw Jackie's Bel Air. The one Ace had wanted to buy. Jackie rolled down his window and waved frantically, and when Ace went over to the curb Jackie snapped, "Get in the fucking car."

Ace opened and closed his fist; his fingers felt unnaturally hot. Jackie reached out and grabbed him by his jacket.

"Get the fuck in," Jackie said. "Now."

Ace went to the passenger door and got in.

"Jesus Christ," Jackie said. He'd been working late and he stank of gasoline and fear. "What the hell do you think you're doing here?"

The dog had come around to Ace's door and Ace was about to let him in, but Jackie stopped him.

"I don't want that dog in my car."

"Yeah, well, it's been nice talking to you," Ace said. He opened the door to get out, but Jackie pulled him back. They hadn't spoken much lately. It hurt just to be together in the same room.

"Stop coming here," Jackie said. "You're just stirring things up."

Ace sat back in his seat, interested. "What kind of things?"

"Just let her rest in peace, understand?"

"Yeah," Ace said. "Well, I'll keep your advice in mind."

"Look," Jackie said, "what's over is over. I'm changed. I'm different. I don't have to pay for this for the rest of my life. You want to keep her dog, fine. But let it be."

"What's the matter?" Ace said. "Afraid of ghosts?"

Jackie took his cigarettes off the dashboard and tapped one out of the pack. "No such thing," he said. His hands were shaking when he got his lighter out, and that was when Ace knew he wasn't the only one who had seen her.

"There is," Ace said.

"Not for me," Jackie told him. He looked scared, though, and he kept glancing at the Corrigans' lawn. "I've got respect for things I never even understood before. Even Pop sees that."

"I'm happy for you," Ace said. He shoved open the door and got out, then leaned back in before he slammed it shut. "I'm real glad you can rest in peace."

Ace stood on the sidewalk as Jackie took off for home. The dog came up and nudged Ace's hand with his nose until Ace petted him, and then they walked home, taking their time, because it was amazing how if you worked it right you could live in a house with your own brother and not say two words to him, whether he was a changed man or not.

Nora knew nothing about him, and that's the way she wanted it. It was enough to know that she wanted him; all she had to do was think of him and her stomach would tighten down low and her breasts would feel full. Sometimes she'd have to take a wet washcloth and run it over her arms and legs, and if the cloth was cold enough, steam would rise up from her skin. He was a desire she had to fit in between doing the laundry and figuring the bills and setting out an afternoon snack for Billy. She had thought she wanted Roger, but that had less to do with her own desire than with a wish to please him, to shine back his own light, at least until the children came and she no longer had the time or energy to wait up for him and do what he liked in bed, or to take his tuxedo and hang it carefully in the closet, after she'd run a lint brush over it to pick up strands of the rabbit's long white hair. She had planned for Roger, she had wanted to trap him, and she'd thought through every moment of her part of their courtship carefully. But with Ace she didn't think at all. If she had she wouldn't be leaving her side door unlocked and watching for him the minute she put the baby down for a nap. As soon as they were finished making love, she wanted him out of her house, but she was letting him stay longer and longer, until the baby grew so used to him he began to look for Ace when he woke up from his nap. Sometimes she had to rush to pick Billy up after school, and still she'd be late and he'd be the only child left. She'd see him standing behind the double glass doors of the school and she'd feel something turn over inside her, the way she had when she was carrying him and he'd suddenly flip-flop inside her. And now she was letting Ace take a shower in her house, even though it was already two o'clock and she had a Tupperware party in Elmont at four and a meatloaf to fix before she got Billy from school.

She was following the recipe for meatloaf from the back of a Hunt's tomato sauce can and she'd set out the chopped meat to marinate in a mixture of tomato sauce, onion salt, and canned button mushrooms. Ace's dog had his nose right up to the counter.

"Don't you dare touch that," Nora told him.

The dog took a step backward and looked at the floor, embarrassed, but every once in a while he'd peek at the meat.

"You're not fooling me," Nora said.

Mr. Popper was trapped next to the toaster, his back arched, ready to spit. If the dog so much as looked at the toaster, Mr. Popper's hair would stand on end and he'd make a terrible snakelike sound.

"You're too big for this house," Nora told the dog.

Rudy stared at the floor and panted. Ace finally came out of the shower, a towel over his shoulders, his shirt and boots in his hands.

"Your dog's got his eye on my supper," Nora said when she heard Ace come into the room. She was at the sink, washing chopped meat and bread crumbs off her hands. When she turned from the sink, Ace was bending over Rudy, scratching the dog's ruff, and Nora felt stricken. It wouldn't be easy to give him up.

"Do you want me to fix you something?" Nora said.

Ace looked up at her; when they weren't in bed he was completely tongue-tied.

"Peanut butter and jelly?" Nora said.

"Jesus," Ace said.

"What?" Nora said.

"I'm not eight years old," Ace said.

"I know that," Nora said. She went to him and put her hands on his chest.

"I've been thinking," Ace said.

"Oh, no!" Nora teased him.

"Sooner or later we're going to get caught," Ace said. "Billy's not stupid. He'll figure it out."

He moved away and put on his shirt and then his boots. Nora tilted her face up and swallowed.

"We can quit right now," she said, to see if that's what he wanted.

"It's not me," Ace said. "You're the one who cares if we're caught, and I'm just telling you we will be."

What he meant was, Leave your door unlocked tonight no matter what—and Nora knew it. She went over to him and put her arms around him.

"You sound like an old man," she whispered. His jeans were tight, but she could get one hand down the front without unzipping them.

"Well, I'm not," Ace said.

"No," Nora said. "You're not."

Ace whistled for the dog, then slipped out the side door and quickly went around to the backyard. He was good at sneaking out unnoticed, and he scaled the fence so easily he left nothing behind, except for his footprints. The dog took the fence in one leap, not caring or even looking where he was going, knowing only that he was beside Ace. As she watched them disappear, Nora knew she could never have made that leap, not in high heels, not burdened down with bottles and frying pans and record albums and twenty-three shades of nail polish. Besides, it was her choice to stand at her kitchen window, watching him disappear through the leafless lilacs and azaleas. But that didn't mean she didn't see that the sky was the color of plums or that the frozen bark of the lilacs was already turning blue or that the boy who was in her backyard only moments ago was now running, fast.

Billy no longer went to the cafeteria at lunchtime. He spent the forty-five minutes in the boys' room, crouched over the toilet, his feet straddling the seat so that no one would see him. He'd wait until the bell rang and the halls filled with children, then he'd take a pack of matches out of his pants pocket and crumple up blank pages from his looseleaf and light a small fire on the floor of the stall. On days when he was lucky, the smoke would set off the fire alarm overhead and the alarm would act as a diversion so he could slip out of the bathroom and get back to class without anyone noticing him.

He'd almost succeeded in making himself entirely invisible at school. He'd read everything about Houdini he could get his hands on and, after weeks of practicing, he could slip his feet out of his sneakers without untying the laces, he could squeeze out of his shirt without touching the buttons, he could force his entire body into a space no bigger than a coffee urn. During gym class he would hide next to the basketballs, in a crevice so small he had to wrap his arms around himself like a straitjacket, and when he finally crawled out his limbs would be weak with needles and pins. He could now hold his breath in the bathtub for two minutes and he was working on tightening his stomach muscles. In the mornings he got up early and did a hundred sit-ups, and another hundred before he went to sleep.

"Go ahead," he'd whisper to James when they were alone together. "Punch me."

But the baby would just lift Billy's shirt and tickle his stomach, so Billy would have to punch himself, making sure to tighten his stomach muscles first.

"Booboo," James would say, and then he'd watch, silently, as Billy hit himself again and again.

He had no choice but to make himself tougher, because even if most of the children ignored him there was a small group, led by Stevie Hennessy, who would not let him be. He would pick up their thoughts just before they got him from behind. They'd pull on his shirt until the seams split; they'd spit on his shoulders and hair. The band of Billy's enemies grew braver all the time, stuffing his looseleaf into the garbage can, ripping his homework in half, writing KICK ME in black ink on the back of his shirt, pouring milk down his collar so that he'd have to sit in a pool of warm milk all afternoon and the teacher would turn up her nose whenever she walked past his chair.

They knew that his mother picked him up after school; they stayed away after the last bell had rung. And that was why, on the fifteenth of January, Billy was less upset to get his report card and find he was failing every subject but penmanship than he was to find out that school was to be let out at noon. All morning there was a lump in his throat. When he went to the closet for his coat and rubber boots after the noon bell rang, he could hear them thinking about what they were going to do to him. He tucked his report card into the waistband of his corduroy pants and took his time with his gloves and his blanket scarf, making certain he was the last to leave and hoping desperately they would forget him.

When the school buses pulled away they left clouds of blue exhaust hanging after them, and when you breathed out your breath made its own clouds in the cold, clean air. The street was deserted when Billy came out and crossed onto Mimosa, except for a group of first-grade girls who held hands three across. As he turned the corner from Mimosa onto Hemlock, Billy picked up the first black snippets. *I'll hold his hands behind his back.* He scanned the street but there was no one to see. Not a sparrow, not a cat. Billy stood on the corner, his looseleaf tucked under his arm, his wool hat low on his forehead. He started to walk because he had no choice; it was impossible to become invisible on the empty street with nothing but bare bushes and black, leafless trees.

They rose up from behind a mailbox when there was no turning back. Stevie Hennessy was out in front, and there were two other boys, Marty Leffert and Richie Mills, both as big as Stevie. They were grinning and they all had rocks in their hands. Billy stood there, mesmerized, and then he did the unthinkable. He turned and ran, letting his looseleaf drop to the cement, and as soon as he did he was fair game and they let their rocks fly.

The first rock hit him as he turned onto Evergreen. The second rock got him as ran up the driveway to a house he'd never been past before. He went up and pounded on the front door.

"Let me in!" he heard himself scream.

He kept pounding on the door, but no one answered and they were getting close to him. The third rock got him on the neck and Billy could feel his blood run down. He raced through the backyard behind the empty house and threw himself over the chain-link fence and into the adjoining yard on Hemlock Street. It was Stevie Hennessy's backyard, and once Billy realized where he was, he ran faster than he thought possible. He made it across the street and to his side yard and stopped, breathing hard, to examine the damage. He took off his coat and bundled it beneath some limp, leafless bridal wreath that hung low to the ground. He wiped the blood on his neck with his hands, and then he heard them, over at Stevie Hennessy's, and because his choices were folding himself into the window well, where there was a family of mice, or going inside, he went in through the side door.

He didn't go any farther than the vestibule that separated the kitchen from the door to the garage. His breath was raggedy and hoarse and he planned to make a dash for the basement before Nora got a look at him, but when he peeked into the kitchen he saw Ace McCarthy sitting there with his boots up on a chair, drinking a Coke.

They looked at each other, startled.

"Jesus," Ace said finally. He dropped his feet to the floor and put down his Coke. "What the hell happened to you?"

Billy didn't answer. He never would have guessed it was Ace, even though he knew his mother had been having someone over to the house; he'd hear them whispering sometimes at night, he'd notice extra towels in the laundry basket, he'd wake suddenly, from the deepest of sleeps, with some man's thought in his head. He didn't know what his mother and this man were doing, but he knew they were doing something, and he knew he shouldn't let on. If he had to go to the bathroom in the middle of the night he would pee into an orange juice bottle he kept in his room.

Ace began to inspect him. "Man," he said. "They really got you good." Ace went to the sink and let the water run. "Come on." He nodded to Billy. "Let's get you cleaned up."

Billy washed his hands and face. His forehead stung. He couldn't bring himself to look at Ace.

"Where does your mother keep the Bactine?" Ace said.

"In the hall closet," Billy said.

"Right," Ace said. "So does mine."

Ace got the Bactine and some cotton balls and cleaned off the back

of Billy's neck. Billy winced and pulled away. He could not understand what his mother and Ace could possibly want from each other.

"Two against one?" Ace said.

"Three," Billy said.

"Fucking animals," Ace said.

"So what?" Billy said, glaring at him. "I don't care."

"Yeah, well, you should," Ace said. He reached for the report card
that was sticking out of Billy's waistband and took a look at it. "You're
a mess," he said. "Tell your mother you got rope burn on your neck
during gym. And don't even bother trying to forge this." He handed
back the report card. "What'd you do, get out early today and you
didn't even let your mother know?"

"I don't have to tell you anything," Billy said. "Where's my
mother?"

Ace swallowed hard. "She's in the shower and I'm baby-sitting."

"Oh, yeah," Billy said.

"I hate fresh kids," Ace told him. Billy leaned against the counter;
he looked so small and defeated that Ace couldn't stand to see it.
"These three guys your friends?" Ace asked.

"Nah," Billy said.

"You don't have any friends," Ace guessed.

"So what?" Billy said.

"So who're you gonna play ball with?"

"I don't play," Billy said.

"What?" Ace said. "Did I hear you correctly?" He got his jacket
and pulled it on. "You're one sick kid, anyone ever tell you that
before?"

"So what!" Billy cried.

They stared at each other.

"Go get a ball and a bat," Ace said, deciding to cut his last class.
When Billy didn't move, he added, "You've got one, don't you?"

Billy went to his room and brought back the ball and bat Nora had
once bought him.

"Jesus," Ace said. The bat was still in a shopping bag. He pulled it
out. "Get a jacket and let's go."

They went through the side yard and then walked down to the
high school, not saying a word. The field was frozen mud, but they
went out to the diamond.

"I'll pitch them straight at you," Ace said. "All you have to do is hit them."

Billy nodded and raised the bat. He missed the first five in a row. Ace walked across the diamond to him.

"I'm a great pitcher," he said. "All you have to do is relax and get loose."

Billy looked up at him, puzzled.

"Stop thinking," Ace told him.

They practiced all afternoon, and by the time they were done it got so that Billy missed only two balls out of every three.

"I didn't think I could do it," Billy said. He was out of breath and had to run to keep up with Ace.

"Yeah, well, you can't," Ace said. "Not yet."

All the way home Ace tried to figure how much the kid knew. He certainly wasn't giving anything away. "I'll be back tomorrow after school," Ace said when they got to Billy's driveway.

"You'd be here anyway," Billy said. "Wouldn't you?"

It did no good to lie to this kid; anyone could see that.

"Not at two forty-five I wouldn't," Ace said. "I'd be long gone by then."

"You don't have to do this," Billy said. "I'll keep my mouth shut."

"Look," Ace said. "I don't have to do anything."

"Yes, you do," Billy said primly. "Everyone has to do some things."

"Did you see anybody holding a knife to my throat out on the field?" Ace said.

Billy had to admit that he hadn't. He swung the bat over his shoulder and watched Ace walk across the lawn. When Billy finally went into his house, Nora was already setting dinner on the table.

"Where were you?" she asked.

"Playing ball with Ace McCarthy," Billy said. He went to the refrigerator, got himself a glass of milk, and filled James's bottle.

"Me bab!" James cried.

"You don't play ball," Nora said.

She was spooning out mashed potatoes that stuck to the spoon like glue. There were pink spots on her cheeks, but other than that she didn't look upset.

"I've started," Billy said.

Nora got out the ketchup and sat down at the table. Her hair was pulled back in a ponytail and she hadn't bothered with makeup. "Anything you want to talk to me about?" she said casually as she cut James's hamburger into tiny pieces.

Billy looked up at her. The cuts on his neck and forehead burned, his coat was rolled up under the bridal wreath, his report card was still in his pants, and he knew something about his mother and Ace that he wasn't supposed to know.

"Nope," he said.

"How's your hamburger?" Nora asked.

She had taken a bite of the meat; it was so dry she had felt as though she might choke.

"Great," Billy said.

Nora watched him douse his burger with ketchup and thought he was a particularly good liar, maybe even better than his father. Roger always grinned too widely when he lied; he used to make physical contact, reach out and grab and then hold on tight, as if he could bodily force you into believing him.

After the meal, Nora got out some cups of Junket she had dotted with maraschino cherries.

"You know you can ask me anything you want, right?" she said to Billy as she spooned Junket into James's mouth. "You can tell me anything at all."

Billy concentrated on his dessert and mumbled, "Yeah."

"Look at me, Billy!" Nora demanded.

So he did and he picked up the word *Lie* from her and he knew he was a dead duck.

"I want the truth," Nora said, praying that Ace had been dressed if Billy had found him in the house.

Billy put down his spoon and pulled out his report card and laid it on the table. Nora looked at the wrinkled report card, puzzled, then flipped it open and saw the Fs circled in red.

"Oh," she said.

"It's not my fault," Billy said.

Nora got a pen and signed her name to the report card. She kissed Billy on the top of his head, and when she asked if he wanted another serving of Junket, Billy ignored the fact that he was completely full and said, "Oh, yes. Please."

7
MERCY

*N*ORA Silk stayed in bed listening to the ice melt on her roof. The cat was curled up at the foot of her bed; the curtains were not completely drawn, and she could see a wedge of blue sky. It was the first of March, a mild, pale day, a good day for hanging laundry out on the line. A year ago today she had been in a Laundromat on Eighth Avenue, a horrible place where the clientele sat hunched over, ignoring each other while their most private underwear flew past the glass in the dryers. She always took the boys and they'd sit there, held hostage by their clothes, because the one time she'd left the laundry and taken Billy out for hot chocolate, they returned to find that someone had stolen all their clothes, which hadn't even been dried. Someone had simply taken the whole sopping mess and left the washer door ajar. On this day a year earlier, Nora had bought Billy every kind of snack food imaginable just so he'd sit still. She kept the baby up on one washer, while she jammed their clothes into another. After she'd slipped her quarter into the washer, she looked up and saw Billy across the room, all scrunched up in one of the orange plastic chairs. He was tapping his feet and popping Milk Duds into his mouth and he had those awful bald spots and Nora's heart had dropped into the pit of her stomach and she thought, Anything is better than this; but now, after six months on Hemlock Street, she wasn't so sure.

She was still waiting for one of the other mothers on the block to drop off a cake or invite her for coffee or suggest that she bring the children over to play. The truth of it was they still wouldn't talk to her when they ran head into her with their carts in the A&P. On the first Monday of every month Nora hired Rickie Shapiro so she could go to the PTA meeting in the school cafeteria, and she made certain to wear flats now instead of her stiletto heels; and still when she raised her hand to speak the board members, who sat up at the first table, refused to recognize her and conversation would stop dead after the meeting when she came up to the refreshment table with an angel cake or a pan of muffins.

Studying the other women in the cafeteria, Nora began to realize that they didn't really talk to each other either, even the ones who saw each other nearly every day. Their mouths were going a mile a minute, but they were lying to each other, and they lied about the smallest thing, whether their children were getting good grades at school, how they felt about their mothers, what their husbands had whispered in their ears, as if any truth would be a horrible admission. Nora could always tell when they were lying because their necks would grow rosy and they'd run their tongues over their lips as if their mouths were dry. And when Nora had finished stirring sugar into her tea and stepped up next to a group and sighed "Jesus Christ, I'm tired," after a day when she'd sold four cartons of Tupperware and fixed supper for the kids and hung out her laundry and done the food shopping and helped Billy with his homework and changed the baby's diaper nine times and reapplied fresh lipstick three times, the other mothers would stare down at the floor, embarrassed, as if she'd made the crudest remark they'd ever heard. And once in a while one of the other women, the younger ones with three or four small children, would say "I am too" before she could stop herself and then she'd look guilty and break into a sweat and forever after avoid Nora like the plague.

On the days when Nora looked out her window and the chain-link fences looked suspiciously like prison gates or when she longed to go dancing or have Ace stay with her the whole night through, she forced herself to think about laundry drying in the fresh air, about her baby's footprints on the grass, and cicadas and lilacs and baseball. She'd give Hemlock Street another month or two or six, two years at the most, because it was worth it for her children not to grow up as she had, isolated and so desperate for people that she fled to Manhattan as soon as she turned eighteen and said yes to the first man who asked her to marry him. She was working in the Joke Store on Lexington Avenue; she'd met Roger there when he came in to buy six exploding cigars, not for his act, but for dinner parties, where they were always a big hit. He told her afterward that what had attracted him most was how completely happy she was, there behind a counter crowded with junk and bad jokes. And why shouldn't she be? When Roger had met her Nora thought it was heaven enough just not to be in New Jersey any longer. She'd been raised by her grandfather, Eli, twenty miles outside of Atlantic City, out beyond the marshes, in a run-down house surrounded by chicken coops. Eli was an electrician, and a good one. He could have lived anywhere, but he happened to despise, or at the very least mistrust, people. You would have thought he'd have some faith in science, would trust the mechanics of his own trade, but when he talked about wiring new buildings he always spat over his shoulder, so as not to jinx the job, and if a blackbird flew over a house he refused to go inside. When Nora was sick he wrapped her cuts in spiderwebs and gave her a mixture of rosemary, horehound, and cherry bark for her bronchitis and never once took her to a doctor's office. He, himself, drank a mugful of his own personal elixir made out of woodruff, nettle, and thyme every day and he lived to be ninety-three, all on his own, taking only Christmas, Easter, and the Fourth of July off from work. He never touched a drop of liquor and he was convinced that cigarettes left tar on your lungs and he never raised a hand to another man in anger. He didn't have to, he had his own ways of righting things when he was wronged, and maybe that was why he liked to live out by the marshes, where the sea grass turned silver after the moon rose and no one complained if you kept some chickens.

When Eli was stiffed on a bill or insulted by a bigger man, he never said a word. But at night he would make small figures out of beeswax and food coloring, which he'd shape with his thin whittling knife, and by morning the dispute would be righted somehow. When she was a girl, Nora begged for some of these dolls to play with and her grandfather, who would have given her the world, or his world at any rate, and who drove ten miles to buy her jelly doughnuts every Sunday, slapped her hand if she reached for the figures he was working on. Later, when she was more interested in climbing out her bedroom window and meeting her boyfriends to drive to Atlantic City, Nora began to think of her grandfather's whittling as quaint, something like folk art or quilting.

When he died, in his own bed during a thunderstorm, Eli left Nora everything, even though he had met Roger twice and despised him, but then who, if anyone, would he have approved of? Nora was pregnant with Billy when she drove down to the house, alone, because Roger needed a good fourteen hours of sleep on days when he performed. She wept in the kitchen and took off her charm bracelet and packed up her grandfather's clothes for Goodwill and the few personal items, his watch and his wedding ring, for herself. Before she left she dug up two orange lilies from beside the house, but they wilted as soon as she entered Manhattan and then died on her windowsill. For two years her grandfather's house stayed on the market and then finally a chicken farmer bought the place, and the three thousand dollars Nora had left after taxes and outstanding bills went into a cigar box. She never told Roger about her inheritance, thinking she would someday surprise him, take him on a trip to Europe or buy him two new tuxedos and a gold ring, but in fact she used part of the money to pay the hospital bills when Billy and James were born, and the rest she used as her down payment for the house on Hemlock Street.

In a way, then, this was her grandfather's house, although certainly he would have hated the neighborhood beyond words. He would have been spitting over his shoulder day and night. He would have known, long before Nora found Billy's bloodstained coat under the bridal wreath, that something was wrong. Nora ran the coat through the wash and dried it in the basement and hung it in Billy's closet without saying a word. She crossed her fingers and waited, she thought good thoughts and experimented with casseroles that contained olive loaf and hoped that would be enough. But it wasn't. Stevie Hennessy just couldn't leave Billy alone. Billy's other tormentors had grown bored, but not Stevie, and he knew no limits. Billy's blanket was now as small as a potholder, he could keep it in his pocket and stroke it when he was nervous, but one day he forgot it in his desk and when he remembered he saw that Stevie had already gotten it and was cutting the piece of material into bits with a pair of scissors. Billy got up to grab it away, but the teacher asked him where he thought he was going and she ordered him to his seat. Billy had to sit back down and watch Stevie destroy his blanket; and he put his head down on his desk, embarrassed, because he was crying. It should have been a good day—Billy had batting practice with Ace to look forward to—but now Stevie Hennessy had ruined everything. Billy cried on and off all day, and at dismissal his eyes burned when he had to look at the floor as he walked past Stevie.

"Baby," Stevie said, rubbing the last remaining scrap of the blanket between his fingers. "Snotface."

Billy walked right past him, out into the hall.

"Why don't you go back where you belong?" Stevie said, following him. "Sewer rat. Your mother is a whore."

Billy turned around and he was so surprised to be facing Stevie Hennessy that he nearly tripped.

"Take it back," Billy said, and hearing his own voice he thought he must really be crazy.

Stevie lost his balance for a moment, then regained it and came closer. He was as big as a fifth-grader; he grinned when he looked down at Billy. "What?" he said.

"You heard me," Billy said. "Jerkface."

Stevie pushed him and Billy pushed back, and when he did Stevie's eyes lit up. He punched Billy hard in the face, and in spite of himself Billy let out a wail, but Stevie pushed him up against the wall and hit him again, in the mouth.

"Who's the jerkface?" Stevie said, and he walked away and left Billy gasping for air. Billy felt dizzy and his mouth tasted like rusty iron. He stood there buttoning his coat, then walked to the front door. The VW was already there, idling in front of the buses, and Stevie was across the street, so Billy had no choice. He went to the car and got in.

"Do you have to be late on the one day I have to drive to Freeport?" Nora said.

Billy put his head down and figured he could not talk or she'd find out everything. He planned to leap out of the car as soon as his mother pulled up in front of the house, then wave good-bye with his back to her.

"I won't be back till six, so when you get home from playing ball you start the baked potatoes," Nora said as she put the car into gear. "Bake at three fifty. Or maybe it's three seventy-five."

"Teddy Bear" was on the radio and Nora turned up the volume and she got that dreamy look on her face that she always got whenever she heard Elvis. In the backseat, James was rattling a bag of pretzels. Billy made certain not to move at all.

"Oh, shit," Nora said.

Billy figured there was something major wrong with the car, because it had begun to buck like a horse and he prayed it wasn't anything too serious because he didn't know if he could talk. His mouth was hot now and he couldn't seem to move his tongue.

"Oh, lord," Nora said and she stopped the car completely.

Billy shifted his gaze from the floor of the car and realized that a pool of blood had formed in his lap. Before he could do anything about it, Nora took his chin with one hand and tilted his face upward.

"What did they do to you?" Nora said.

Her fingers felt like ice, but maybe it was because his mouth was burning hot.

"Open your mouth," Nora said.

Billy wrenched away from her and faced the window and began to cry. Nora took his chin in her hand and tilted his head back again, and when she did his front tooth fell into her hand.

"Who?" Nora said.

Billy lowered his eyes and rubbed one hand over his mouth; the places where he had pulled out patches of hair in the fall had grown back in wild, unmanageable tufts. "It doesn't matter," he said.

Nora looked across the street. She saw Stevie Hennessy watching and instantly she knew.

"That little shit," Nora said.

"Why do I have to be this way?" Billy said.

He had such fine bones and long, delicate fingers and all his shirts were too small; his sleeves didn't reach to his wrists. Nora pulled him over to her, onto her lap.

"I have a headache," Billy said, turning away from her.

"Every morning when you wake up you tell yourself you're just as good as everybody else. Tell yourself that three times. You hear me?"

Billy nodded and put one thin arm around her neck.

James was jumping up and down in the backseat, shaking the car. Nora leaned her head close to Billy's.

"Who's my best boy?" she whispered.

Billy shrugged and put his hot cheek against hers.

"Who?" Nora said.

"I am," Billy said in a small, froggy voice.

Nora drove him straight to the dentist, who immediately set to work making the mold for a cap. While Billy was in with the dentist, Nora ran out to the pay phone on the corner and canceled the Tupperware party in Freeport, saying there'd been a death in the family and she was immediately flying to Las Vegas; then she called Marie McCarthy and left a message for Ace that Billy was too sick to play ball. By the time they got home it was dark and James was whimpering for his supper and there was no time to bake the potatoes, so they had TV dinners and Kool-Aid and Nora let Billy stay up late to watch *The Untouchables*. When he went to bed, Nora tucked him in, something she hadn't done for a long time. Billy liked the weight of his mother on the edge of the bed; he liked the way she smelled—a mixture of Kool-Aid and Ambush. He fell asleep holding her hand, and Nora sat beside him for a long time and then went into the kitchen. She cleaned up the dishes and put cold cream on her hands, so they wouldn't wrinkle. Then she took four white candles from the drawer next to the refrigerator and put two in holders, lit them and shut off the light. She held the two unlighted candles over the flames until they were soft enough to mold. She stopped working only long enough to fix herself a cup of Sanka and then she kept at it, until she had formed the figure of a boy. She got a flashlight and went outside and searched until she found the perfect stone, one she could easily mold into the boy's hand. Her Sanka was cold by then, but she drank it anyway. Her grandfather used to do that too, he used to drink cold coffee and eat a stale jelly doughnut before he cleaned his whittling knife of wax. The cat came and sat by Nora's feet; he curled up and Nora could feel him purr. She couldn't bring herself to switch the lights back on, so she sat there by candlelight, smoking a cigarette and turning the wax figure over in her hand. And before she went to brush her teeth and clean her face with cold cream, she held the boy over one of the lit candles and let the wax drip from it, until it formed a white pool on the kitchen table.

In the morning Stevie Hennessy didn't realize anything was wrong, not even when he pulled on his jeans and found he had to roll the cuffs up three times. When he went to eat breakfast, his mother asked him if he was feeling all right and she touched her lips to his forehead. Stevie said, "I feel great," even though he wasn't so sure. He felt off balance, as if he had a fistful of marbles in one pocket. He forced himself to eat a bowl of Kix and drink a small glass of orange juice.

"He looks like he's coming down with something," his mother told his father when he came in for coffee. Joe Hennessy put his jacket on, then felt Stevie's forehead.

"Perfect," Hennessy declared.

"I told you so," Stevie told his mother, but all the same he felt weird as he walked to school. He went to the coat closet and quickly hung up his jacket so he'd have time to make up a good store of spitballs before gym. He'd been a little nervous last night, afraid that little jerk Silk would spill his guts and his mother would call up and then Stevie would have to hope that his father would go easy on him. When he'd gotten into his pajamas and she still hadn't phoned, Stevie figured he had it made. He grinned to himself now as he made spitballs, and when it was time for gym he made sure to stand right behind Billy Silk.

"Hey, babyface," he jeered under his breath.

Billy turned around and Stevie backed up. It seemed as if Billy had grown overnight, but he was still the same height as Abbey McDonnell, who stood in front of him on line. Stevie Hennessy, who had always been the tallest boy in the class, refused to believe that if Billy hadn't grown, he himself must have shrunk sometime during the night. He could believe whatever he wished, but even Stevie Hennessy could see that if he ever wanted to hit Billy Silk in the mouth again he'd have to find the nerve to strike upward.

Now Billy played baseball with Ace after school and he handed his homework in each morning and he wasn't punched in the face once.

But he kept hearing things he shouldn't, a buzz of words inside his head that he just couldn't shake. Down at the candy store he heard Louie complain about his wife, when all he wanted was a pack of Black Jack gum. He heard his mother adding up figures and Rickie Shapiro worrying about the shape of her eyebrows and late one night he heard someone crying out in pain. The cry was so awful, in a wordless way, that Billy got out of bed and pulled the blinds up and he heard much more than he'd ever heard from anyone's silence before.

It took a long time for him to fall asleep after that. He woke at dawn and was already in the kitchen, eating Frosted Flakes, when Nora woke up. He ate the whole bowl and watched as his mother set the kettle to boil and opened a pack of cigarettes, and then he told her he had seen Donna Durgin. She'd been wearing a black coat and standing outside her house, weeping.

"Did you see her face?" Nora asked. When Billy shook his head no, Nora suggested that the woman could have been anyone.

"It was Mrs. Durgin," Billy said. "I heard her."

"I've told you half a million times not to listen in to people," Nora said, stubbing out her cigarette and getting up to shut off the whistling kettle. She had a heavy day booked at Armand's and lately she was uncomfortable about having Rickie Shapiro baby-sit; she had the feeling that when she was gone Rickie was snooping around, trying on her dresses, slipping on her bangle bracelets. "It's going to drive you crazy," she told Billy.

"All right," Billy said, "but I know where she is."

Nora thought it over while she had her coffee and put on her makeup and got dressed. She was still trying to decide when she left, as Rickie fiddled with the radio and Billy held James back from the storm door, while the baby cried and held out his arms to Nora, just as he did every Saturday when she left him. She started the Volkswagen, and as it warmed up she decided she wouldn't be betraying Donna if she told just one person, so she let the car idle and crossed the street. Nora was checking her purse for matches and change when Stevie Hennessy opened the door. He was still in his pajamas and he'd slept scrunched up on his pillow so his hair stood up in a cowlick. When he saw Nora his mouth dropped open, and Nora stared back at him, just as surprised. Since he had stopped tormenting Billy, Nora had forgotten all about him. Now she noticed he was at least a good head shorter than Billy.

"I need to talk to your father," Nora said through the storm door.

"Who's at the door?" Ellen Hennessy called from the kitchen.

Stevie Hennessy stared at Nora, unable to move.

Nora rapped on the storm door impatiently. "Your father," she said slowly, as if talking to a complete idiot. "Is he home?"

Ellen came up behind Stevie and opened the door wider. She stopped when she saw Nora on the stoop.

"Oh, hi," Nora said. "I know it's early, but I've got to see your husband."

"My husband," Ellen said.

"Joe," Nora reminded her. Nora grabbed the handle of the storm door and opened it. "I've got to be at Armand's by nine, otherwise I get backlogged and my regulars go nuts."

She came inside and Ellen Hennessy put both hands on Stevie's shoulders.

"I could do you for half price," Nora said. "Come in any Saturday."

"I never have time," Ellen said weakly. She couldn't take her eyes off Nora's red nails and her long, bare fingers.

"Make time," Nora said. "Or I could come over here. Your cuticles could really use it."

Ellen looked down at her own nails just as Hennessy came out from the bathroom, showered and shaved and ready to take Ellen and the kids to her sister's in Rockville Centre. When he saw Nora talking to his wife in his own living room he stopped and put one hand on the wall.

"Joe!" Nora said when she saw him. "I really need you."

Hennessy looked at his wife and their eyes locked.

"I'll make coffee," Ellen said. "Sanka?" she said to Nora.

"I can't," Nora said. "I've got to run. What I have to talk to him about is kind of personal. Police business."

"Oh." Ellen gave Hennessy a look, then guided Stevie into the kitchen.

"I hate to barge in on you," Nora said.

"You're not," Hennessy said.

"It's about Donna," Nora said.

Hennessy was staring at the gold-plated chain Nora wore around her neck. Sometimes when he imagined Ace and Nora together he thought he would go crazy. He knew there were love bites on her throat, that Ace was screwing her all night long. God, when he was seventeen he was dating Ellen, and he had kissed her probably only half a dozen times.

"Billy overheard something she said, he knows where she is, and after I thought it through I decided I'd better tell you."

"Look," Hennessy said. "No one knows where she is."

"Well, Billy does," Nora insisted. "She's at Lord and Taylor."

"Lord and Taylor, the department store?" Hennessy said.

Nora and Hennessy stared at each other and then started to laugh.

"It's not exactly like running off to France," Nora said.

"I guess this means Robert didn't chop her up into pieces and hide her in the basement," Hennessy said.

"Oh, God." Nora was holding on to the storm door because she had a stitch in her side from laughing. "Well," she said finally, "I hope I'm doing the right thing."

"You are. I'll take care of it."

"Boy," Nora said. "If I had a husband like you, I'd still be married."

"I would have never let you go," Hennessy said.

Nora almost laughed, but then she looked at him and thought better of it. "I'm glad I told you," she said before she left. "I just hope Donna is."

Hennessy watched her cross the street and get into the idling VW, then pull out of the driveway and go right over the curb. He realized then that his wife was standing behind him.

"I've got to go to work," Hennessy said.

He went past Ellen into the bedroom for his sport coat and his gun. When he turned from the night table to fit on his holster he saw that Ellen had followed him.

"I swear," Hennessy said. "I'll meet you at your sister's."

"Don't bother," Ellen said.

"I'll be there by dinnertime."

"You do what you want," Ellen told him.

Hennessy stopped for coffee and the paper on his way to Garden City. As he drove on, the houses got bigger and broader, with rolling lawns and tall, glossy rhododendrons. He pulled into the empty parking lot of Lord & Taylor so he could see the door; he finished his coffee, then opened the glove compartment for the Pepto-Bismol. By now, he figured he knew the Durgin kids as well as anyone; Melanie always ran right to him, and he kept lollipops in his coat pockets for her. Last time he'd visited he'd brought over some of Suzanne's old clothes for her, little dresses with lace collars, corduroy overalls. He sat parked, reading the newspaper, and at a little before ten the lot started to fill up. He watched the sales clerks arrive; they parked in the last row or walked over from the bus stop, wearing sheer stockings and high heels and scarves knotted tightly to keep their hairstyles in place. They were well-dressed, and Hennessy figured they had to be. If Donna Durgin had been among them he would have spotted her a mile away; she would have stuck out in her lumpy cloth coat, with that coy, rolling gait of a fat woman. At ten the shoppers began to arrive and Hennessy was glad Ellen wasn't here to see the way they dressed or what they drove up in. They were pleasure shoppers, and as far as Hennessy could tell there was nothing they needed, especially the ones who got out of their Cadillacs and Lincolns and buttoned their camel-hair coats against the wind.

He sat in his car till eleven, thinking that Billy Silk wasn't the most reliable witness in the world, what with his unruly hair and the way he sat on the front stoop lighting matches when his mother couldn't see him, with his baby brother beside him, much too close to the flame. He knew Billy's type, the oddball who always got picked last for any team, and then only because the gym teacher insisted. And actually, Stevie was becoming a little that way. He used to spend all his time with a gang of friends, and now Ellen complained that he came straight home after school and switched on the TV. He seemed somehow punier to Hennessy, as if all the fight had been taken out of him. But just when Hennessy was about to leave and drive to Rockville Centre, even though he was fairly certain Ellen wouldn't talk to him for the rest of the day, whether he showed up or not, he got that feeling along the back of his neck, and he knew that something was about to happen.

When he went in, it seemed to Hennessy that he was the only man in the store. He felt like an ox, making his way past the swinging display of handbags, over the thick carpeting. He made a circle around the first floor, and once he held up a long black evening dress studded with sequins and imagined Nora Silk wearing it in the dark,

barefoot, with her hair pulled back and around her throat the gold
chain that moved slightly when she breathed. He didn't see any signs
of Donna, but the sensation on the back of his neck felt even
stronger. He went upstairs to the credit department and got a form
for a charge card that he filled out and brought back to the window.

"Won't your wife be delighted," the clerk said to him.

"You bet," Hennessy said. "You've got the best clothes in the world.
The best salesgirls, too. My wife was telling me about one of them.
Donna Durgin."

"Oh, Donna," said the clerk. "She certainly knows her lingerie. You
forgot your place of employment."

Hennessy filled out the name and address of a law firm where one
of the divorce lawyers he knew was a partner. "Send the card directly to my firm," he told the clerk, and then he made his way back
downstairs. His head started to pound as soon as he walked into the
lingerie department. He picked up a black satin slip and rubbed it
between his fingers. He figured there must be a special department
for fat ladies where Donna worked, a department kept out of sight
where wide, white underpants were hidden in cabinets, where thick
brassieres with wire hooks were kept in boxes. He took the black slip
to the register and waited while a woman paid for three pairs of lace
panties. Hennessy made certain not to look at the woman who
bought the panties, but he blanched when he heard that her total was
twenty-four dollars. The saleswoman who finally helped Hennessy
was a tall redhead who had doused herself in heavy perfume.

"Birthday present?" she asked.

"Anniversary," Hennessy said as he took out his wallet, carefully, so
his holster wouldn't show.

It was eighteen twenty-five for the slip, including tax, more than
Ellen paid for most of her dresses. But it was worth it, because while
the saleswoman was wrapping the slip in tissue paper, Hennessy
heard Donna Durgin's voice. He was sure of it; her small, little girl's
voice asking if the silk bathrobes had been hung up for display.
Hennessy saw a group of saleswomen lift bathrobes out of a carton;
tangerine-colored silk, and pink, and a pale, shimmering blue, the
color of robins' eggs. Donna wasn't there, but as Hennessy watched
he saw her emerge from the tent of silk. Her eyes, her mouth, her
pale blond hair, swept up now into a French knot, but if he hadn't

heard her voice he would never have found her. Not in a million years. She was thin now and truly beautiful as she joked with the other saleswomen and lifted up the pale orange silk to model against her white skin.

Hennessy took his package and went outside. He felt dizzy in the fresh air and he leaned against the brick wall, and he stayed there until the sales clerks began to take their lunch breaks. Donna came out at twelve thirty wearing a good English raincoat over a black dress. She was with a group of four women, and when they passed Hennessy, he ducked his head and inhaled the mixture of perfumes they wore.

As he followed them to a coffeeshop called the Village Grill, he thought about the dust balls under the furniture at the Durgins' house, and the wiseguy looks on the boys' faces when Robert called and they refused to come in at suppertime. Hennessy stood at the cigarette machine, eavesdropping as the women talked about customers and weekend plans. Donna ordered a chef's salad and iced tea, but when her food arrived she played with it, obviously more interested in talking to her friends than eating. What Hennessy needed was a good cup of coffee, but he thought about the woman from the domestic, the one who had moved to New Jersey, and when he remembered how he'd left her there, grateful he could walk away, he didn't think he could stomach coffee. He went directly to Donna's table.

"Donna," he said.

She was holding her fork and listening to the woman across from her complain about her mother, and as she glanced up at him the smile on her face froze.

"I'd like to talk to you," Hennessy said.

Donna's gold earrings made a tinkling sound, even though she didn't move.

"Donna?" one of her friends said, concerned.

"I'd like to have a cup of coffee with you," Hennessy said. "That's all."

"Donna, are you okay?" the woman next to Donna asked, looking over at Hennessy.

"Sure," Donna said to her friend. She grabbed her purse and squeezed past the other women. "I'll be right back."

Donna walked to the rear of the coffeeshop, where there were tables for two, and Hennessy followed her. She sat down and watched him carefully as he sat across from her.

"Thank God for coffee, right?" Hennessy said. He picked up the sugar dispenser and tapped his fingers on the glass. Donna Durgin was waiting, and finally Hennessy said, "You sure look different. You look great."

Donna continued to watch him; she sure as hell wasn't making it easy for him.

"People have been worried about you," Hennessy said. "I mean, Christ, Donna, what happened?"

"I can't explain it."

"Well, look," Hennessy said patiently, "a woman doesn't just get up one day and decide, What the hell, today I'm leaving my husband and my kids and my house and I'm not saying a damned word to anyone. You obviously knew what you were doing. No one forced you, right?"

"You wouldn't understand," Donna said.

"Well, Christ, Donna, try me!" Hennessy said. Donna looked down at the table and bit her lip and he knew she was weakening. "Just try me." Hennessy reached into the Lord & Taylor bag and brought out the black slip. "I mean, for God's sake, I already spent eighteen twenty-five on a slip."

Donna laughed in spite of herself. When the waitress came over, Hennessy ordered black coffee. As he turned back to Donna he noticed that her nails were pink and that she wore a silver bangle bracelet.

"No wedding ring," Hennessy said.

"You won't understand," Donna said. "I was dead."

"What about your kids? You haven't even asked about them."

"What good was I to them?" Donna asked. "I was disappearing more each day. Is that what life is supposed to be?"

Hennessy looked at her blankly.

"Is it?" Donna said.

"I guess it is," Hennessy said. "That's the way life is."

"Not for me," Donna said. "Not now."

Hennessy's coffee came, and when the waitress had left he leaned forward. "How would it be if everyone walked away? How would it be if I just up and left Ellen and the kids and the mortgage and just took off?"

"I don't know. How would it be?"

"God," Hennessy said. "I wish I knew."

They stared at each other and then Donna said suddenly, "I will have coffee."

"Good. I hate to drink poison alone."

He ordered for her while she went to tell her friends she'd meet them back at the store. Hennessy could see that they were excited for her; they thought he was a love interest, or at least a possibility.

"They think you're cute," Donna said when she returned. "I go back sometimes," she added. "I look at the house and it seems as if I never even lived there."

"So what do we do?"

Donna took two saccharin tablets out of her purse and dropped them into her coffee. "I don't know. That's up to you."

"I brought over a box of clothes for Melanie yesterday," Hennessy said. "He doesn't know anything about dressing girls. He had her wearing the boys' old jeans."

"Oh no," Donna said.

"He had her in high-top sneakers that were two sizes too big."

Hennessy watched, feeling nothing as Donna started to cry.

"Well, hell," he said. "What did you expect?"

"You bastard," Donna said.

"Yeah," Hennessy said.

They both pushed their coffee cups away.

"So," Hennessy said. "Do you want to see them?"

Donna Durgin stared him right in the eye; she stared him down. "More than anything," she said.

By the time Hennessy had paid the check it was agreed they would meet a week from Sunday at Policeman's Field, a big windy lot used for baseball games on the edge of town. There was a small playground beside the fenced-in field and Hennessy would be there, with the children. Donna would borrow a friend's car and watch from the street. It was not clear to either one of them how or why Hennessy had decided not to turn her in; he simply couldn't do it. He didn't go to Ellen's sister's in Rockville Centre that night. He made himself a sandwich and watched a game on TV and then he went into the bathroom, locked the door, and wept. When he was through, he went out to the car, got the bag from Lord & Taylor, and put it on his wife's bed, just beneath her pillow.

Donna had a one-room apartment in Hempstead, and although there wasn't much furniture, not even a rug, she had spider plants balanced in every window and a row of coleus on the shelf behind the sink. She had brought nothing with her, and the clothes she'd worn when she left she had thrown down the incinerator chute. She had only a couch that pulled out to be a sleeper and a coffee table she'd found in the trash and had painted white and a closetful of good clothes. Every night for supper she ate tunafish with no mayo and a salad made with iceberg lettuce and chunks of tomatoes, even though she was now at her perfect weight.

On the day she went to see her children Donna wore black stretch pants and a thick wool sweater and her English raincoat. She borrowed her friend Ilene's car, and before she left for Policeman's Field she slipped on dark glasses and tied a chiffon scarf over her hair. She didn't think she was particularly nervous, but when she was in sight of the field she wondered if she might be having a heart attack. It wasn't as if she hadn't thought of her children while she'd been gone, but she had been pretending they were with her. She often went to the children's department at lunch break and looked through the blazers and the velvet dresses, planning what she would buy. When she potted plants she imagined the look on her children's faces when they saw her kitchen filled with colorful plants, all bending toward the sun.

Donna pulled over and parked across the street from the muddy field. She rolled down her window so that the crisp March air came in and slapped her in the face. Hennessy was sitting on the edge of the sandbox; he hadn't had the least bit of trouble getting the children— Robert had been grateful for a morning off. Now he watched as Melanie made sand pies and cakes. She was wearing a blue sweatshirt Donna had never seen before and pink corduroy pants that had once belonged to Suzanne Hennessy. The boys were on the monkey bars, not wearing their sweaters, just jeans and long-sleeved T-shirts that were wrinkled and showed the base of their spines when they flung themselves, hand over hand, along the metal bars.

Donna wished then she hadn't come. She had expected them to be exactly the same as they were when she'd left, and to stay that way until she could reclaim them. But already they had changed, they'd grown taller without her. Still, she couldn't take her eyes off them. She didn't even notice that Hennessy had left the playground until he appeared at her window.

"They're great kids," Hennessy said.

Donna Durgin nodded.

"Come see them."

"What?" Donna said.

"I've been thinking it over. You can get visitation rights. If Robert bothers you, you can get a restraining order. Get a divorce, if that's what you want, but you still have rights."

"You know an awful lot about divorce," Donna Durgin said.

Hennessy opened the car door and Donna looked at him, then got out. Watching her walk into the playground, Hennessy thought that there was nothing the same about her, except for her voice, and he was amazed when her children recognized her instantly; they ran to her and grabbed hold of her raincoat, nearly toppling her in the wind.

At a little after eleven that night, after they'd all gone to bed, there was a pounding on the Hennessys' door. Hennessy hadn't been sleeping, though; he'd been waiting and watching the sky through his window.

Ellen sat up in bed and grabbed her blanket to cover herself. "What is that?" she said.

"Don't answer it," Hennessy told her.

Ellen turned and looked at him in the moonlight. The pounding went on, harder and fiercer.

"Joe?" Ellen said, scared now.

"He'll go away," Hennessy said, hoping he was right.

"Who will?" Ellen asked.

Hennessy listened to the pounding. "Robert Durgin," he said.

Ellen looked at him, then got out of bed and grabbed her robe. Hennessy stayed where he was, listening to Robert shouting and the low murmur of Ellen's voice; then he got out of bed and pulled on some clothes. He considered slipping on his holster, but only for a minute.

"You lousy bastard," Robert Durgin said when Hennessy came out to the living room.

"Why don't we talk it over tomorrow?" Hennessy said.

"Are the children all right?" Ellen asked.

Robert didn't answer; he pushed her aside and Ellen gave a little gasp and then looked at him as if she didn't know him.

"Calm down," Hennessy said.

"You fucking lousy bastard," Robert growled.

Suzanne peered out of her bedroom, clutching her doll.

"Mommy?" she said.

"I'll go tuck her in," Ellen said, but she waited for her husband to nod before she made a move.

"You know where she is," Robert said once Ellen had gone. "Melanie woke up with a nightmare and told me she was crying because she knows she's not supposed to lie but Mr. Hennessy and her own mother told her maybe she'd better. I thought you were on my side!"

"I'm not taking sides," Hennessy insisted.

"Then tell me where she is," Robert said.

"I can't do that," Hennessy told him.

"Can you even tell me why she left?" Robert said.

"I don't know," Hennessy said, because he didn't have the heart to tell Robert the truth. "I can take them to see her every other Sunday until you get the divorce proceedings going."

"Oh, shit," Robert said.

"Accuse her of anything you want," Hennessy said. "She doesn't care as long as she gets visitation rights."

Robert sat down heavily on the couch.

"For your own sake, Robert," Hennessy said, "let it go."

Ellen was watching from the hallway. She'd put on some clothes and combed out her hair. She came in and sat next to Robert. "Let me make you some coffee," she said to him. "I'll make some sandwiches."

Robert nodded, and they had ham-and-cheese sandwiches and coffee together, at the coffee table, so they could look out the front window and keep an eye on the house where Robert and Donna's children slept. After he'd gone home, Ellen cleaned up the dishes without a word, but when they were both in the bedroom she turned to Hennessy and said bitterly, "Why you and not me? Why didn't Donna call me?"

"She didn't call me," Hennessy said. "I tracked her down."

"But she could have called me," Ellen said, crying now. "She was my friend."

Joe Hennessy watched his wife cry; then he sat down next to her on the bed.

"I didn't even know anything was wrong," Ellen said. She looked up at Hennessy. "And now," she told him, "I do."

8
GOOD BOYS

$\mathcal{A}$T the end of March Phil Shapiro packed up his Caddy and drove to Manhattan, but at least he had the decency to wait until after midnight, so that none of the neighbors would see him. He had a new job at Best & Co. and an apartment off Lexington, and he'd stacked everything in the world that he cared about into twelve brown boxes. It was, Rickie and Danny had been told, a trial separation, but anyone could see that it was the end, because Gloria Shapiro immediately started cooking like crazy. She made fudge brownies with cognac and chicken à l'orange and she even went over to Nora Silk's and bought an entire set of Tupperware; Gloria spooned her concoctions into the plastic tubs and shoved them into the freezer until it was no longer possible to shut the freezer door. She made it clear to her children that they were to discuss their personal crisis with no one; if asked, they were to say that their father was on a business trip, which in a sense he was, and that their mother, who had never learned to drive, now walked to the A&P and back with a shopping cart not because her husband wasn't available to take her but because she needed the exercise.

Rickie Shapiro cried a lot in the girls' room on the second floor of the high school, but she was emotional lately anyway because she had just begun to go steady with Doug Linkhauser, who was the captain of the football team and whose father had bought him a brand-new

Corvair, white with a blood-red interior. Even though Doug was crazy about her and she was crazy about him right back, she still felt like everything around her was falling apart. What had happened to her parents? Nora Silk was the only divorced person Rickie had ever met, and clearly Nora deserved it. Rickie could tell that Nora had a man now; when she was looking through Nora's jewelry box she'd found cigarette butts from someone else's brand in the ashtray on the night table, there beside the bed for anyone to see. She'd picked one of the pillows off the bed and the pillowcase smelled like sweat and tobacco, and she'd dropped it on the floor, disgusted. She couldn't even stand to baby-sit for the Silk boys anymore. Some Saturdays she phoned Nora and lied and said that she was sick, and Nora would be all flustered because then she would have to call up Armand's and say that she was sick, too. Rickie no longer took Nora's advice; she started to set her hair on big wire rollers again instead of leaving it wild, and as it turned out, Doug Linkhauser thought she looked beautiful in pink.

When she tried to figure out what had gone wrong with her parents, she came up with nothing; they didn't even fight. It wasn't like them to humiliate Rickie and make her keep such an awful secret from everyone, even her best friend, Joan Campo. Danny was useless; he refused to talk about their parents at all, and the whole thing literally made Rickie sick. Her mother was cooking so much that the kitchen was always burning hot; you'd start to feel faint the moment you walked through the side door. On Sunday nights, Rickie couldn't see Doug because Phil would drive from the city and take Rickie and Danny out to Tito's Steakhouse on the other side of the Southern State and they'd all order steak and French fries and onion rings and then no one would eat. Rickie had to make conversation the whole time because Danny wouldn't talk, and then when they were dropped off at home, Gloria was waiting to quiz them. Rickie actually began to make lists of everything they had ordered at Tito's and everything her father wore, just so she'd have something to tell her mother. On Friday and Saturday evenings, when Rickie got dressed to go out with Doug, she could hear her mother outside in the backyard, thinning the pachysandra. It was a horrifying sound, like a wild animal rooting around, but Gloria kept at it and she didn't stop tearing out pachysandra by the roots until there was a tall pile next to the back patio.

"God, you're perfect," Doug Linkhauser would whisper as he kissed Rickie when they parked in the Corvair behind Policeman's Field, and she would just want to crack his head open. Oh, she loved him, she was crazy about him, and why shouldn't she be? Everyone wanted to go out with him—it was just that sometimes she found herself thinking about Ace when she kissed Doug, and then she would pull away from him and feel the color rising in her face.

Nothing was perfect, Rickie Shapiro could see that now. What had her best friend said when Rickie finally broke down and told her about her parents' separation? "God, that's awful, your family's destroyed." She could have kicked Joan, but she couldn't let on that she was hurt. Everything seemed to be on shaky ground now, silt really, that gave way when you touched it with your toe. Rickie had been taught to respect and follow all the rules, at any cost, even losing her chance with Ace, and now it seemed there was a possibility that she'd been tricked. Parents like hers weren't supposed to split up; a boy as smart and handsome as Danny should have been popular, instead of spending all his time locked in his room; even Joan Campo, who had been her best friend for six years, had deceived her. The rules had always been that you could let a boy kiss you and touch your breasts over your bra, but now Joan had more or less admitted she had gone all the way with Ed Laundy and she was probably going to do it again. When Rickie had seemed shocked, Joan had laughed at her and asked, "What do you think everyone's been doing at Policeman's Field?" and Rickie had been too embarrassed to admit that she'd thought everyone was doing what she was doing, being a good girl, and if she hadn't thought that she would have been with Ace instead of being scrunched up in the backseat of the Corvair on Friday nights, letting Doug Linkhauser put his tongue in her mouth.

Something had happened, like a split in the universe, and you couldn't depend on anything being the way you'd planned. And even though Rickie started off convinced that everything would return to normal and she'd know what was expected of her, she soon started to wonder if it would ever change back. Her mother was finished with the pachysandra and had stopped cooking, and now all she did was smoke cigarettes and watch TV, which Rickie knew she didn't approve of. Gloria went out only in the afternoons when she had her driving lessons, and the driving lessons were the worst of all. Gloria had never needed to drive, Phil had taken her anywhere she needed to go, and now the lessons and the fact that she was pricing Fords made the separation more permanent; when Gloria passed her driver's test there seemed no hope at all that their lives would return to normal.

Actually, everyone in the neighborhood seemed a little haywire, especially the mothers. Marie McCarthy, for example, who had spent every day of her married life taking care of her house and her family, suddenly found herself with a job. She went to Armand's once a month to have her hair tinted and cut, but she always avoided Nora. Sure, she saw Nora out of the corner of her eye, but during her last appointment, when Marie was back at the sink with a rubber cap over her head, she noticed that Nora had the baby in a playpen that was jammed into the utility closet. Armand had noticed too, and as Nora sneaked in to give the baby a cheese Danish, he followed her and told her that he didn't give a damn if her baby-sitter was unreliable and that in fact he needed her at least two weekdays or he'd have to find a new manicurist. After he'd stormed out of the utility closet, Nora stood there in the doorway, nibbling on the Danish and holding her baby. Before Marie could look away, Nora spotted her.

"Hi, Mrs. M.," she had called, and she came out to sit on the chair next to Marie's. "The world is not made for women with children," Nora had said darkly.

The baby leaned over and grabbed Marie's silver bangle bracelets, and he scooted out of Nora's grasp and into Marie's lap.

"Hi!" he said to Marie.

"What am I supposed to do?" Nora said. "Put my kids into suspended animation?"

"I could take care of him," Marie found herself saying.

And that was that. She opened her mouth and Nora was only too glad to fire Rickie and take the baby over to the McCarthys' on Wednesdays and Fridays and, along with Billy, on Saturday mornings. So there Marie was, with two little boys in her house again, only this time she was getting paid, and the truth of it was she enjoyed it much more this time around. She bought an old highchair at a secondhand store and she taught James how to use a spoon and a fork and how to say bye-bye and one, two, three. She took him to Lynne Wineman's and Ellen Hennessy's and showed him off, and even they had to admit he was darling. "Marie," James said one afternoon when he woke from his nap, and Marie quickly pronounced him brilliant as well as being sweet as pie.

John McCarthy and Jackie were nervous about having a baby in the house; they thought he was too much for Marie. But Ace didn't seem to mind in the least, and he took an interest in the older boy, taking him out to play ball or to walk the dog; and although it took some time for Marie to win Billy over, she finally did, fixing him noodles with butter and cream, playing mah-jongg and gin at the card table, teaching him to crack open pistachio nuts with his teeth.

Marie didn't notice that when she got together with the other mothers they might admire the baby, but the questions they asked were about Nora. Lynne wanted to know where she shopped for clothes and if she had a boyfriend, but Ellen Hennessy was interested only in how Nora managed to take care of her children and work. Every weekday morning, between getting Stevie to school and Suzanne to Lynne Wineman's and going food shopping, Ellen was taking a typing class. It was a five-week class and, because she was almost done, she'd already begun applying for jobs. There was one job she wanted more than anything, as a receptionist in a nearby orthodontist's office. On the day of her interview she actually took Suzanne and went over to Nora Silk's house to get a manicure. Nora was in her bathrobe when she answered the door, but she smiled right away and led Ellen into the kitchen. The house was a mess, worse than any of the women on the block would have imagined, and Nora set out fingerpaints and paper on the floor for Suzanne and James and then had to clear cereal boxes and clay off the kitchen table before she could get to work on Ellen.

"Boy, I'm just crazy about your husband," Nora said to Ellen once she had her hands soaking in warm, soapy water.

"Oh?" Ellen said. She looked down and saw that Suzanne had already smeared fingerpaints all over her forehead.

"My ex didn't know how to fix anything the way Joe can," Nora said. "He couldn't even set an alarm clock."

"Pale pink," Ellen said when Nora brought out her bottle of nail polish.

"Try the fuchsia," Nora said. "Trust me."

"I'm thinking about getting a job," Ellen blurted out. "An orthodontist's office on the Turnpike."

"That's great," Nora said. "You'll probably get a terrific discount if either of your kids needs braces."

"You think so?" Ellen said, pleased. She took her hands out of their soaks and watched as Nora cut her cuticles. "I'm just worried about the kids."

"You'll be doing that after they're grown and gone," Nora said. "Mind some music?"

Nora went into the living room and put on a stack of 45s, then came back, lit a cigarette, put it in the ashtray, and uncapped the fuchsia polish.

"Don't you worry when you're at work?" Ellen asked.

Nora took some graham crackers out of a Tupperware bowl and handed them to the children without bothering to clean their hands.

"Oh, of course," she said. "I worry about them all the time."

When Ellen Hennessy got the job, the first person she called was Nora.

"That's so fabulous," Nora said. "But I can tell you're thinking about not taking it."

She let James creep into a kitchen cabinet to play with the pots and pans. Ace was on his lunch hour and he had grabbed a Coke to drink before he climbed back over the fence and returned to school for eighth period.

"What do I tell Joe?" Ellen said.

"It doesn't matter what you tell him," Nora said. "What matters is where."

Ace put his empty Coke bottle on the kitchen counter, then came up behind Nora and put his arms around her.

"Tell him in the bedroom," Nora said.

Ace kissed her neck, then went to the baby and crouched down beside him.

"See ya, buddy," Ace said to James.

Nora turned and put a finger to her lips to hush him.

Ace got up and made a mocking little bow, then whistled for his dog and went out the side door. In the kitchen across the street, Ellen Hennessy sat down at her table, confused.

"I don't know what you mean," she said, embarrassed. For a moment she thought she must have been completely crazy to have called Nora and confided in her.

"You know what I mean," Nora said.

"Nora," Ellen said.

"Well, you do know what I mean," Nora insisted. "Give him something more important to think about than whether or not his wife works."

Joe Hennessy had too much on his mind already. All week he'd been working on a case he hated, staked out in the evenings outside the hardware store, which had been burglarized three times already this month. Not a damned thing happened during his stakeout, except for the one evening he went to the diner to get himself a hot turkey sandwich. When he came back he discovered that someone had thrown a brick through the plate-glass window during his absence and made off with six transistor radios. He hated the case even more then, because it was so obviously kids, and kids would probably outgrow it, unless he arrested them, but of course he looked like a fool now down at the station because he'd somehow been had.

And then one evening, twenty minutes before Johnny Knight was due to relieve him, Hennessy got a call on his radio and he knew right away it was going to be bad, even before he was told that there was a possible homicide over on Mimosa. He put on his siren and pulled out onto Harvey's Turnpike just as the deep blue in the sky began to turn black. When he got to 445 Mimosa three other detectives were already there, including Johnny Knight, who met him in the driveway.

"Take my advice," Johnny said as he offered Hennessy a cigarette and a light. "Turn around and drive the other way now."

They walked up to the front stoop together, smoking their cigarettes in the dark.

"Bad?" Hennessy said.

"Unbelievable," Johnny Knight said. "Christ."

Hennessy knew the family who lived here, at least well enough to greet Roy Niles down at the Dairy Queen he owned whenever Hennessy brought his kids there in the summer. If he remembered correctly, Niles's wife's name was Mary and there were two kids, a girl in junior high and a boy who worked at the Dairy Queen in the summer. As soon as they went into the house they could hear a woman screaming, so Hennessy knew that the wife was still alive.

"We just got a call from the hospital that he was DOA," Knight said. "The guy. Niles."

Hennessy's shoes had mud on them and he wiped them on the mat in the front hallway.

"You're here to talk to the kid," Knight said. "Raymond."

"How'd he get it?" Hennessy asked.

"A knife," Johnny Knight said. "Eleven times."

"Christ," Hennessy said. "Any suspects?"

"We've already got him in custody. It's the kid. His mother and sister are in the bedroom screaming their heads off. He did it down in the basement. Did you know that Niles had a complete bomb shelter down there? Cans of food to last six months. A ham radio. Water. Everything."

"Is that where it happened?" Hennessy asked.

Knight shook his head. "In the laundry room. It's a mess."

The kid was in the kitchen, sitting with his head between his knees. Hennessy greeted the two other detectives and a pathologist who had been sent over from Hempstead.

"He's off his rocker," one of the detectives, Ted Flynn, told Hennessy. "You want to try talking to him, fine, but we're taking him down to be booked and then over to Pilgrim State."

Raymond had just turned seventeen, he was a junior in high school, like Rickie Shapiro, but she didn't even know he existed. He was thin and his hair was in a fuzzy crewcut; you could see his scalp. His skin, which was usually pale, was ashen now. He was wearing a brown shirt and tan slacks and white sneakers and he looked as if he might throw up at any minute. Hennessy took one look at the boy and he thought, Why the hell is this one mine? He asked for ten minutes alone with the boy, and when the others had gone into the living room, Hennessy opened the refrigerator and took out two Cokes. He sat down across from Raymond and opened both bottles, holding one toward the boy.

"Drink this," Hennessy said. "It'll settle your stomach."

The boy looked up at him and swallowed hard. He stared at the Coke as if he were dying of thirst. Hennessy put it on the table.

Raymond grabbed it and drank half the Coke straight down, then put the bottle back on the table.

"They think you're crazy," Hennessy said. "They think it's open and shut and you don't even have a story to tell."

The boy shuddered and looked down at the floor, but Hennessy could tell he was listening.

"Like maybe it was self-defense. Or maybe just an accident. Or maybe it wasn't even you, and these idiots just want the easy way out."

"It was me," Raymond said.

Hennessy took a sip of his Coke. "You want some cookies?" he asked. Raymond shook his head, but Hennessy got some from a tin on the counter anyway. He felt sick, too, but he forced himself to eat one. "That's your mother and sister crying in the other room," he said.

"Leave me alone," Raymond said. "Just let them take me wherever they're going to take me."

"Eleven times," Hennessy said.

"What do you want!" Raymond said. He was just a skinny, nothing kid no one even noticed.

"I want your story," Hennessy said. "I want to hear your side."

His side began down in the laundry room, where his father always took him when he wanted to beat him up. He'd make Raymond wait, a day or maybe two, and then he'd let him have it. Only this time Raymond had decided it wasn't going to happen; he thought all he'd have to do was wave the knife at his father and he'd let him go, but his father went crazy at the sight of the knife, and then he couldn't back down. And when he stabbed his father once he couldn't stop himself, so he figured he was crazy and he wanted to go anywhere where he couldn't hear his mother crying.

"Finish your Coke," Hennessy said when the boy was through talking.

"No one would believe me," the boy said. "My mother always turned on the radio so she couldn't hear it."

"I believe you," Hennessy said.

He left the boy in the kitchen and joined the other detectives.

"His father beat the shit out of him," Hennessy said.

"Yeah?" Johnny Knight said. "So he stabbed him eleven times?"

"He didn't plan it," Hennessy said. "It just happened."

"Come on," Ted Flynn said. "You buy that? He just happened to have a knife on him?"

Some people in the neighborhood, especially the boys in Raymond's gym class who had seen bruises up and down his legs and back when he undressed, bought it, and some people didn't. And in the end it didn't matter because there was no proof and no one to stand up for the kid except Hennessy, so they took Raymond to Pilgrim State. The news of what had happened spread fast. That very same night fathers in the neighborhood couldn't sleep and mothers studied their little boys' faces for signs of trouble. How was it possible for this to have happened, that's what people asked themselves, waking and in their dreams. Parents and children were excessively polite to each other, as if they expected someone else to snap and they wanted to make certain it was no one in their own house, certainly not themselves. You could hear a murmur between the hedges, but no one talked about the Niles family out loud. Hennessy spent three days interviewing teachers and relatives before he realized he was getting absolutely nowhere. They canceled appointments with him, they gave one-word answers, and even the guys down at the station didn't want to hear about it; they were actually avoiding him. When he finally turned in his report, which had nothing, not one incriminating word, against the kid's father, Johnny Knight invited him to a poker game, and when Hennessy arrived the other detectives hit him on the back and offered him cigarettes, relieved he had given up and more than ready to welcome him back as one of their own.

He won fourteen dollars and he didn't come home until after midnight. Usually he just fixed himself a sandwich if he got in this late, but when he came into the kitchen he found Ellen had made a late dinner for him. There were lamb chops and carrots cooked with butter and a baked potato with sour cream.

"I just felt like cooking," Ellen said defensively when Hennessy stared at the dinner.

"All right," Hennessy said finally. "Great."

Ellen sat down across from him and watched him eat. "Do you want to talk about it?" she asked.

Hennessy stabbed his baked potato and shook his head.

"Maybe you need to talk about it," Ellen said.

Hennessy looked at her then. She really meant it. "Thanks," he said. "I can't."

More than anyone, Ellen had been waiting for Hennessy to give up on the Niles case. When he grabbed a beer and went to sit down on the couch, she went into the bedroom and her hands shook as she undressed. She switched off all three lights on the pole lamp, then put on the black satin slip. It had been three months since she had made love with her husband, and her heart had certainly not been in it. She went to the bureau and brushed her hair in the dark, then she took the jasmine oil Nora had given her and sprinkled three drops on her pillow.

When Hennessy finished his beer he turned off all the lights in the house. Ever since Donna Durgin had disappeared, Ellen had asked him to lock the doors at night, and by now it was a habit, even though something closed up in his stomach each time he turned a lock. He checked the children and covered them with their blankets, which had fallen onto the floor. He thought about the kid drinking Coke at the kitchen table, he thought about how pale the kid was, and how limp his hands were, and how desperately thirsty he seemed. He thought about the woman he hadn't helped who'd been fixing hamburgers after she'd been beaten, and the look on Donna Durgin's face when she saw her children get out of his car every other Sunday. Tomorrow he'd probably find himself staked out in front of the hardware store again, and this time he wouldn't complain about the job. He'd read the newspaper as he sat behind the wheel, and he'd drink coffee, and if the stupid kid who'd been breaking and entering dared to show up, Hennessy would lean down on the horn to frighten him off.

When he went into his bedroom the scent of jasmine made him dizzy, and for a moment Hennessy felt as if he'd wandered into the wrong house. Ellen had switched on the dim night-table lamp and her back was toward him; one of the straps of the black slip had slid down. He could see a white shoulder. Hennessy undressed and put his clothes in the hamper.

"Why don't you come over here," Ellen said as he started for his own bed.

He sat down beside her on the bed, and because she seemed to be waiting he ran his hands over the satin slip. He was actually afraid to kiss his own wife, because the last time he had wanted to make love she had turned away. But now Ellen put her hands on his face and drew him to her, and after she started to kiss him Hennessy knew she wouldn't turn away. He made love to her as if she weren't his wife, and when she moved down to take him into her mouth, Hennessy thought he might explode. She had never done this before, she wouldn't even listen when he asked for it in the past, begged for it, really, and now she was doing it all on her own. Afterward, when she moved on top of him, Hennessy made love to her as he'd never dared to before, but he knew she didn't want him to stop because her arms were fastened around his neck and she was kissing him.

They fell asleep in the same bed while the moon rose in the sky, and in the morning they woke early, before the children, and they dressed in silence, as if stunned by what had gone on between them after all these years of marriage. Ellen found the black slip tangled in the sheets; she folded it carefully and put it in her top drawer. And when she told him, after breakfast, that she'd decided to take a job, Hennessy was too confused to argue with her. He spooned sugar into his first cup of coffee and stared at her for so long that Ellen leaned up against the sink and laughed, and if the children had not already been awake and calling for their clothes, she would have taken her husband back to bed.

There was a calculus exam on April Fool's Day, for those few seniors who were allowed to take advanced math. The exam was more a matter of personal pride than anything else; all twelve students in the calculus class would be getting their acceptances to college in only a few weeks. That's why it was particularly odd when Danny Shapiro didn't show up on the day of the exam. The math teacher, Mr. Bower, waited until ten minutes past the bell, and finally had to distribute the exam booklets. It was a test Danny would have had no trouble with, he would have placed first in his class, but by the time Mr.

Bower was handing out the number-two pencils, Danny Shapiro was already on his way to the bus terminal in New York City.

If he had thought it over he probably wouldn't have left, but he didn't stop to think. On Saturday he had smoked some marijuana and was sitting in his room, listening to the radio play in his sister's room while she dressed for a date with her latest moron. Danny had known she wouldn't have the guts to stay with Ace McCarthy and he pitied her for not having the courage to do anything more than what people expected of her. He pitied his mother as well. She had become something of a lunatic on several subjects. If anyone happened to innocently mention Lucy and Desi's impending divorce, she would lambaste Desi, using language Danny hadn't even guessed she knew. She despised cars and car salesmen. She'd insisted that Danny go with her to test drive a new Ford Falcon, and she screamed at the salesman, crying out that he was trying to cheat her, and finally Danny was so mortified that he dragged her to the auto parts department and begged her to stop.

What really got to Danny was not just that his father had left but that he had dumped everything on Danny. After their first Sunday dinner at Tito's, Phil had waited until Rickie was in the ladies' room and had told him in all seriousness that he was now the man of the house. Well, who had asked for that? He hadn't applied for that job, hadn't wanted it, but his father acted as if it were a kingship and Danny was the next in line. Like it or not, he could now change the fuses and wait up to make certain Rickie got home on Friday nights. Danny had actually been excited when he first heard his father was moving to Manhattan. Columbia was Danny's first choice, he had dreamed of getting to the city, and he thought he could save some money if he moved in with his father. He had been stupid enough to help his father carry his boxes out to the car, and while he was watching Phil arrange them in the trunk he approached him about moving in with him after graduation. Right away Phil began to explain why that wasn't a good idea; Danny would miss out on dormitory life, the apartment wasn't big enough, it just wouldn't work out, and then Danny knew that his father wasn't escaping just from his marriage but from all of them.

And so he pitied his mother and sister, because he could see their blind faith, their belief that they were doing what they were sup-

posed to do, and it was getting them nothing. He watched them after
supper, washing the white dishes with the band of gold around the
edge until they shone, chattering about nothing, absolutely nothing,
like birds fluttering their wings and plucking their own feathers, and
he grew to despise them. When Raymond Niles stabbed his father
and the whole damned neighborhood clammed up about it and acted
as if the Nileses were complete strangers, Danny felt something
inside him turn off for good. He couldn't bear to be where he was, the
neighborhood was suffocating him, and when he saw Rickie wearing
Doug Linkhauser's I.D. bracelet he felt like breaking her wrist.
When she had walked beside Ace along the parkway, her long red
hair trailed behind her like a stream of fire. Now she seemed smaller,
contained within crinolines and I.D. chains, and each time she
walked through the hallways with Doug Linkhauser's arm around
her he seemed to block her out completely.

On the day before he left, Danny had waited for Linkhauser after
school in the students' parking lot. He stood by the new Corvair like a
maniac, and even Linkhauser could sense his fury.

"Hey, Danny," Linkhauser said easily.

Danny had left his books in his locker; but he was holding a baseball
bat in one hand.

"You're going out with my sister," Danny had said.

"Well, yeah," said Linkhauser, confused. Everybody knew that.

"And?" Danny said.

"And," Linkhauser had repeated stupidly.

"What do you plan to do about it?"

"Oh," Linkhauser had said and he'd leaned up against his car to
think it over. He was planning to go to the state college in Farming-
dale and live at home, so of course he'd still be seeing Rickie. "I guess
when I finish school I'll ask her to marry me."

He looked over at Danny and smiled, thinking he'd said the right
thing. His father owned a chain of carpet stores and he'd never
thought about what he planned to do because he always knew he'd
go into the carpet business. Now he felt as though he'd been put to
the test and had done rather well. There were worse things than
marrying Rickie Shapiro.

"God almighty," Danny said.

"What?" Doug Linkhauser was alarmed.

"Maybe you'll want to be a race car driver," Danny said.

Doug Linkhauser stared at him.

"Maybe you'll want to join the foreign service and Rickie won't want to travel to Italy or Syria, did you ever think of that, Linkhauser?"

"I think you're nuts," Doug Linkhauser had said.

Danny had leaned up against the Corvair. "Yeah, maybe I am."

And standing there in silence with Doug Linkhauser, staring at the blue sky and the windows in the gym, Danny Shapiro had felt a pain shoot through his left side, up into his shoulder and his arm. He wished he were twelve years old again, and he could meet Ace McCarthy in the field for baseball practice, he wished he could just block out everything he was feeling, but he couldn't, and on his way to school the next morning he walked up to the Chemical Bank by the A&P and withdrew all his savings. He didn't even bother to go home and pack.

The sky was bluer once the bus passed through New Jersey, and it grew wider and bluer with every mile. In Washington the azaleas were starting to bloom. Danny had two seats to himself, until some guy in his late twenties got on in Richmond and folded himself into the seat next to Danny's. The guy lit up a cigarette and took out a deck of cards.

"You play poker?" the guy asked Danny, and when Danny shook his head, he asked, "Twenty-one?"

"I don't play cards."

"Yeah?" the guy said. He had a thick accent and Danny had to strain to understand him. "What do you play?"

"Baseball," Danny said.

"Shit. Baseball's for kids."

"Not where I'm headed."

"Where's that?" the guy asked, and he put out his cigarette in the ashtray between them so that smoke spiraled up into Danny's face.

"Spring training," Danny said. "Yankees."

"No shit? And you travel on a Greyhound bus?"

"Sure," Danny said. "Get to see the country that way."

Right then all they could see was the dark highway and a line of shacks beyond a metal fence.

The guy's name was Willie and he was going to Clearwater, Florida, to visit his mother, whom he hadn't seen in something like seven years. "She won't recognize me," he kept saying to Danny. "I was a baby when I left. Younger than you."

They slept just a little and in the morning they got off together when the bus stopped south of Greensboro for breakfast. The sky was so wide open Danny felt dizzy with joy. He had almost been swallowed up by his hometown and now he was ready for the world, not some safe, constricted suburb, or even a protected campus, like Cornell, his second choice. When he got to St. Petersburg he'd buy himself some new clothes, maybe even some cowboy boots, like Willie's. But what he wanted now was the biggest breakfast he'd ever had, pancakes and eggs and two glasses of orange juice.

"We'd better get washed up first," Willie told him. "Otherwise the waitresses will run in the other direction."

Danny laughed and while the other passengers headed for the restaurant, he went over to the outside restroom.

"Hey, not there," Willie called to him. He came and got Danny, grinning. "You really are one of the Yankees. That toilet's for niggers."

A black man came out of the restroom and looked straight at Danny, and Danny wanted to explain that he wasn't really with the moron by his side in the cowboy boots, but he didn't. He followed Willie into the restaurant and went to the restroom behind the counter. He washed up and peed and combed his hair and he realized he was feeling sick. Willie ordered breakfast for them both and Danny couldn't even force himself to eat his platter of biscuits and eggs, and when they got back on the bus he didn't feel like talking anymore. The air grew sweeter as the bus drove on, and after a while Willie found an empty seat where he could stretch out and take a nap and later he found some sucker to play poker with and that was fine with Danny. Willie didn't know shit about baseball or anything else, and all Danny wanted was to get to Florida.

He had the sinking feeling that he should have thought more carefully about leaving home. He looked out the window and felt as if he were hurtling through space, weightless and completely at the mercy of gravity. When they crossed the Florida state line a whoop went up in the bus and the driver banged on the horn, but Danny felt sicker than ever. He'd been to Miami with his parents several times, but this didn't feel like the same state, or even the same country. Everything looked washed out, the fronds of the palm trees were brown instead of green, the earth looked like plain old dirt. He didn't have any luggage, so he went looking for a place to stay as soon as he got off the bus, and he found a motel two blocks down from the bus station. It had been a long time since Danny had eaten. After he washed up he went to a little market and bought some Scooter Pies and a bottle of Coke and had them standing out in the street, starving and wired and wishing he had a pair of sunglasses because the glare out here nearly blinded him. The air was warm and wet and pushed down on you and made you sweat even when you weren't doing anything but standing still. When he went back to the motel it was even hotter in his room, and he couldn't sleep all night; he didn't even bother to try.

The first day at training camp he just watched through the fence. He'd bought three new T-shirts and a pair of dark glasses, and after seeing some of the rookies he felt so pumped up he did three hundred sit-ups before he went to bed, and all that night he saw pitches the way he'd seen headlights whenever he'd fallen asleep on the bus. In the morning he did more sit-ups to get loose, then went back to training camp, early, when the heat wasn't yet grinding him down. He realized then that he wasn't the only one waiting for the office to open; there was a group of hopefuls by the fence, junior-high kids and grown men, some of whom had brought their own bats. Danny Shapiro figured he had to make his move. The skin on his nose was sunburned and if he stayed down here much longer his hair would turn platinum. He headed for the office as soon as he saw the lights go on, but he was stopped just outside the gate by a guard, a middle-aged black man in a blue uniform.

"I have an appointment for a job interview," Danny told him.

"Come on," the guard said. "You expect me to believe that?"

"I'm a CPA," Danny said. "Certified public accountant."

"Prove it," the guard said.

"What do you want?" Danny said. "For me to do your taxes?"

The guard laughed and motioned for Danny to come inside the gates. He walked him to the front office, then said, "Wait here."

The dust from the field went up Danny's nose as he stood outside the office. His hands were sweating, so he wiped them on his dirty blue jeans and looked up at the sky and tried not to breathe too fast. The guard brought out an older guy who wore a black wool suit that was much too heavy for Florida in any season.

"This the accountant?" the guy said.

"That's him," the guard said.

"What's your name?" the guy asked.

"Danny Shapiro." Out here the sun could blind you even if you wore sunglasses.

"Of Hebrew extraction?"

"Look," Danny said. "I play ball."

"What a fucking surprise," the guy said. "Who doesn't?"

"Yeah," Danny said, "but I'm good."

"Who told you that? Your high-school coach?"

Danny swallowed hard and wiped his hands on his pants.

"CPA." The guy laughed. "That's a hot one. That's one I never heard before."

He nodded and Danny stood stunned, realizing that he was meant to follow. Over by a bench near the batter's cage three rookies who had shown up early for practice were leaning back against a wooden wall. The guy yelled out a name and a tall kid, not more than nineteen, with long, nervous arms, immediately stood up.

"How about pitching a few to my accountant," the guy said.

"Sure, Mr. Reardon," the rookie said.

When the rookie nearly bowed to Mr. Reardon, Danny realized that the guy was on the coaching staff. But the rookie looked Danny over only once, disinterested, as if Danny didn't mean more than a piece of pie.

Danny slipped off his sunglasses and put them in his pocket, then grabbed a bat and went up to the plate. The sky looked white now, and amazingly close to the earth. Out in the field, the rookie was winding up his long, jerky arms. Danny closed his eyes and imagined Ace out on the pitcher's mound. He heard the crickets the way they always sang in summer, and the groaning sound Ace made whenever he started to pitch. Danny missed the first two pitches completely. He started to think about the way the garbage cans were lined up on Hemlock Street and the way lawns turned green at this time of year, and he hit the next ball as hard as he could and he felt as if his heart were going right up with it. He kept on hitting them, and on the last pitch he knocked a sparrow out of the sky, and it fell to second base with a thud. Danny walked back and handed the bat to Mr. Reardon. He was shaking so hard that if he had tried to run the bases he would have fallen on his face.

Mr. Reardon lit a Pall Mall and studied the field. "You're good," he said to Danny. "But I see a dozen boys as good as you every week."

"You just saw me once," Danny said.

"Look," Mr. Reardon said, "just thank me for giving you the chance and get off the field."

Danny got out of there as fast as he could, but once he passed the guard at the gate he had to double over just to breathe. Then he went to stand in the shade of a gumbo-limbo tree and he could see through the fence that the rookie who had pitched to him was now pitching to another rookie, a real joker who stuck his tongue out at the pitcher. And as soon as the rookie threw a curveball Danny could see that the pitcher had gone easy on him, because now the ball went faster than seemed imaginable and the kid up at bat hit it farther than Danny Shapiro could have if he had hit balls for the rest of his life. The rookie batter was a nothing, a nobody, he probably wouldn't even make the final cut, but as soon as he hit the curveball Danny knew he didn't have a chance. Not now. Not ever.

He used almost all that was left of his money to buy a one-way plane ticket to La Guardia and a box of oranges for his mother. He never had the chance to buy a pair of cowboy boots and he left the sunglasses on the shelf above the sink in his motel. When he got back to New York he took a cab home and he told his mother it was nothing, he just had to get away, and he told the same thing to Mr. Hennessy, who came over to talk to him because Gloria Shapiro had filed a missing-persons report. He wasn't missing at all, he told Hennessy as they sat across from each other in the Shapiros' living room, and Hennessy assured Gloria that all boys had a wild week in them, it was natural, it was better for them to let it out and take off than to end up like Raymond Niles. They had oranges all through April, cut into quarters and made into thick, pulpy juice. On garbage nights Danny always took the silver cans out without having to be asked, and he listened to the sound of the Southern State as he lined them up on the curb, and when he got into both Columbia and Cornell, he sent back his acceptance to Cornell without thinking twice.

9
WHEN THE LILACS GREW

ᒍACKIE McCarthy didn't see his friends much anymore. He worked down at the station until closing, he avoided bowling alleys and movie theaters, he never took joy rides. He washed the kitchen floor for his mother on Saturday mornings and he watched TV every evening, sometimes falling asleep to it, and he was devastated when Lucy and Desi's divorce became final.

"Ma!" he called when he heard it on the six o'clock news, and Marie had come rushing in from the kitchen, waving a wooden spoon, afraid he'd fallen off the couch and hurt himself. He even sent a present for Little Ricky to the TV studio in Hollywood, a model of a race car he'd put together and painted on Saturday nights. Marie urged him to go out at night. Go to a movie, she suggested. Get yourself a date. Jackie smiled and insisted he had better things to do, but the truth was he was afraid of the dark. He was afraid of more things than he'd ever thought possible, including his brother's dog, who was now full grown and huge, a hundred and twenty pounds. Whenever Jackie and the dog were alone in the house the dog bared his teeth and made a horrible sound, as if he had swallowed a chain saw. If anyone else in the family was home, Rudy kept his head on his paws, but the ruff around his neck stood straight up and his eyes never left Jackie. Sometimes, late at night, Jackie would hear a rapping at the window.

"It's no one, man," Jackie would whisper to himself, but then he'd look and see that the dog was staring at the dark window, his head tilted to one side, listening.

Jackie vowed to be even better, purer. When anyone left a car to be worked on he'd drive the customer to his job and pick him up again in the evening, and he'd deliver every car with the ashtray cleaned out and the front and back windshields washed. In that first week of May, when the buds of the maples looked yellow and then green, depending on the angle of light, Jackie hung up his black leather jacket in the basement and went to Robert Hall's to buy a blue suit, just like the one the Saint wore every Easter. He went to the barber, and the Saint nodded, surprised and pleased, when he came home with his hair cut short. They didn't talk much while working side by side at the station, but they didn't have to. Every morning, Jackie would make coffee in the aluminum percolator. Every evening, at closing, he'd sweep the garage and the office. They had a calm, wordless routine, disrupted only on Saturdays, when Ace came to work. Most of the time Ace just pumped gas and came into the office to make change, but whenever he ventured into the garage, Jackie couldn't work. He'd feel Ace staring at him, he'd start thinking about ghosts and bad blood and he'd get clumsy and screw up his jobs, and he'd find himself cursing under his breath, which wasn't like him at all anymore.

One Saturday in May, when the wisteria was blooming and the lilacs in the backyards were filled with tight buds, Jackie couldn't stand it anymore. Ace's eyes were burning into his back, and when he got up from the dolly he'd been sitting on he shouted, "Cut it out."

Ace just kept staring at him, so Jackie got up, grabbed his brother, and pushed him up against the wall.

"Stop looking at me!" Jackie shouted.

Ace kept right on looking, a satisfied grin on his face, as though Jackie had just proved him right in his opinion of him. Ace didn't fight back, but the dog rushed in from the shadows of the gas pumps with all his hair on end, stopping in front of Jackie and barking like a dog from hell.

"Get out of here," Jackie told him, but Rudy circled around the brothers, getting closer all the time. Jackie let go of Ace and backed off, but the dog kept circling, catching the leg of Jackie's uniform pants in his teeth.

"Hey!" Jackie cried, panicked.

Ace watched his brother blankly.

"Call your goddamn dog off," Jackie said.

"Rudy," Ace said.

The dog stopped barking and came to stand beside Ace, but he was still growling and his eyes didn't leave Jackie. As soon as Jackie took a step, the dog moved forward, barking again, and Jackie cried, "Oh, shit!"

Ace watched for a moment, then grabbed Rudy by his collar.

"I told you I'm different," Jackie shouted. "But you don't want to give me a goddamned chance!"

The Saint had come from the office and stood now in the doorway into the garage.

"That's about enough from you," the Saint said.

The brothers both turned to face him, uncertain, each hoping their father was reprimanding the other.

"You," the Saint said to Ace. "Take that dog out of here and don't bring him back."

"Pop," Ace said, and his voice broke and he felt betrayed and burning hot.

"We can't live with a vicious dog," the Saint said.

"He's not the one who's vicious," Ace said.

"That's enough," the Saint told him.

"Pop," Ace said, pleading now. "Whose side are you on?"

"I'm not on anyone's side," the Saint said, but he looked at Jackie, and maybe because his father and brother had gone to the same barber and were wearing the same uniform, Ace felt a shiver along his spine.

He took the dog out and tied him to the air pump; then he went back into the office, where his father was going over the records. The Saint didn't look up when Ace came in.

"Maybe I shouldn't be working here," Ace said. Now that it was just the two of them, all Ace needed was a sign, the slightest smile, a nod, anything, and he'd know which side his father was on.

"That's up to you," the Saint said without looking up. "But you've got to work somewhere."

As if he were the son who needed to be told what his responsibilities were.

"I can get a job at the A&P," Ace said, desperate for his father to tell him not to, to tell him he'd always planned for Ace to be the one working beside him.

"If that's the way you want it," the Saint said.

"Yeah," Ace said tightly. "That's the way I want it."

He got a job as a cart boy, bringing in the shopping carts that had been left in the parking lot, helping older women or those who were too pregnant to lift their own groceries by carrying their bags out to their cars. He worked on Saturdays and after school. Instead of going home afterward, he'd swing by to pick up Billy Silk for a late practice and Nora always insisted on feeding him dinner. The days were longer now, Ace and Billy could play later, and soon Billy could hit whatever Ace pitched him; he could hit a ball over the fence that had been repaired and showed no sign that Jackie's car had ever crashed through.

They walked home side by side in the dark, sweaty and smelling like grass, the dog beside them. It would be late enough for James to have had his bath and gone to sleep and Ace would watch TV and drink lemonade until Billy had finished his homework and gone to bed. Nora let Ace keep the dog at her house during the day, and when they went into her bedroom the dog always followed, and he lay down in the far corner while they made love. Ace usually got home near eleven, after Jackie had gone to bed. Sometimes Marie was in the kitchen folding laundry or having a cup of tea. She knew there'd been some trouble over the dog and she was thankful that Nora had offered to take him in, and that she'd taken Ace in like one of her own, too. Before he came in, Ace would always leave the dog in the backyard; then he'd get himself a soda from the refrigerator as Marie watched him.

"Over with the Silk boys?" she'd ask him.

"That's right," Ace would say easily.

Marie knew he took a special interest in Billy and she liked to hear about Billy's baseball progress.

"Better than Danny Shapiro?" she'd always ask and Ace would smile and say no, not yet, there hadn't been anyone in the neighborhood born who could come close to Danny. Marie would show Ace the fingerpaintings James had done if she'd baby-sat for him that day or the cupcakes she'd made for the boys if it was a Friday night and she was to have them both the next morning. When at last Ace went into his room he'd open his window and whistle and the dog would climb up on the rim of the window well, then jump through the window. He'd lie on the rug and watch as Ace stripped and got into bed and sometimes he'd pick up his huge head and touch Ace's hand with his nose. Those were the times when Ace felt like weeping, but he never did. Instead, he'd rub the dog's head with his open palm and then fall asleep, curled up, knees to chest.

On Sundays, Jackie McCarthy drove his mother to church. He never went to Mass with her, but he waited, parked in front of St. Catherine's, wearing his blue suit. He saw Rosemary DeBenedict one Sunday as she stepped outside to pin a lace kerchief over her hair. She was a senior in Catholic school and she wore a plaid skirt and plain black pumps and her hair was dark and straight. She was there with her mother and two younger sisters, and as soon as Jackie saw her he knew she was the right girl. He thought she looked over at him, but he wasn't sure. She had wide blue eyes and didn't wear any lipstick, although she had on small pearl earrings and a gold locket.

When Marie got into the car after Mass she smelled like gardenias and incense. She slipped off her shoes and sighed. Jackie started the car, but he kept on looking for Rosemary.

"My knees are killing me," Marie said. "I'm getting old." She laughed. Then she looked over and saw that her boy was staring at a girl on the steps of the church and realized it was true. She had a son who was old enough to fall in love.

The following Sunday Jackie borrowed a tie from the Saint and he got out of the car to wait. After Mass his heart grew larger in his chest when he saw Rosemary walk away, and he grinned like crazy when Marie came and told him Rosemary would be happy to sit next to him when he came to church.

He hadn't been inside a church for years, other than at Christmas and Easter, but he didn't feel nearly as uncomfortable as he thought he would. He couldn't take his eyes off Rosemary when he sat next to her, not even afterward, when he was introduced to her parents and her sisters, and by the time he got up the nerve to ask her out he had completely forgotten the boy he used to be.

As soon as he could, Jackie started saving to buy Rosemary an engagement ring. She would graduate in June and, aside from working in her father's bakery, hadn't thought much about what she'd do next, although certainly there would be a husband. She quickly accepted Jackie as that man. There was a dinner at her parents' house to celebrate. The Saint and Marie brought wine and almond cookies. Rosemary didn't look at Jackie all night, but when he was leaving she let him kiss her for the first time. Then Jackie knew it was settled between them.

Marie went with him to Goldman's Jewelers in Hempstead on a Tuesday afternoon, after Jackie had made certain to ask his father for two hours off. They picked out a ring that was small but surrounded by sparkling diamond chips, and Marie wept as Jackie paid the jeweler, cash, and then she put her arms around him so tightly he thought he wouldn't be able to breathe. He gave Rosemary the ring that evening; he got down on one knee, and as he slipped the ring on her finger he realized that she smelled delicious, like a cake in her father's bakery, and he realized, too, that he would spend every day of the rest of his life trying, and failing, to be good enough for her.

On Jackie's twenty-first birthday the bridal wreath bloomed in big, white clumps, which attracted the season's first bees. Cathy Corrigan had been dead for nearly six months, but it might as well have been six years as far as Jackie was concerned. He still had bad dreams, but everybody did, now and then. And, yes, he was terrified of dogs, small poodles and beagles made his heart jump, but anyone who'd been attacked by a monster like his brother's dog would have had the same phobia. And the dark, well, that seemed to be getting worse, and because of this he took to carrying a flashlight. On the night of his birthday he'd have to go out after dark because Rosemary had made him a special cake at the bakery, with cherries and marzipan and chunks of chocolate. When he woke on the morning of his birthday, he could smell another cake baking already, his mother's vanilla fudge cake, the one she made for both her sons every year.

Ace hadn't planned to be around for the celebration at dinner, but Marie had begged him and he'd grudgingly agreed. They all sat down at half past six. Marie had made stuffed shells and garlic bread, fruit salad with pink grapefruit slices, and the vanilla fudge cake. She felt a little depressed about the cake, even though Billy Silk had been over that afternoon and had licked out the frosting bowl and declared it the best he'd ever had. Still Marie knew it wouldn't be as good as whatever Rosemary baked. She couldn't quite believe that her first baby had turned twenty-one, although when she tried to imagine him as a baby she kept seeing James's face, and she had the urge to hold James and feel how warm he was when he woke from his nap.

Still, she served the stuffed shells with a flourish. She'd saved some in a Tupperware bowl for James's lunch the next day, and she'd decided to take an extra pan to the Durgins because she knew Robert loved her sauce. The Saint and Jackie were grinning. The Saint picked up a bottle of Chianti and three wineglasses. Ace watched his father and his heart sank; they were all so used to his not being at their table that the Saint didn't realize he was one glass short until he began to pour. He looked at Marie and she quickly got an extra wineglass down from the cabinet.

Jackie kept glancing at his father, waiting for the time to be right. Just before they left the station to come home for supper, when Jackie was sweeping out the garage, the Saint had stood in the doorway to watch him.

"Hey, Pop," Jackie had said. "Clean enough to eat off of."

The Saint had come over and handed him an envelope.

"Pop?" Jackie had said nervously, but the Saint just nodded and Jackie had to read the document enclosed twice before he could believe it. It was the deed to the station. The Saint had gone to a lawyer and had made Jackie an equal partner.

Now the Saint nodded and Jackie cleared his throat. "We've got a little news," Jackie said, and he handed his mother the deed.

Ace kept his eyes on his food; if he was at Nora's now he'd be having franks and beans and a Coke with ice, he'd be watching the way her hands moved as she cut up James's portion.

"Good Lord," Marie said, and she put her arms around Jackie and hugged him.

Ace looked up and saw the document. "What's this?" he said.

"Pop and I are partners," Jackie said.

Ace ignored him and turned to their father. "Pop?" he said. "What the hell is this?"

"Hush," Marie said. "Don't talk that way."

"What about me?" Ace said. "Where am I in all this?"

"You weren't interested," the Saint said. "Jackie is."

"Oh, right," Ace said. He pushed his chair backward so that it scraped against the linoleum. "You just give it all to him? You forgive him for everything?"

"That's right," the Saint said. "I do."

"Well, I don't," Ace said.

He got up and grabbed his jacket. He pushed open the side door and kept right on going. When Ace went to let the dog out of Nora's yard he saw that the lilacs were in full bloom beside her fence. Rudy came over to him and pushed his nose against Ace's leg to be petted, but Ace gently shoved the dog away. From where he stood he could hear the clinking of dinner plates inside his own kitchen, and it was an odd thing to hear at the moment when he stepped into his own future. There was less than a month of school left, and Ace had always assumed he'd be working at the station after graduation; the job at the A&P had been temporary, but now he realized that if he worked pushing carts around the parking lot much longer he might be doing it forever. All he wanted was to make love to Nora and not have to think. But it was still light out, and Joe Hennessy was mowing his lawn and the neighborhood kids were out playing kickball, and it just didn't seem right to walk in on Nora with a future like his hanging over him.

Ace stood beside the lilacs. They were amazingly sweet. He could see Billy Silk practicing out in the yard with the batting tee Ace had made for him out of one of Mr. Olivera's old sawhorses and he wished he were the same age as Billy. He wished he could crouch in the grass until dark watching to see if the fireflies had returned. Instead he started to walk down Hemlock Street. Rudy snapped up a tennis ball from Nora's yard, then followed Ace. The dog ran ahead, then turned back and laid the ball at Ace's feet, looking up at him expectantly.

"No, boy," Ace said, and he picked up the ball and put it in his pocket.

Ace could smell Nora's lilacs halfway down the block. The street-lights came on automatically, even though it wouldn't be dark for a

while. When they got to Cathy Corrigan's house Ace and Rudy
stopped at the driveway. Mr. Corrigan was out, unloading empty
crates off his truck. Ace watched him for a while; then he went to the
truck and grabbed a crate. Mr. Corrigan looked over at Ace, and
although he didn't speak, he didn't stop working either, and he didn't
tell Ace to go away. After Ace had carried half a dozen crates into the
garage Mr. Corrigan said, "Don't lay them on their side," as they
passed each other. Ace straightened out the crates and saw that in a
corner there was a white dressing table, with a skirt of rose-colored
material around it.

"She always wore too much damned makeup," Mr. Corrigan said.

Ace hadn't known Mr. Corrigan was standing beside him and he
jumped when he spoke.

"Eyeliner," Mr. Corrigan said.

He shook out a cigarette from his pack of Marlboros and offered
Ace one. It was cool in the garage, and against one wall were full
crates of soda and seltzer. From where they stood, smoking their
cigarettes, they could see Rudy sitting near the driveway.

"You've got that dog trained pretty well," Mr. Corrigan said.
"What do you do, just tell him to stay and he does?"

Ace knew Rudy wouldn't come near this house for anything, but he
said, "Hand signals." He put his hand up like a policeman to show Mr.
Corrigan the stay command.

"I'll be damned," Mr. Corrigan said.

When they finished their cigarettes there was a high keening
sound. Mr. Corrigan froze, then realized it was only the dog, out on
the sidewalk with his head back, howling.

"Rudy!" Ace shouted.

The dog looked at him and was silent.

"Jesus," Mr. Corrigan said. "The cry of the banshee." He stubbed
out his cigarette on the garage floor. "She was too kindhearted," he
said. "I see that now."

Ace reached into the pocket of his leather jacket and took out the
dog's tag with Cathy's name on it and handed it to Mr. Corrigan. Mr.
Corrigan turned it over in his hand, then gave it back to Ace.

"My boss is stopping my route," he said. "People don't want their
soda delivered anymore. I'm going to Maryland. More jobs down
there."

"What about the house?" Ace said. He now realized there was the faint aroma of perfume in the garage, as if someone had scented the skirt of the dressing table.

"I'm selling it and everything in it," Mr. Corrigan said. "I told my wife I'll buy her everything brand new." He stared at the dressing table. "Let someone else throw out her stuff, let the new owners do it. I can't."

Ace looked beyond the dressing table and saw that it was still all here in the garage. Everything Cathy had owned, cartons of notebooks and bags of skirts and dresses, boxes of sneakers and high-heeled shoes. It was garbage night tonight and after their kickball game was over, boys all up and down the block would be pulling out trash cans.

"I'll do it," Ace said.

"Don't do me any favors," Mr. Corrigan said.

Ace nodded but when Mr. Corrigan looked at him they both knew he would. After Mr. Corrigan had locked up his truck, Ace stayed in the garage and had another cigarette, and when he was through it was finally dark. It was the soft darkness of late spring, a violet-colored darkness that felt warm and damp. Now Cathy's mother wouldn't have to look outside and see what was set out for the trash. Ace carried out the dressing table first and then he worked on the boxes, stacking them neatly on the curb. Rudy edged over, closer and closer, until he finally came to lie down on the grass strip between the sidewalk and the gutter. Cathy must have saved everything; there was a box filled with stuffed animals and dolls, there was a box of old makeup, all tossed together in a jumble, and all the bags of clothes, some of which felt like bodies when Ace picked them up and held them to his chest. When he was done Cathy's belongings stretched from the driveway to the large elm that marked the end of the Corrigans' property. Ace sat down on the curb and he put his head down, like a man who's been drowning and then finds himself propelled to the surface for no good reason other than the fact that his body was stronger than he'd ever imagined. He whistled for Rudy. The dog came over to sit beside him, and when Ace put his arm around him he realized the dog was shivering.

It was the time when the youngest children were already in bed and the older children took their baths or begged to watch one more

TV program. Cathy Corrigan used to set out her clothes carefully for
the following morning at this time of night. Among the looseleaf
notebooks and the comic books and romance novels, Ace had found a
notebook of the weekly sheets she made up, completely planning
each day's outfit, including accessories. She never wore the same
thing twice in a single week. Half the money she earned at the A&P
went to her mother, and the other half she used for herself, mostly to
buy earrings and shoes. The largest of the boxes was filled with shoes;
the leather ones were all polished and the sneakers had special pink
laces.

Ace looked into the dark and listened to the hum of the parkway.
He had his arm around the dog's neck and he could feel the low
vibration of a growl before he actually heard it. There, in the middle
of the street, was a pair of Cathy's shoes. Rudy would have bolted and
run after them if Ace hadn't grabbed his metal collar and held on
tight. He pulled the dog back onto the curb and forced him to stay as
the shoes began to walk. They were red high heels with a strap and a
small buckle; Rudy could have easily fit both of them into his mouth if
Ace had allowed him to go fetch. Left alone, the shoes continued
down Hemlock Street, and when they reached the far corner, past
Nora Silk's house, the asphalt beneath them turned a silvery blue,
like tracks made of phosphorescent dust, and as soon as the shoes
disappeared the tracks dissolved into the calm May air.

Ace loosened his grip on the dog, now that it was impossible for
him to fetch the shoes. Rudy whined, then he tilted his head back and
made a soft howling sound, and the howl went right through Ace, it
cut him in half. There were stars in the sky now, and the lights in
living rooms along Hemlock Street were turned on. Ace sat where he
was for a little while longer, and by the time he got off the curb and
headed back to his parents' house, he knew he didn't live there
anymore.

When Nora came back from Armand's, Marie McCarthy let her put
her feet up and she made her a cup of Sanka while they waited for

the baby to wake from his nap. There was a blueberry pie in the oven and the smell of it made Nora feel sleepy. She popped two saccharin tablets into her Sanka.

"No wonder he's sleeping so good," Marie said proudly. "He must have climbed up and down the basement stairs fifty times when I did the wash."

Marie took the pie out of the oven and the crust was so perfect that Nora got to her feet. She stood next to Marie at the stove and watched the steam rise from the golden pastry.

"How do you do that?" Nora said, awed.

"The secret of a pie is in the crust," Marie confided. Her daughter-in-law to be, Rosemary, was such a good baker that it gave Marie the greatest pleasure to have Nora admire her pie.

"I can bake everything except pie crust," Nora said. "Mine are always white. They look like glue."

"You use butter," Marie guessed.

"Butter and sugar," Nora said.

"Never," Marie told her. "Use Crisco instead."

"Ah." Nora nodded.

Nora and Marie looked at each other and smiled.

"Prick the top with a fork seven times after you flute the edges," Marie said.

Nora put her arms around Marie and thanked her.

"What's a pie crust?" Marie shrugged.

"You know what I mean," Nora said.

It wasn't just that Marie took care of the boys; she had also introduced Nora to all the other mothers in the neighborhood and, as a friend of Marie's, Nora had been accepted. Now it wasn't just Ellen Hennessy who called Nora on the phone but Lynne Wineman as well. Lynne had been terrifically impressed when Marie brought Nora over and Nora got rid of her daughter's wart. All Nora had done was tie a string around the wart; she attached the other end of the string to the handle of the toilet and flushed once, then threw the string into the bowl and flushed it away, just as her grandfather, Eli, had always done. In the morning, the wart had disappeared and Lynne Wineman phoned to invite her over for lunch.

Nora had been elected head of the playground committee at the last PTA meeting after she vowed to have the dangerous old slide replaced with a newer model, and she got a lot of support when she suggested tulip bulbs be planted all along the blacktop in September. Sometimes, when Nora was waiting outside the school for Billy at two forty-five, a stone would come skittering along the sidewalk and Nora would jump, but it would be nothing more than a pebble rolling down the incline of the sidewalk. She was not someone children threw stones at now.

Nora felt closer to Marie than to anyone else in the neighborhood, and sitting there eating warm pie and drinking Sanka she thought to herself, I am sleeping with this woman's seventeen-year-old son, and she felt dizzy and had to fan herself with her hand.

"Let's go peek," Marie said, and they tiptoed into the living room, where the crib was set up. Marie thought that James wasn't a proper name for a baby and, even though she tried to call him that, he was Jimmy as far as she was concerned. As he slept he clutched an old bear that had yellow glass eyes.

"He loves that bear," Marie whispered.

"Googa." Nora nodded.

Earlier that day Marie had thrown Googa into a pillowcase and washed him in the delicate cold-water cycle. James sat by the washing machine, patiently waiting for his bear to be washed clean of jam and mud. Marie had stopped judging Nora. So what if Googa was filthy, or if the little sneakers Jimmy wore had holes in them? So what if she let Ace's vicious dog live in the house with her children, or if she listened to Elvis—although actually, Nora had confided that ever since Elvis had gone into the army his charm had been wearing thin. He just wasn't the same in those uniforms.

"What do you hear from your ex?" Marie would sometimes ask.

"Zippo," Nora would usually say, but once in a while she'd admit that she'd gotten a postcard and that Roger was playing in a motel not far from the Sands or that he'd sent an envelope with a twenty-dollar bill tucked inside for the boys. She would have loved to tell Marie the truth, that it wasn't her ex she thought about but Ace and that the real reason she had stopped listening to Elvis was that his voice made her feel so sulky that she could let dinner burn in the oven. Sometimes Ace wasn't able to sneak over and get his dog at night. Nora would watch the dog waiting by the front door and she'd sit by him and take his head into her lap and stroke him between his eyes and along his ears and she'd know sooner or later there'd be a time when Ace wouldn't come back. At least, not for her.

On the nights they dared to be together Ace was so fierce as he made love to her that Nora forgot where she was. When they weren't in bed he almost never spoke to her now; but Nora often caught him looking at her, when he thought she didn't see, and she knew that something had happened inside him and that he wasn't the same. The dog knew it too, and when Ace was around, he followed him more closely than ever. But even with Rudy beside him, Ace was alone. The only one he felt comfortable with was Billy, and that was only out on the field. He'd decided that Billy was going to make the Little League team, and during the week before the tryouts they practiced every night until ten. Billy insisted they keep the tryouts secret from Nora. He didn't want her worrying, sitting there snapping her gum while he was working hard to concentrate. But he definitely wanted Ace there with him.

"You don't need me," Ace told him.

"I do," Billy insisted. "I'm not that good, but if you're there, maybe I won't strike out completely."

"Listen," Ace told him. "You are good."

"Oh, yeah, right," Billy said. "As good as Danny Shapiro?"

Ace thought it over. "No," he said. "Better."

On the day of the tryouts they walked to Policeman's Field together, and all the way there Billy had a lump in his throat. He kept thinking about what Ace had said to him until he believed it. The day was hot and beautiful and blue. There were so many boys trying out that the bleachers were filled with parents. Billy stopped at the gate to the field. He had holes in his dungarees and he'd forgotten to comb his hair. Without thinking, he reached out and grabbed Ace's hand.

"Go on," Ace said. "You think you're so special they're gonna wait for you?"

Billy dropped his hand, embarrassed. "Maybe I'll skip it," he said.

"Go on," Ace said. "I'll be right here watching you."

Billy walked into Policeman's Field alone. He just hoped to God they wouldn't put him in with the Pee Wees, first- and second-graders he wouldn't want to be caught dead with. He waited his turn on the bench with the other new kids, most of them younger than he was. When it was his turn at bat he looked back toward the fence. He saw Ace McCarthy nod and he hit the ball just as hard as he would have if Ace had been pitching. The ball flew up, high and long; it sailed over the outfield and over the fence that separated the park from the Southern State.

"Great!" one of the sign-up coaches shouted to him as Billy ran back to the bench.

Billy felt so happy he didn't think he could keep it all inside. If someone had touched him he would have burst open. He didn't even notice Stevie Hennessy until Stevie had walked right up and sat beside him.

"You're not bad," Stevie said.

"Oh yeah?" Billy said cautiously.

"They might even put us on the same team," Stevie said.

Out in the field the dust had risen up and it smelled sharp and sweet. There was the sound of traffic and the boys shouting out on the field and maybe that was why Billy couldn't hear a thing when he tried to listen in to what Stevie was thinking.

"Seeing we live on the same block," Stevie explained.

"Yeah," Billy said. "They might." He couldn't hear a thing inside his head. Just one of the coaches out in the field shouting and a plane overhead.

"I was on the Wolverines last year," Stevie said. "We could have used you."

Billy put both hands on his head. The constant hum he heard was gone and with it the headache he always had when he picked up anyone's thoughts. Out by the gate, Ace's shadow looked long and thin as a scarecrow's as he turned and began to walk home. And really, there wasn't any reason for him to stay. Billy had made the team, anyone could see that; when they called out his name he ran to the team sign-up sheets so fast that his sneakers didn't leave any tracks in the dirt.

10

THE SOUTHERN STATE

$\mathcal{I}$T was terribly hot on graduation day; steam had begun to rise from the streets. Some of the graduates, who had to stand out in the sun for over two hours, fainted and others had to drink quarts of ice water after the ceremony was finally over, and still others put their arms around their classmates and cried salty tears that were hot enough to mark their cheeks with tiny red burns. Danny Shapiro gave the valedictorian's speech, just as everyone always knew he would, and Ace McCarthy graduated, as few would have guessed. The tradition of going to Tito's Steakhouse for graduation dinner begun by the very first graduating high-school class six years earlier continued, and Gloria Shapiro drove Rickie and Danny there in her new Ford Falcon. Phil had shown up late for the graduation and had left early, missing Danny's speech, because he hadn't wanted to run into Gloria.

"I could wring his neck," Gloria said as their steaks were brought over. "I could watch him eat dirt."

"Mom," Rickie Shapiro said, "please."

Rickie's eyes were red because she had broken up with Doug Linkhauser and she still didn't know why. Everyone said he wanted to marry her, they said he was already looking at rings, but the last time he had tried to kiss Rickie she had gotten all panicky. She started to avoid his calls, and finally she mailed him his I.D. bracelet, which was the coward's way out, but a way out all the same. Sometimes she'd look out her window at night. She'd watch the Mc-Carthys' house and she'd try to wish Ace into coming to her window, but it never worked and she knew it wouldn't. Once, on a clear night, she'd opened her window and thought about climbing out, but then she'd seen Ace cutting across his front lawn, coming home from Nora Silk's house. She had leaned her elbows on her windowsill and some of the first of the season's fireflies caught in her hair, forcing her to brush her hair hard, so hard that her scalp hurt all through the night.

Danny sat across from his mother and sister, wearing a white shirt and a blue suit and a new silk tie. After his speech, several of the parents and teachers had come over to congratulate him, and he'd thanked them politely, but the truth of it was he couldn't even remember what his speech had been about. Hope, he thought. Belief in the future. He watched his mother call the waiter over to order a gin and tonic and he knew he'd have to drive them home from Tito's. He planned to work at the lab this summer, to earn extra money for whatever his scholarship at Cornell wouldn't cover. He was already registered for two advanced math classes, even though he didn't care much about math anymore. He wasn't certain if he cared much about anything other than getting to a place where there were green fields, and where, in the winter, the snowdrifts would be deep enough to cut him off from the rest of the world.

"Ace isn't here," Rickie Shapiro announced after scanning the room.

"Why should he be?" Gloria said. "They passed him through his classes because they wanted to get rid of him."

Danny looked around the restaurant. "Nope," he agreed. "They couldn't drag him here." He smiled. He looked at his sister across the table as their mother stirred the ice in her drink. What an idiot she was to have listened to his advice, but then she'd always been that way. He wished someone would slap her, just to wake her up.

"Miss him?" Danny asked Rickie meanly.

Rickie took an onion ring off her plate. She studied her brother and suddenly realized they were not as different as she'd always thought they were. The restaurant air conditioner was turned up so high that her fingertips were blue. "Not as much as you do," she said, and instantly she regretted it because she could see it was true.

Ace had refused to go out to dinner, although Marie had begged him. Instead he went to Nora's house, without bothering to get out of his suit and tie, and he didn't care who saw him. He went right up to the front door, even though Lynne Wineman was out in her front yard clipping back her hedges.

"You're not supposed to be here," Nora said when she opened the door and it was so true, and had been so true all along, that they both laughed.

Nora brought him into the kitchen, where his present, not yet wrapped, was on the table. It was her grandfather's pocket watch. Ace picked it up and turned it over in his hand.

"I can't take this," he said. "It's gold."

"Plated," Nora said, and then she closed his fingers over the watch.

For weeks she had been knitting him a sweater, before realizing it wasn't what she wanted to give him. She had found the watch in the bottom of her jewelry box, and she knew this was the right present as soon as she saw that it was ten minutes fast and always would be.

Billy came in and he whistled when he saw Ace. "You're supposed to be at Tito's. Your mom made reservations last week."

"Yeah," Ace said. "Well, I'm not hungry."

But he managed to eat two servings of the macaroni and cheese Nora had made, and then two cupcakes and ice cream for dessert.

"How does it feel?" Billy said, while Nora was clearing the plates.

"Like lead in my stomach," Ace joked, and Nora turned around from the sink and made a face at him.

"To be free," Billy said. "Just think. You never, ever have to go to school again."

James came over and climbed onto Ace's lap, and Ace bounced his leg up and down without thinking, to give the baby a horsey ride.

"It doesn't feel the way you'd think it would," he said finally.

Nora sat down at the table. "Your mother made a cake," she said.

Ace looked at her, angry. The nerve along his jaw twitched. "Yeah?" he said. "How come everybody knows so much about my goddamned life?"

"It's vanilla fudge," Nora said.

Ace grinned in spite of himself. "Oh, really?"

"Listen, go home," Nora said. "She worked on it all day yesterday.

She had the oven on even though it was ninety-six. She put it in the cabinet over the refrigerator so you wouldn't see it."

Ace put the baby down on the floor and stared at Nora. "Are you kicking me out?" he asked.

"Do I have to?" Nora said.

"Does she?" Ace asked Billy.

Billy looked at his mother and tried to hear what she was thinking. He strained to pick something up over the sound of James rattling pots and pans and the dog barking in the backyard, but nothing came through. His mother looked calm as glass; she had her hands around a tumbler of cold lemonade and she was staring at Ace.

"She won't kick you out," Billy said, hoping it was true.

"That just goes to show how much you know, buddy," Nora told Billy. She thought about the Laundromat on Eighth Avenue and the wild lilies from her grandfather's yard that had refused to grow on her windowsill, she thought about her children asleep in their beds when the stars came out, and then she realized that she no longer heard the drone of the Southern State, it had become the sound of a river, smooth and constant and blue. She closed her eyes when Ace got up from the table, and after the first few steps he took across the kitchen floor, she couldn't even hear him anymore.

It was dark now, but the temperature was still just as high as it had been at noon. Ace noticed the car as soon as he stepped out of Nora's house, and he stood there on her stoop, wondering why it was parked in his driveway. He saw that his father was leaning up against the front grille. The light of the Saint's cigarette looked like a firefly. The car was a blue Ford with whitewall tires. Ace loosened his tie. He'd put Nora's grandfather's watch in his pocket and it was heavy, like a stone. He cut across the lawn and grass stuck to the soles of his shoes.

"Your mother's been waiting," the Saint said when Ace walked to the driveway. "She made a cake."

"So I hear," Ace said.

He went to the driver's side and ran his hand over the paint.

"Four on the floor," the Saint said to him as he smoked his cigarette.

Ace nodded and looked inside the open driver's window.

"Eight-cylinder," the Saint said. "I rebuilt it."

Leaning against the car, the Saint looked smaller than usual, more clenched up, as though you could see his muscles working under his skin.

"Pop," Ace said.

"I know you wanted a Chevy, but believe me, you'll get better mileage on this," the Saint said.

Ace wanted to put his arms around his father, but instead he came to stand beside him and leaned on the car's grille. They could see the lights inside the house; the globes of the pole lamp in the living room formed three perfect white moons.

"I always thought you'd be the one to work with me; that's what I wanted, but that's not the way it turned out," the Saint said.

Ace could hear that his father's breathing was strained.

"Look, Pop," he said. "I've been saving up for a car. I've got enough money."

The Saint threw his cigarette on the ground and stomped on it. "It's the one thing I can give you!" he said.

"All right," Ace said, frightened.

"Jesus Christ!" the Saint said, turning to look at him, and looking at him so deeply that Ace took a step backward. "God damn it," the Saint said, wounded. "Can't you just take the damn car!"

Ace put his arms around his father and noticed what he would have known long before if he had only looked; after all this time he was now taller than the Saint.

Sometime after midnight James woke up. He opened his eyes, but he didn't make a peep. His stuffed bear was with him in the crib, and he stroked the bear's face and his glass eyes. Through the screen window he could hear the first cicadas; he could see a few bright stars. He closed his eyes and the stars disappeared; he opened them and there they were again, set into a black bowl above his house.

James was now twenty months old, and he loved to dance. Whenever his mother put on her Elvis records James clapped his hands and lifted first one foot and then the other; when he was very daring, he would pick up both feet at the same time and hop like a bunny and then his mother would scoop him up and kiss his neck and tell him he was wonderful. He had a passion for lime-flavored Jell-O and graham crackers and hiding behind doors, especially when he heard his mother calling to him and he could see her in a crack in the door as she looked worriedly for him. He liked to get the deck of cards when he went to Marie's house to be baby-sat and let all the cards fall to the floor in a storm, then carefully pick them up, one by one. He liked to sit on Marie's lap and have her sing "Clap hands, clap hands till Daddy comes home" in her smoky voice that sounded like a friendly frog. He could now understand everything that was said to him, even when he made a mess in Billy's room and Billy said, "Bug off, buster!" He understood "sweetie pie" and "Bring me your shoes." He could speak, but aside from a few words—*Mama, Marie, doggy, Twinkie, nose, hi, butter, one two three*—everything he knew refused to come out as words, and whenever that happened he stamped his feet and lay down on the floor clutching Googa, and then he would feel much better.

He loved to look around his room, especially through the wooden slats of his crib. When he woke early, or in the middle of the night, he always made sure that everything was still the same. Still the lamp on the dresser, the toy box in the corner, the red-and-white rug in the center of the floor, the fringes of which he liked to chew on some-times, when no one was looking. Tonight, while everyone else was asleep, his room was exactly as it had been when he'd gone to bed. Because it was still dark, he knew that if he called out his mother wouldn't give him a bottle, he was too old for that. She would only come to the doorway and say *Ssh*, but he experimented by banging his hand against the crib. He banged harder, then began to kick with his feet. He heard someone get up, and then footsteps in the hallway, and he knew from the sound of nails clicking on the wood that it was the dog.

Rudy stood outside the door, breathing hard and listening, so James kicked harder against his crib, and finally Rudy pushed open the bedroom door with his nose. The dog's nose was wet and black and his fur was black and wheat-colored. James sat up in his crib, holding onto Googa and his blankie, and when the dog came over he stuck his fingers through the slats. Rudy let himself be prodded, then stuck his nose between the slats and pushed the baby's hand away. James took his blankie and threw it over his own head.

Rudy stood on his back legs and leaned into the crib to pull the blanket off with his teeth, then he dropped the blanket onto the mattress. The dog sat down beside the crib and let the baby touch his big, black nose.

"Nose," James said.

They stared at each other in the darkened room. The sound of the Southern State was faint, almost watery. Rudy nudged the baby until he lay back down. James reached for his blankie and hugged it, still staring into the dog's eyes. James smelled good, like milk, and the dog licked his face through the slats.

Cool night air came in through the window, and the grass smelled sweet. When the neighborhood was a potato farm, rabbits used to appear between the raised rows at dusk, and they stayed until long past midnight, digging in the soft earth for their supper. Now there were only stuffed bunnies in toy boxes, although sometimes when Rudy went into Nora's backyard he dug deeper and deeper until he found a potato that had grown in spite of the lawn above it.

Rudy sat by the crib until the baby moved his thumb into his mouth and closed his eyes. Then he got up and went to the rug and circled until he found the exact right spot and he lay down, his head on his paws. He kept his eyes open and listened to the sound of human breathing, a sound so helpless it could make even a dog shed tears. Beneath the sound of breathing was the rustle of moths hitting against the window screen, the creak of the floorboards settling, the sound of a window shade in another room flapping against a wooden sill. Sometimes, on nights when there was a full moon and the whole world turned silver, or on black nights, when he could have slipped through the shadows and in between the parked cars more quickly than any human feet, the dog felt something in his blood that urged him to run. He could have scooped up those bunnies between the rows of potatoes with one snap of his jaws and eaten them whole. He could have outrun any car on the Southern State and if anyone had tried to hold him back he could have cracked a femur in two, so that pieces of bone flew into the air. If he'd wanted to, he could have leapt up and knocked out the screen window with one push of his huge head and the fences in the backyards could never have held him back. But the sound of human breathing made him stay on the red-and-white rag rug. It didn't matter that he could run faster than any man, or if somewhere there were still rabbits who put down their ears and trembled in the dark. Even when he was asleep he was ready for the whistle or the clap of human hands that might wake him. He longed for the call; in his dreams when he was running only inches away from the moon, a full moon, white enough to blind a man in seconds, he was ready to be claimed by the person he belonged to.

In the bedroom, where he lay beside Nora, Ace knew that he would never love another woman the way he loved her. She was asleep, but he couldn't leave her alone. He ran his hands along her arms, her breasts, and then her belly. There were stretch marks across her belly and hips from carrying her children; bands of devotion Ace could not, and might never, understand. When he asked her to go with him, she told him to shut up and kiss her and stop wasting their time. And he supposed she was right; now that he had her grandfather's watch he was amazed to see how quickly time passed.

The night before, when he had cleaned out his room, he'd found only enough possessions worth taking to fill one small suitcase. The Saint and Jackie had stayed late at the station, sharing a pizza out of its box and cleaning the windows in the office with Windex. This way there would be no good-byes, and Ace understood that, he actually appreciated it. His mother was not so easy; she wept in the kitchen as she fixed him two roast beef sandwiches and a tin of cookies to take along. She threw her arms around him when he came in with his suitcase and pretended she wasn't crying. When Marie finally let him go, Ace packed up the Ford the Saint had given him and, with Rudy beside him, drove to a field beside Dead Man's Hill. He'd planned to leave right then, but when he saw the entry ramp to the Southern State, he left the car parked and walked back to Nora's. Her door was unlocked and she'd been waiting for him in the kitchen with the glass of water she hadn't given him the first time he'd come to her house.

Now it was morning, just dawn, but morning all the same. He'd done it, he'd stayed the whole night through and seen the way she looked before she opened her eyes, the way her black hair streaked along the white pillowcase. He watched her sleep, then got up and pulled on his clothes. He went to the window and lifted one slat of the venetian blinds to look at his house; his mother was probably already fixing coffee, his father was in the shower, Jackie was reaching for his freshly pressed uniform, which hung in his closet. As far as they were concerned, Ace was already gone. But he wasn't. He got himself a cigarette and sat down on the edge of the bed. He would think about Nora every time he saw a woman wearing a charm bracelet, every time he had his lunch at noon or took off a woman's blouse, and when he drove across the desert on his way to California, he would pull over to the side of the road and stare into the purple dust and say her name out loud.

He went back to the bed and Nora woke and sat up. She put her arms around him and leaned her face against his back, then reached for the cigarette in his hand and took a drag, before stubbing it out in the ashtray on her night table.

"Nora," Ace said.

"I'm going to plant sunflowers today," Nora told him. "All around the patio. I'm going to do the laundry and then I have to go food shopping. We have no bread."

She kept her arms around Ace and he leaned back toward her, until she pulled away.

"Whole-wheat bread," Nora said.

All through June there had been a troop of large black ants in Nora's kitchen and she couldn't seem to get rid of them, not even when she washed the counters with a mixture of garlic and wild marjoram, the way her grandfather always did. The ants were fearless; they'd jump into the sugar bowl or even into your coffee cup, and Marie McCarthy had told Nora that everyone in the neighborhood had them in June and that the only way to be rid of them was to put out ant poison and be done with it. So Nora had put out poison in the little tins she saved from frozen chicken pot pies, making certain that the tins were far out of the baby's reach, and the ants started to die right away.

It was amazing how fast they could die and how many of them there were; she had to sponge them off the counters and sweep them into a dustpan so James wouldn't pop them in his mouth. The man at the hardware store had promised Nora that all her ants would be dead in twelve hours, but she had expected them to slink off somewhere and die quietly, not turn onto their backs and wave their legs and litter her floor and make her feel like a murderess. It was clear the ants knew something horrible was going on, because the ones who were still mobile were frantic, ignoring the sugar bowl and the sticky cookie James had left on his highchair. They made a line along the window ledge above the sink, racing back and forth. Nora got a newspaper and rolled it up, planning to kill them all quickly, and then she realized what they were doing. The healthy ones and the ones who were already in the grip of the poison were racing back and forth to their nest in the window ledge, trying desperately to save their eggs. All along the counter by the sink there were tiny yellow eggs, translucent as rice paper, delicate enough to disintegrate as soon as Nora touched them with her finger.

Nora stood at the counter and wept as the ants dragged more and more unsalvageable eggs out from their nest. She wept as she brushed the eggs into a paper plate and took them out to the backyard, where she mixed them into the earth in the place where she would plant her sunflowers. She sat out there for a long time, perched on the border of bricks Mr. Olivera had carefully placed around the patio, and when she was done crying she knew she'd be able to watch Ace put on his boots.

When he forced himself to leave the bedroom, he found the dog waiting for him by the front door, and Ace snapped on his leash. They went through the backyards and along the fences, and because they traveled as the crow flies they got to the parkway in no time. Ace let Rudy off his leash, and they took off for the Ford parked on the other side of Dead Man's Hill, running until they finally reached the place where there were no more chain-link fences, where the air was as sweet as it used to be when there was clover and tall, purple lupine and Dead Man's Hill was covered with small wild roses that bloomed for only one week out of the year.

On the last Sunday in June, Nora and James went into the backyard with two spoons and a packet of sunflower seeds. It was a beautiful day, hot and clear, with high, white clouds that looked like popcorn. After a lunch of tunafish and chocolate milk, Nora settled James in his stroller, to let him nap while they walked. When she stopped in the driveway to light a cigarette she saw Donna Durgin pull up in an unfamiliar car. Donna honked the horn three times and looked at her old house, but nothing happened. Donna leaned on the horn again, and Nora headed for the car and went around to the driver's window. She tapped on it and Donna jumped. When Donna recognized Nora, she rolled down her window.

"You're wearing black," Nora said. "You look fantastic."

Donna smiled and adjusted her black headband. She had on a black cotton sweater and tight black slacks; her blond hair was cut short and curled around her face.

"I'm picking up my kids," Donna said.

"Good for you," Nora said.

"I get them every Sunday and he knows I come at one."

"He probably wants to make you squirm because you look so great," Nora said. Nora reached her hand into the car and pressed down on the horn and didn't let up. "That ought to get his attention," she said.

Robert Durgin opened the front door and pushed the screen ajar. He was wearing an undershirt and jeans and he yelled for Donna to hold her goddamned horses.

"See what I mean?" Nora said.

Donna got out of the car to wait for her kids. She knelt down and tickled James under his chin. "I got lost coming here today," she said. "I got all confused and forgot what street I was on."

Donna straightened up and she and Nora leaned against the car and looked at the house.

"I always wanted to have an arbor right in front of the stoop," Donna said. "I wanted red roses growing up it."

"Roses are a pain in the ass," Nora said, as she stubbed out her cigarette under her shoe. She was surprised when Donna Durgin laughed. "Well, they are," Nora said. "You've got to spray them for aphids and fertilize them like crazy and cut them back before winter and then pray that your kids don't prick their fingers on the thorns. Sunflowers are better. Come over in August and you'll see. I'll have a whole forest of them, they'll all be six feet tall."

Both women smiled to think of a ring of yellow flowers, all moving their heads toward the sun.

"I'm going to get my children, too, you know," Donna said.

Donna's kids were at the screen door, but Robert was holding them back, giving them some last-minute advice.

"Suddenly he knows everything," Donna said. "He writes me notes telling me what they should eat for dinner. As if I didn't feed them their dinner all those years!"

"Tear up the notes when the kids aren't looking," Nora said.

"I will." Donna grinned before she went up the driveway to meet her children.

Nora watched them for a while; then she turned and walked toward Harvey's Turnpike. By now she knew the name of every street, and the peculiar turns each one took, which one was a dead end, which looped up toward the turnpike. On each block there were men out mowing grass, and the smell was so sweet it made you want to curl up, right then and there, on somebody's front lawn. James fell asleep in his stroller, with his hands on his knees and his head drooping on his shoulder. Nora navigated carefully over the curbs, and when she got to Policeman's Field she slipped a sun hat over the baby's head. She greeted some of the mothers she knew and waved to Lynne Wineman, who was high up in the bleachers.

Nora wheeled the stroller to the bleachers. She was still wearing the old Bermuda shorts and sneakers she wore for gardening, and her hair was pulled back into a ponytail with an elastic band. She sat down on the lowest row; she might not have the best view, but this way she could let James go on napping. Across the field, in the dugout, the Wolverines sat on a wooden bench in their blue uniforms. Nora took a cigarette out of the pack in her pocket, lit it, and leaned back.

"Hey!" she called out, when she saw Joe Hennessy. He was leading Suzanne through the crowd and carrying a large container of popcorn. When he heard Nora shout he turned, puzzled. "Joe!" Nora called and she patted the spot next to her.

Hennessy stood for a moment, straining to see who had called him, blinking until he recognized her. He had to sweet-talk Suzanne into going over before they backtracked toward Nora.

"She wants to sit at the tippy top," he explained to Nora.

"I don't blame you," Nora said to Suzanne. "Where's Ellen?" she asked Hennessy.

"She had to work late yesterday. She's taking the afternoon off. Now I get kid duty on Saturdays and Sundays."

"I'll bet you're great at it," Nora said. She stubbed out her cigarette in the dust and grinned up at Hennessy.

"No," he insisted. "I'm not."

"Daddy," Suzanne said, pulling on his hand. "You promised."

"I did," Hennessy admitted to Nora.

"Onward, Wolverines, right?" Nora said.

"Right," Hennessy said, not moving. "You okay?" he asked.

"Sure," Nora said. She grabbed at her Bermuda shorts and smiled. "I just look this way because I've been gardening."

The light was thin and yellow, and because of it Nora's skin looked golden.

"That's not what I mean," Hennessy said.

In his stroller, James turned his head and slipped his thumb into his mouth and sucked hard, the way he always did just before he woke.

"I know what you mean," Nora said.

Nora and Hennessy looked at each other, then laughed. Hennessy lifted Suzanne and began to carry her up to the top of the bleachers. Nora watched them, then realized James had woken up and was staring at her.

"My sweetie pie," she said, and she took him out of his stroller and held him on her lap.

The boys from the opposing team had started to come onto the field and when Nora shaded her eyes and stared hard she could make out where Billy sat on the bench in his new uniform. The baby on her lap was still heavy from sleep; he turned and sat up on his knees to put his arms around Nora's neck. Above the baseball diamond the sky was a clear, luminous blue, and in the east there was a line of red, a promise of continued good weather. Nora blew on James's sweaty neck and then kissed him. She leaned against the bleachers and pointed upward so that the baby could see the first ball rise into the outfield, far above them, where the moon hung suspended, white and full, appearing in the sky hours before dark.